I0579518

The Shaman's Son

Jane Glatt

The Shaman's Son

Jane Glatt

TYCHE BOOKS LTD.

The Shaman's Son
Published by Tyche Books Ltd.
www.TycheBooks.com

Copyright © 2017 Jane Glatt
First Tyche Books Ltd Edition 2017

Print ISBN: 978-1-928025-69-6
Ebook ISBN: 978-1-928025-70-2

Cover Art by Niken Anindita
Cover Layout by Lucia Starkey
Interior Layout by Ryah Deines
Editorial by M.L.D. Curelas

Author photograph: Eugene Choi
Echo1 Photography

All rights reserved. No part of this book may be reproduced or transmitted in any form or by any means, electronic or mechanical, including photocopying, recording or by any information storage & retrieval system, without written permission from the copyright holder, except for the inclusion of brief quotations in a review.

The publisher does not have any control over and does not assume any responsibility for author or third party websites or their content.

This is a work of fiction. All of the characters, organizations and events portrayed in this story are either the product of the author's imagination or are used fictitiously.

Any resemblance to persons living or dead would be really cool, but is purely coincidental.

This book was funded in part by a grant from the Alberta Media Fund.

Alberta
Government

Thanks as always to everyone at Tyche Books and especially Margaret Curelas.

Chapter One

"HE'S THERE," ARIC said. "I can feel him. Or her."

"Him," Fae replied. "It's a man. Wailes was only looking for men."

"Yes," Aric said. "Foolish of him." There was another flash of . . . something in the magic, and he gripped Fae's hands tighter.

Keetley Kellen's journal was clear that women had never been selected as conjurer's apprentices—that was one reason why the bloodlines had been lost until now, lost until Fae. But she didn't seem to have any trouble learning how to create spells, and Aric had to wonder if conjurers had always been so blind to the abilities of women.

He felt another, stronger wave of magic, and he concentrated on it, on probing it, trying to feel its purpose.

"A making spell," he said. "A big one but I can't tell what it's creating." The magic—the spell—completed doing whatever it was created to do, and Aric opened his eyes against the bright glare of the sun.

"I felt that last one too," Fae said. "I think he was making a fire. At least it felt the same as when I do that."

Aric tried to recall the feeling of Fae making a fire but . . . he shook his head. "I couldn't tell," he said. "Maybe I'll never be able to tell."

"Maybe not," Fae agreed. "Zevach writes that shaman talents

were generally based on family, but that didn't mean other abilities couldn't show up unexpectedly."

"And I'm not sure which family I belong to. It would be nice to know what abilities I can expect to have," Aric said. *And how to use them*, he finished silently.

He stared out across the waters of the Dark Sea. For the past two weeks, he and Fae had stayed close to the mouth of the Aberhayle while they tried to figure out what they could about their respective abilities. But it was frustrating. Both the shaman and Kellen journals had instruction and explanations but so much knowledge had been lost that they often struggled to understand what some terms meant.

And even as they were exploring their talents, they could feel the other conjurer learning to use his own.

Initially the other conjurer used magic sparingly—small spells performed with long stretches of time in between them. Now the spells were more powerful—and more frequent. And it made *their* task so much more urgent.

From what they'd read they knew it used to take years, decades even, for conjurers and shamans to master their powers. He and Fae had only had a few weeks, and at the rate the other conjurer was progressing, they feared that they only had a few more.

But they had discovered that for some reason, when they worked together they could do things that neither one could do alone. They'd looked through the books very carefully but none of them mentioned anything about combining efforts to increase power and control.

Aric assumed that if a conjurer and Riverman shaman had ever worked together, it was so long ago that even the authors of their journals had forgotten.

Conjuring was a solitary endeavor—at least how it was practiced today. A conjurer taught their apprentice what they knew and the apprentice carried out their tasks alone.

From what little Aric's mother had told him, shamans learned in much the same way. Pooling talents and strengths wasn't something they did. According to Fae, conjurers didn't trust each other enough to work together. And his mother had been the last shaman—there hadn't been anyone for her to work with.

"We know more about magic than he does," Fae said.

"True," Aric replied. *For now*, he thought. They'd argued about this too often for him to say it out loud. Fae knew how to create new spells but the new Wailes conjurer—whoever he was—had dozens of books full of old spells. Did he even need to create new ones when he had so many to choose from? And many of those older spells were the work of powerful conjurers in their prime. Fae assumed they had a significant advantage for weeks to come—he didn't think they should count on it.

"I'm going to make us some cold drinks," Fae said. She rose and went into the boat's cabin.

Aric closed his eyes and concentrated and . . . there! There was a yell from inside, and he smiled. He felt another wave of magic but he ignored it.

A few minutes later, Fae came back outside.

"Nice trick," she said from behind him.

"Couldn't resist," Aric replied. He'd taken her spell of cooling and changed it so that it heated instead. "I wanted tea with the ice."

"Here's some ice."

"Hey!" Something cold dripped down his back and Aric jumped to his feet. He grabbed Fae's cold hand and forced it onto her bare arm.

Laughing, she danced away from him. He took a step to follow then stopped.

"Fae," he said. She giggled, took another step back.

"Fae!" he repeated, louder. "A big spell. Grab my hand. I'm going to try to change it."

Fae grasped his outstretched hand and then the magic washed over him. This was a formidable spell—and the intent! His knees buckled, and he felt Fae pull him closer to her. Wrapped in her arms he *looked* at the intent of the spell. Destruction. Devastation. Death. It was such a terrible spell. And powerful. Could he even change it? The spell was building, intensifying, and he concentrated his entire being on it, trying to force his will onto it. He breathed out once, then he whispered.

"Life."

Power—magic—exploded, pummelling him, and with a groan, Aric dropped to his knees, pulling Fae down with him. Her arms went around his shoulders and then something else enveloped him, blocking the magic, keeping it away from him until it faded.

"What happened?" he panted. "There was a backlash but it didn't reach me, couldn't reach me. What did you do?" He looked up and met her eyes. They were ablaze with power.

"I tried to protect you," Fae said. "I put up some kind of . . . I don't know, a magical barrier of some kind, to keep the magic away."

"It worked," Aric said. Shaking, he sat up. He raked a hand through his hair. "I think you saved my life."

Fae dropped down beside him and grasped his hand. "I think I did too."

After a few shaky breaths, Aric turned to look towards the mouth of the Aberhayle.

"That was a killing spell," he said. He shivered. He could still feel the horrible intent of the spell. "It didn't take long for the new Wailes to decide to kill with magic." And it had been deliberate: he'd felt not just the intent of the spell, but the intent of the one casting the spell.

"He didn't kill anyone," Fae said. "At least not yet, because of you. And with luck you turned that spell back on him and killed him."

"Let's hope so," Aric said, even though his shaman senses told him that hadn't happened. The new Wailes was still alive.

HEWITT LOOKED UP as Oleda Burrage barged into his office.

"You have to come!" she shouted before she turned and hurried out.

Startled, Hewitt got up too quickly and almost tripped when one of his oversized feet wedged behind the leg of his chair. He untangled himself and rushed out his open front door and along the cobblestones to Conjurers Hall. Not a single Bridger barred his way and by the time he reached Wailes' office he was uneasy.

He stepped through the open door and paused, uneasiness turning to dread as he surveyed the scene.

Oleda Burrage knelt beside her son, who lay on the floor. She leaned over him, smoothing his hair.

Across the room, Wailes slumped in his chair, the ropes that kept him upright taut. Tymm hovered over him, shifting from foot to foot, softly whimpering.

Shiv detached himself from the half-dozen Bridgers who huddled near the door, staring at Wailes and Graylon Burrage, and walked over to stand in front of Hewitt.

"We don't want no trouble," Shiv said. He looked over his shoulder. Hewitt followed his gaze to Oleda, who must have sensed him looking. She turned and glared at Shiv, before her eyes landed on Hewitt.

"Conjurer Hewitt," Oleda said. "Help. Graylon was doing magic when he collapsed."

Hewitt knelt on the other side of Burrage, across from Oleda. He was pale, and when Hewitt gently touched his wrist, his skin was clammy. But there was a strong pulse.

"Some water might help," Hewitt said. "And then we'll move him somewhere more comfortable." He turned his head. "Shiv? Can you send someone to fetch water?" Shiv eyed Graylon before glancing over at Wailes. "I'm sure they can both use some water," Hewitt continued. Shiv nodded—a single lift of his chin—and one of the Bridgers hurried out the door.

"Give him small sips when the water gets here," Hewitt said to Oleda. "I need to see to Conjurer Wailes."

He got to his feet and slowly approached Wailes. "Tymm," Hewitt said. "Please let me look. To help."

Tymm moaned but took a step back. Hewitt bent down to look at Wailes. He was breathing, but just barely.

"What happened to him?" he asked Shiv, who had followed him.

"Ask them." Shiv gestured to Oleda and her son. "They were arguing with Wailes. *She* was arguing with him, then she told her son to *do something* about the Head Conjurer. Burrage started reading from a book, there was a big flash, and then they were both knocked back by . . . something. Burrage landed on the floor but Conjurer Wailes stayed in his chair."

Hewitt looked at Oleda, who still hovered over her son. Had his mother asked Burrage to hurt Wailes? Maybe even kill him? And if she had, would they blame Hewitt if the older man lived? He sighed. He hated Wailes, but he couldn't simply let the man die.

"Tymm, take your master to his bed." Hewitt straightened while Tymm fussed over Wailes, undoing the ropes that held him upright and gently lifting him. He backed out of the room with the conjurer's tiny body cradled to his chest.

"What are you doing?" Oleda said. "He tried to kill my son."

"He's barely alive," Hewitt replied. "And Tymm is unpredictable right now. I thought it safer for Graylon if Tymm was elsewhere."

"Oh, yes," Oleda said. She smoothed a hand across her son's forehead. "We must protect Graylon. Thank you. But Wailes tried to kill us. He needs to pay for that."

Hewitt met Shiv's eyes and raised an eyebrow. The other man shrugged. There was no way Wailes tried to kill anyone—the man couldn't even keep himself upright. Besides, that was not what Shiv had said happened.

Was Burrage ready to get rid of Wailes? It had been a few weeks since Burrage had read the spell and lived, and Wailes, although Head Conjurer, had so much less magical ability than him. Had the younger man decided that he could no longer take orders from Wailes? Hewitt looked over at Burrage and his mother. Or had it been Oleda's decision?

He'd assumed Burrage would simply let Wailes fade away. It wasn't as though he was going to live much longer—in fact, he'd already survived far longer than Hewitt had expected him to. But maybe that was the problem—they were impatient for him to be dead.

No doubt Burrage expected to replace Wailes as Head Conjurer. As would Oleda. And really, he was the only one with true power. But he didn't know their ways. The others had to vote Burrage as their leader, but would they?

The Bridger returned with water and Oleda spent a few minutes dribbling it onto her son's lips. When she would allow it, Bridgers moved him off the floor and onto a settee. Hewitt handed her a small pillow, and she tucked that under Graylon's head before standing up.

"That horrible little man needs to pay," Oleda said sharply. "For what he's done to my son."

"He's old and very frail," Hewitt replied. "He will not recover, at least not much. I'm more concerned about your son's full recovery." He held her gaze, trying to look worried for her sake. She needed to understand that *her* place depended on her son recovering more than just his health: he needed to be able to do magic again. Eventually Oleda paled and looked away.

With a nod to Shiv, Hewitt left.

Oleda Burrage might think she had the right to make demands

but she was not a conjurer. And if her son didn't recover, or didn't recover enough to cast spells, neither Oleda nor Graylon Burrage would have any say in what happened on the bridge. *Hewitt* would. He already had the confidence of the other conjurers: he expected it would be a simple thing to convince them to vote him Head Conjurer.

Hewitt headed for the door and home. He could remain at Conjurers Hall; it would allow him to stay close to Oleda, to display his concern for her son's recovery. But he had to be careful not to choose a side, not until he was certain whether Burrage would recover or not. And the rest of the people on the bridge—especially his fellow conjurers—needed to see that he had authority and autonomy, however small a measure.

FAE WATCHED THE sun set and sighed. Even so far from the bridge, they weren't safe. Aric had almost died today. He would have died if she hadn't been able to protect him.

Now she was trying to figure out exactly what she'd done because she needed to be able to do it again. She'd acted instinctively and now, trying to relive it, trying to recall her actions, all she could remember was her fear and terror when Aric had been in danger.

She flipped Keetley Kellen's journal over and stared at the cover. She'd been through this book enough times to know that there was nothing in it about a protective spell like the one she'd created. She hadn't even used words. But all spells were made up of words, weren't they? At least they were according to Keetley Kellen. And why else had all those spells been written down in books?

But Aric's shaman abilities didn't require words. They helped him focus, he said, and could give more force to his thoughts, but it was his *thoughts* that directed the magic, not words.

Had the conjurers gotten it wrong all those generations ago? Or did her magical talent work differently because she was a woman? Or . . . she studied her hands, spreading her fingers. Did she have some tiny amount of Riverman blood in her, something that carried shaman abilities?

She didn't think so. Even a tiny amount of Riverman blood would mean she'd be affected by the curse: she wouldn't be able to breathe either on the bridge or on land.

She closed her eyes and concentrated on what she could remember: using magic to keep Aric safe. She created a spell that enveloped her, concentrating on it protecting her. Was that it? Had she produced a protection spell without any words?

The boat rocked as Aric climbed on board, and her spell slipped away. She'd work more on this spell later. It was too important to ignore or forget.

Aric had been fishing, but not with a net or a line. Instead he was using a sharpened stick.

She worried about him being underwater: what if he had a premonition and stopped swimming? But Aric had told her not to worry, that Rivermen never drowned and a premonition wasn't going to change that.

He dropped down beside her, his wet skin gleaming. He held the pointed end of the stick up to her. Three fish were skewered on it.

"Dinner," he said. He shook his head and drops of water landed on her. "I'm going to tell Rand about spear fishing." He grinned. "It's fun."

"We need to go back," Fae said abruptly.

Aric's smiled faded to a thin line. "Yes. We do." He let out a loud sigh. "I don't want to but I feel that it's time: that it's what we *need* to do." He stood up. "I'll make dinner."

"Thank you." Fae sighed and stared out towards the river mouth. She didn't want to go; didn't want to have to confront what was happening on the bridge. But there was no one else to do it—no one else who *could* do it.

She sighed again. But if she didn't, if *they* didn't, Quillan Wailes would have the new Wailes complete the curse and she would lose Aric. She didn't need shaman abilities to tell her that.

HEWITT SWUNG HIS feet out from under the blankets and placed them on the floor. He usually tried not to look at his feet. For some reason, they—more so than his hands—reminded him of the price he'd paid for being a conjurer. He snorted. And he wasn't even a real conjurer—could *never* be a real conjurer.

He dressed quickly but paused after grabbing his shoes. He reached back into the wardrobe. There. He pulled the old shoes out—the shoes he had worn when he'd started his apprenticeship—and placed them beside his current pair. They were so small that he could hardly believe they'd ever fit his feet.

He placed one old shoe in front of the other. Twice the length. His feet were now twice the length they were when he'd first come to live here all those years ago. And more than twice the width.

He sighed and shook his head. All so he could do small spells that were almost useless. He'd wasted his life up until now. The only way to make all his sacrifices worthwhile would be to restore conjurers to their full power and glory.

He'd been certain that Burrage would be the one; that he could forget about Faelin and concentrate on helping Graylon Burrage become a conjurer as powerful as any who had ever lived. But now the lad was hurt and his ability to do magic possibly ruined forever—all because his mother hated Wailes too much to let the old man die in his own time.

He was almost certain that Graylon had used magic to try to kill Wailes. The Head Conjurer wasn't relevant anymore, didn't the lad see that? All he had to do was master his magic—that would make him the most powerful conjurer in memory. Shiv and his Bridgers would do whatever he asked—including killing Wailes if that was what Oleda Burrage so desperately wanted.

Now a spell had somehow backfired and who knew if Burrage would even recover? And so *he* had to keep looking for Faelin. Initially she might be reluctant do his bidding but she had a kind heart. He didn't think she would waste her time and talent on revenge.

When he arrived at the hall a Bridger politely opened the door for him. Had Shiv told his men to treat him with respect? He must be as unsure as Hewitt about who would eventually be in charge. Was there a way he could he use that to his advantage? He had so few that he couldn't afford to ignore any.

He picked up his pace. Unless the Bridger knew something had happened to Burrage. Had the man recovered? Had he died?

"Oleda my dear," Hewitt said when he spotted her up ahead. "Your son, is he well?"

"Conjurer Hewitt. I have very good news. Graylon woke up this morning ravenous. He has a slight headache but other than that he seems fine. He's resting now." She gestured to the door a few steps away. "I'm afraid I can't have anyone disturb him. Not even you."

"Of course," Hewitt replied. "With your care, I'm sure he'll be back to his studies in no time. Please tell him I wish him a speedy recovery."

"I will," she said. "You've been so kind to us both. Even before."

"I do my best," Hewitt said. So, it seemed that Burrage would recover: he had to assume that meant his magical ability would too. He nodded, thankful that his earlier actions—small kindnesses that had never increased his own danger—were paying off with Oleda and her son. He turned and headed back the way he'd come. Now it was time to see to Wailes.

Quillan Wailes was in even worse shape that he'd expected.

Tymm hovered over the small lump that was the Head Conjurer. He lay in his bed, numerous pillows surrounding him, propping up various parts of his twisted body. Hewitt had to lean in close before he was certain that the man was breathing.

He straightened up and shook his head. He thought Wailes would have preferred to die quickly instead of lingering like this. If he told Burrage and his mother that, would they let Wailes die naturally? He couldn't advise them not to kill Wailes—he wouldn't put his own position at risk for the sake of a few days of half-life for the man. But Wailes' murder could cause trouble with the Bridgers and Hewitt needed them on his side. He couldn't pin all his hopes on Graylon and Oleda Burrage so he needed Shiv's help finding Faelin.

ARIC LOOPED THE line over a tree limb that stretched out over the river. They'd come in at night with the tide. Now dawn was lightening the sky and the tide was going out. A few boats had come out early to fish the marsh ponds, and Aric had almost run them aground trying to stay out of sight. Now he was tying them up as close to shore as he could, hiding them under a canopy of willow branches.

This boat couldn't be seen—it had supposedly been scuttled after the death of his mother. And he still didn't want his and Fae's presence to be known. At least, not by everyone and especially not by anyone on the bridge. One Riverman had already betrayed his mother to Bridgers and Conjurer Wailes; they couldn't take the chance that another one would betray him and Fae.

He brushed a willow frond away and stared out at the river.

He recognized the boats there, of course, but he didn't see the one he was hoping for.

"Any sign of Rand?" Fae asked. She crouched beside him in the stern and held out a mug of tea.

Grateful, he took it, feeling the warmth from the mug spread to his fingers. A chill had settled into him while he waited and watched the river.

"No," he replied, taking a sip. "There are too many boats anyway." They needed to approach Rand alone. Only Rand and Pax knew he and Fae were alive and on his mother's boat.

"If we don't see him, I'll go at dusk," Fae said.

"We talked about this," Aric replied. He didn't want Fae to walk into the Riverman village alone, but he couldn't go with her by land. They should have brought a dory with them when they'd left.

Not having a smaller boat hadn't caused any problems when they'd been out at sea: fishing off the larger boat—casting nets or using a rod—had been simple, and once he'd figured out how to fish with a spear it had been even less of an issue. But now they had no way of reaching the village unseen.

"I never actually agreed to your plan," Fae said. "I know you're a strong swimmer but the village is too far away."

"I'll find a log," Aric replied. "Like when we went past the bridge."

"We almost didn't make it."

"I . . ." Aric paused. "We don't have to decide this minute," he said. "Let's hope we see Rand out in his boat sometime today."

"All right," Fae said.

He looked at her: he wasn't convinced she was as persuaded as she seemed. He sighed. One of them had to go find help and there was no way to know which one should do it. Or was there?

He drained his tea and handed his mug to Fae.

"I'm going to try something," he said. "I'll just be a minute." Nothing in the books he'd inherited from his mother indicated that premonitions were controllable. But what if they were? What if he could trigger one? What if he could trigger a premonition specific to the dilemma they were facing and then *sense* the best option?

Aric sat down facing the riverbank and dangled his feet over the water. He breathed out—one long breath—and concentrated.

He tried to see himself swimming out to Rand's boat but he couldn't even picture it, never mind get a sense of whether or not this was the best course of action. He could see himself sitting by the side of the boat staring out at the river, but he couldn't see himself actually in the water.

Did that mean they didn't see Rand today? That he didn't come this far downriver to fish?

What if Fae went by land? He sighed and pictured her leaving the boat. He felt the distance between them increase and he sensed that it was the right thing to do. But it wasn't what he wanted.

Could they wait another day? He let that thought settle but a twinge of fear swept over him. Trouble if they waited, he thought, but there was no way to know how much.

Aric sighed again and rose to his feet. Fae would be happy. Well, not happy, but she would appreciate him finally agreeing with her. But he would worry about her the whole time she was out of his sight.

HEWITT BECKONED TO Shiv. They were just outside of Wailes' office. Both Graylon and Wailes were still recovering in their own rooms, but Oleda had made herself comfortable. She was sitting behind Wailes' desk, sipping tea and staring out the window towards the Riverman village.

"Head Conjurer Wailes is very weak," Hewitt said when the Bridger came close. "I suspect that he will not live very long."

"Will you take his place?" Shiv asked, and Hewitt thought he heard a hint of worry in his voice. "Conjurer Wailes never said what would happen when he died."

"I expect he planned on outliving us all," Hewitt replied. "And whether I replace him or not very much depends on how fully Graylon recovers." Shiv frowned slightly, more expression than Hewitt had expected him to show. "In either case, I will do my best to keep things steady. For everyone on the bridge, including your people."

"I appreciate it," Shiv said. "We've not always treated you well."

"No, you haven't," Wailes said. "But you can make it up to me. I know Wailes had you searching for the bookbinder's daughter, Faelin Keetley. I want you to continue looking for her. If she's alive, I want her found. And Burrage can't know."

"Master Burrage . . . *Conjurer* Burrage told us to give up that search," Shiv said. "Said it was old Wailes who wanted her dead. Although I think his mother wouldn't mind seeing the girl suffer."

"Faelin is not to be harmed!" Hewitt said.

"Why? What's she to you? And why should I risk my place here for this girl?"

"She's the daughter of a very dear friend," Hewitt said. "And I had asked her to be my apprentice, something that even the Head Conjurer cannot overrule. And that offer still stands." He wasn't about to tell Shiv that Faelin was the only one who might be able to defend them all against Graylon Burrage and his mother. He didn't think the Bridger actually cared who was in charge of the bridge, or what he had to do to be on their side, as long as his people were allowed to stay. The man had been willing to kill his own daughter-in-law so that his son could marry Faelin.

"A female conjurer," Shiv said. "She was a pretty one." Shiv gave him a look that said he thought Hewitt had more than teaching in mind with Faelin. Hewitt kept his expression blank. Let the man think whatever he wanted, as long as he found Faelin.

"I think I can do some looking," Shiv finally said. "This means you owe me."

"Yes," Hewitt said quickly.

"Good," Shiv said. He stepped aside to let Hewitt pass him. "When I have news, I'll let you know."

"Thank you," Hewitt said. He shuddered as he stepped into the room. He hated that he would be in debt to Shiv, but if he found Faelin safe and sound it wouldn't matter. With Faelin—a true conjurer—by his side, Hewitt would be able to control Shiv and his Bridgers.

"Oleda." Hewitt stopped a few paces from the desk where she sat. "I trust that your presence here means that all is well with Graylon?"

"He's resting comfortably, Conjurer Hewitt," Oleda said. "I took him some soup earlier and his appetite was good."

"Excellent." Hewitt took a chair across the desk from her. "But I am concerned about the cause of his collapse. Could he have been overtaxing himself? Or perhaps he misstated a word in a spell?"

A frown flitted across Oleda's face. She carefully put her cup down and looked up at Hewitt. "I do think Conjurer Wailes has been pushing him hard," she said. "It's all so very new to Graylon that he doesn't know when he's been asked to do too much."

"That's probably it," Hewitt said. Wailes had been trying to coach Graylon, although Hewitt expected he'd thought to control him as well. "I've been to see Conjurer Wailes. Do you know what happened to him? Was he too close to Graylon when he recited a spell?"

"That despicable little man!" Oleda said. "He hates that my son has real power. Don't trust anything he says."

"He didn't tell me anything," Hewitt said calmly despite his surprise at the hatred and anger in Oleda's voice. "I'm very much afraid that Head Conjurer Wailes will never say another word in his life." And now he was certain Burrage had been trying to kill Wailes at his mother's request.

"Good," Oleda said. "He has not been kind to either me or my son. He would have been happy if we'd both died so I see no reason to pretend I am not happy now that the circumstances are reversed."

"Understandable, Mistress Burrage," Hewitt said. "Wailes was no friend to me."

Oleda met his gaze and her chin dropped. "That's why I told Graylon to do it," she said. "When he told me about the spell he'd found. I thought he should test it, to make sure it worked, and Wailes deserved what was coming. A killing spell, it was called."

"A killing spell," Hewitt repeated, ignoring Oleda's confession. He was more interested in knowing how much power one must have in order to wield such a spell. And who had created it? "But it did not kill."

"No," Oleda's voice was bitter. "At least not who it was supposed to. It almost killed my son."

"Perhaps when he's well he'll show me the spell," Hewitt said. And the book it came from. Would Burrage be too afraid to try such a spell again? Or would he simply wait until he was stronger—maybe practice with less powerful spells—before he tried it again? As cruel as Quillan Wailes was, he'd never had such terrible power.

"You don't seem shocked," Oleda said quietly. "About what I asked Graylon to do."

"You were protecting your son," Wailes said, trying to sound as sincere as possible. He couldn't risk Oleda seeing him as an enemy. "As any mother would."

"Exactly," she replied with a smile. "I knew you would understand."

Hewitt nodded because he *did* understand. Oleda Burrage held grudges and did not hesitate to retaliate against those she felt had wronged her. And Graylon seemed happy to use his abilities to do whatever his mother asked.

He would have to be very careful to make sure that Oleda didn't find a reason to hate him, or he would be on the receiving end of her vindictiveness.

Shiv had to find Faelin. She may not want to help him, but he didn't think she would want Graylon and Oleda Burrage in charge of the bridge. She'd grown up here—she still had friends on the bridge. If Oleda and her son weren't reined in, sooner or later one of Faelin's friends would end up dead.

Chapter Two

FAE CAREFULLY FELT her way through the tangled roots, testing each step. It was slow, but so little moonlight filtered through the trees that all she could see were shapes and shadows. She couldn't afford to twist her ankle or fall and hurt herself, not when there was so much she and Aric needed to do.

At this rate, she would barely make it to the Riverman village by dawn. Rand hadn't taken his fishing boat out all day, at least not as far downriver as where they'd been hiding, and Aric said that could mean he'd head out at dawn. If Fae didn't reach the village in time—if she missed him and Rand had already left in his boat—she would have to wait until dusk. She sighed. It would mean a long, uncomfortable day along the riverbank making sure no one saw her.

Fae skirted the trunk of a large tree and stepped into a narrow, moonlit meadow that paralleled the river. Willows lined the side of the meadow closest to the river and on the other, pine trees clung to a steep hill. She hurried out into the moonlight, moving more swiftly now that she could see where to place her feet.

She would never say anything to Aric but she'd missed the feel of solid footing, of just walking and not having to steady herself against a rolling deck beneath her. The springy earth wasn't the same as the hard stones of the bridge, but it was stable—and comforting.

She could live on a boat—she *would* live on a boat, with Aric—but there would be times when she would crave something more solid beneath her feet.

The meadow ended and she was back among trees, once again slowly feeling her way forward. The moon was still visible when she finally peered out at the Riverman village.

Rand docked his boat on the outer edge of the village, Aric said, in order to keep his fishing dory close to where he lived. That meant Fae should be able to reach his boat without being seen.

She tentatively stepped down from the bank and into the river. It was cold and her bare foot sank into the muddy bottom. She took a deep breath, placed her other foot in the water, and stared at the village.

She was looking for a blue boat with red trim, but in the dark, the colours were muted; she'd need to be close before she could identify Rand's boat.

Fae waded a few steps before the riverbed fell away and she was forced to swim. Even though the current was sluggish, she struggled to keep from being swept downstream. Her arms were tiring by the time she made it to the outer boats of the village.

The fourth boat she touched was painted the right colours. Fae swam to the closest dock and heaved herself up onto it. The moon was barely visible now, and there were a few streaks of pink in the sky off to the east.

A sliver of light sliced across the deck of a boat in front of her, and Fae froze. The light swung back and forth a few times then it retreated, as whoever carried it headed away from her. She heard the sounds of wood bumping against wood a few moments later and then the light receded.

Once she was sure no one else was around, Fae stepped onto the boat that she hoped belonged to Rand. Keeping to the shadows, she crept towards the small cabin door.

"Rand?" she called softly. "Rand?"

"Who's there?" A voice came from behind the door.

"Rand?" If it wasn't him, if she'd chosen the wrong boat, she'd have to jump back into the river and hope no one saw her.

"It's me. Who's there?"

"Fae," she replied softly. "Aric and I need your help."

The door cracked open, and faint light spilled out onto the deck. "Well, get in here."

Fae scrambled through the door, bumping into Rand. He backed down the stairs, giving Fae enough room to close the door; then she followed him down into the cabin.

"Hang on a second," he said. The light bobbed lower and then a second lamp glowed.

Rand cleared some fishing nets off a bench, and Fae sat down, sliding behind a small table.

"I'll make tea," Rand said. "Too early to hear bad news without it."

He busied himself at a small stove, lighting a flame and setting a pot on the top. He grabbed a mug from the counter and another from the small cupboard above the stove.

The layout of Rand's boat was much the same as Aric's. A few steps led up to the door, and a table, fixed to one wall, was flanked by benches. Across from the table was a small kitchen with stove, sink, and a few cupboards, and beyond that was a door that led to what she assumed was a bedroom. Behind the stairs was a cluttered set of shelves instead of Aric's old bunk.

But in Rand's boat every inch of surface space was covered. Nets, mostly, and ropes that were frayed in places, and what looked like a rolled-up sail on the floor. Rand didn't seem to notice that his bare feet kept bumping into it as he rooted through the items that were strewn across the kitchen counter.

"Tea'll be ready soon," Rand said. He placed the mugs on the table along with a jar of sugar before taking the seat across from her. He met her gaze and nodded. "Not bad news, then. Where's Aric?"

"Not good news either," Fae said. "Aric's on his mother's boat. We couldn't bring it into the village."

"Not when it's supposed to be at the bottom of the sea."

"But we didn't have anything smaller to use to get here," Fae said.

"Berhalla's tits," Rand said. "Excuse my language. We didn't think of that, did we? Shoulda hidden a boat for you so's you could get back here without anyone seeing you. I'll fetch him first thing."

"Thank you," Fae said.

"Sure." Rand poured hot water into the mugs. Black tea leaves floated to the surface. "I might need to stay out a while. So's I actually have some fish to show for taking the boat out."

"Of course," Fae said. She took a sip of tea, its warmth chasing away some of the chill from her damp clothes. But when she put the mug back down, it rattled against the table top as a shiver wracked her body.

"Berhalla's . . ." Rand stopped. "Where are my manners? I'll find you something dry to put on." He slid off the bench and headed towards the door at the back of the boat. In a few moments, he returned with a wrinkled shirt and a pair of faded navy trousers.

"These are clean," Rand said. He patted his stomach. "Don't fit me no more but I keep them around hoping that someday . . . well, they'll do for you until we can get your own clothes washed and dried. Can't hang them outside, though."

Rand gulped the last of his tea and put his mug by the stove. "I'm off to get Aric," he said. "Feel free to use my bed." He nodded and headed up the stairs.

Fae had already peeled off her wet clothes by the time she felt the boat dip as he stepped off it.

Once changed, Fae settled with her back against the hull and her blanket-wrapped legs stretched out across the bench. She closed her eyes and ignored her rumbling stomach.

She'd decided not to use Rand's bed because it felt too intrusive, so she'd opted to stay out here. Besides, she was tired enough that where she slept didn't matter.

HANDS HIDDEN IN the sleeves of his robe, Hewitt looked around the room. Burrage had only been out of his sick bed for a few hours and he'd already made some changes to Wailes' office. The desk had been moved closer to the window, and the only books on the bookshelf had the Wailes binding. He'd have to find out what had happened to the rest of the books. Faelin would need the Kellen spells, once she was found.

"Are you going to follow the tradition?" Hewitt asked.

Burrage looked up from the book he was studying and blinked. "Tradition?"

"Yes," Hewitt continued. "It's tradition for a conjurer to take the name of one of the original Seven. And it would be even more appropriate in your case, since you truly have Wailes blood."

"If you had said that to me before I found this book I would have been angry," Burrage said. "The current Wailes does not deserve the honour of me taking his name. But this Wailes." He tapped a finger on the page in front of him. "This Wailes was incredibly powerful."

"Following the tradition would help legitimize you," Hewitt said. "In the eyes of the people who live on the bridge."

"Placate them, you mean," Burrage said.

Hewitt inclined his head. "If you prefer to call it that. It's important to show that things are getting back to normal, after so much upheaval. Too much change is not good for business."

"Why should I care about business?" Burrage asked. He jabbed a finger at the page before him. "Do you have any idea how powerful these spells are? How deadly?"

"A little," Hewitt said. "Because trying to use one of them almost cost you your life. And business is what keeps people fed and occupied. Do you really want the Bridgers bored and hungry? They're barely controllable now."

"I don't care," Burrage said. "They won't hurt me or my mother."

Hewitt plastered a smile on his face and forced himself to remain calm. The boy didn't even see how easy he would be to kill. Yesterday he'd been too feeble to get out of bed, let alone perform a spell. Did he think Shiv hadn't noticed? Did he think that because he had strong magic everyone else was completely powerless?

Wailes had been terrorising the bridge for years without much more than the ability to speak. And control the Bridgers.

"That's true," Hewitt said. Doing anything other than agreeing with him would only antagonise Burrage. He had no wish to die today. "You asked to see me?"

"Yes," Burrage said. He ran a hand across the book in front of him. "I think I found what Wailes was looking for."

"What Wailes . . ." Hewitt stopped and stared at the book on the table. Wailes had been looking for a cure to his affliction. Had Burrage really found it? Could it help him or would it only help a Wailes? But a true Wailes—a conjurer with the blood—wouldn't need the cure, would he? Could he convince him to use it on him?

"In this book?" Hewitt asked. "Are you sure?"

"Yes," Burrage said. "It was a Wailes curse; even the old Riverman shaman said that." He smiled. "Right before she died."

"A curse," Hewitt repeated. Not the cure: Burrage wasn't

looking for ways to help people; he was looking for ways to hurt them, to control them, to exact his revenge on them.

He wanted—*needed*—Burrage to be a great conjurer: a conjurer who would leave behind works of huge importance, who would have a legacy of creation, not destruction. The bridge itself was a lasting symbol of the most powerful conjurers of the past; conjurers whose names had never been forgotten—men of power who weak men had named themselves after for generations.

Could he convince Burrage to aspire to that rather than waste his talents by destroying the Rivermen and reciting killing curses? And if he couldn't, was there a way to stop him, even without Faelin?

"I don't think it's the exact curse," Burrage said. "But it's close. It could be an earlier version of it. This book is filled with such elegant, powerful . . . useful spells." He met Hewitt's eyes and Hewitt had to supress a shudder. "But I will need help," Burrage continued. "Someone who can read and document all of the spells in this book." His gaze sharpened. "Someone who knows better than to try to use one of them."

"Of course," Hewitt said. He paused. "But there are few left who can read. Shall I see if the Tadlow apprentice is available?"

"Make him available," Burrage said. "I am not interested in waiting for him to finish whatever pitiful work he is doing for his master."

"I will see to it," Hewitt said. There was an opportunity here, he could sense it. He'd have a conversation with Meade Tadlow before he sent him to Burrage. At the very least it would be helpful to have another set of eyes at Conjurers Hall. And give him time to understand how to use this to his advantage. He quickly left Wailes'—no—*Burrage's* office.

Aric *knew* Fae was safe—not only had Rand told him but he'd *felt* it. But he was still relieved when he saw her sleeping on the bench. He dropped some fish by the sink and turned to watch her.

Her head leaned against the hull, at the back of the bench, her hands clutching a blanket. When he gently pulled the blanket up to her chin, Fae stirred, but didn't wake.

He was tired as well. He hadn't slept since she'd left the boat— hadn't even tried—not when she'd been out in the dark, alone.

Just before dawn, Rand had rowed into his view, and Aric had quickly swum out to meet him. Then he'd spent hours huddled in the bottom of Rand's boat, hiding while he fished. Finally, Rand decided that his catch was big enough that he could to return to the village without arousing anyone's suspicions.

He understood Rand's caution, but waiting those extra hours to see Fae; to have proof that she was safe, had made him worried and tense.

He sniffed his shirt. He stank. The tarp he'd hidden under also covered the catch. After helping Aric sneak onto his boat, Rand left to finish some chores and then find Pax. And now that it was day, Aric and Fae would need to stay hidden below deck.

He opened the door to the bedroom. Rand had said to help himself to clean clothes so he did, rummaging through a cupboard for some trousers and a shirt. They were too big on him, but they were dry. He brought his damp clothes out into the main room and tossed them on top of Fae's. He'd wash them all later.

Fae was still asleep so Aric picked a knife up off the cluttered counter. He'd wake her once he had the fish gutted and cleaned. They couldn't risk a fire—couldn't risk anyone noticing smoke coming from Rand's boat when he wasn't on it. But they didn't have to, not when Fae could cook using magic.

"You should have woken me when you came in," Fae said from behind him.

"You needed the sleep." Aric grabbed a cloth and wiped his hands on it before turning to her. He lifted Fae's feet and sat down on the bench with her feet in his lap.

"So do you," Fae replied. She yawned as she sat up and leaned against the hull of the boat.

"After we eat," he said. "I've done my part. Now you need to cook the fish. Unless you want to try it the Riverman way?" He'd grown up eating raw fish—some types of fish were even better raw—but Fae hadn't. "And there's water in the kettle. Can you heat it for tea?"

"All right." Fae pulled her feet off him and gently pushed him off the bench. "Let me up."

"When is Rand due back?" Fae asked him.

"I'm not sure. He was going to talk to Pax but he had to get him alone."

They'd eaten and Aric had tidied up. And more than just the mess they'd made cooking and eating.

Rand's boat had been cluttered, although it had been reasonably clean underneath his scattered gear. Now the main cabin was organised and he was just finishing laundering his and Fae's wet clothes. He twisted his wet shirt, wringing as much water out of it as he could before hanging it beside Fae's on a hook near the door.

"Should we try to look for the conjurer?"

"We can," Aric replied. He sat across from Fae. Her hands were on the table and he picked them up and held them. "Just to see if he's alive or not."

"Let's hope not," Fae said.

Aric concentrated on the feel of Fae's hands in his as he cleared his mind. He felt a whisper of power—Fae had created a small spell. He tried to follow it as it sped off, but it was too fast. He felt a sharp tug, and then his connection to both the spell and Fae was broken. He looked down as she pulled her hands from his.

"He's still alive," she said.

"I'm not surprised," Aric replied. "If he was dead I think I would have sensed the lack of danger."

"So." Fae pulled a blanket up to her chin. "I suppose I'll be going to Waglenn Landing after all."

"When you're ready," Aric said.

"I have to go," Fae said.

"I know. I'm not simply trying to delay you. I'm trying to make sure you return to me." He'd already lost this argument with her. She would go—because he couldn't—but he wanted her to be prepared.

To him, that meant that she had to create spells that would keep her safe. He also wanted them to explore—and hopefully strengthen—their magical link. And he wanted them both to have all the news from the bridge and both towns that they were able to get.

They had time, he sensed that.

THE BOAT LISTED to one side and Fae met Aric's eyes across the table. Someone had just stepped on board. When there was no corresponding dip of someone leaving, of someone simply using

Rand's boat to get from one place to another, he gestured to Fae, and she slid off the bench, taking the journal with her. She stepped into the small bedroom and closed the door, leaving it open just enough for her to see Aric.

Someone spoke too softly for her to understand but she heard Aric's quiet reply, and she opened the door wide enough to see Rand come down the stairs, followed by Pax Oldham.

"You can come out, Fae," Pax said, his voice low. "We have news."

Aric slid along the bench, making room for her, and she sat down beside him.

"From the bridge?" she asked.

"From Bridgers," Pax replied. "Asking about you."

"Just me? Do they think Aric is dead?" The reason they'd pretended to scuttle Sigrun's boat was to make everyone— including the Rivermen—think he'd disappeared after his mother's death.

"Just you," Pax replied. "And it were an odd request. Word was sent through the fishmonger. Well, not the actual fishmonger. A Bridger was sent to pick up the catch. I was there personally, just as I have been since . . . Well, since one of our own betrayed one of our own." Pax frowned and shook his head. "Never thought to see that happen. Anyway, I been going every day, and every day the fishmonger is there to inspect and pay for his catch."

"But not today," Fae said.

"Not today," Pax agreed. "Today it were a Bridger. An important one too. Always hanging around Wailes. He was there *that* day."

Pax didn't need to explain what day he meant. "It was probably Shiv," she said. "He's in charge of the Bridgers. Or one of his sons."

"Didn't tell me his name, just that he'd kill me if I told anyone on the bridge what he was asking about. He wants you, Faelin Keetley. Called you by your full name, too."

"He told you not to tell anyone on the bridge?" Aric asked. He turned to Fae. "What do you think?"

"It has to be Hewitt," Fae said. "If it was Wailes, Shiv wouldn't care who knew he was looking for me. And Wailes was looking for *both* of us, not just me. Pax, do you know what's happened on the bridge? Is Wailes still in charge?"

"That's the odd thing," Pax said. "I been talking to the fishmonger, and he says the old crippled conjurer hasn't been seen in a while. That there's a younger man who seems to be in favour. He was on the stairs the day Sigrun . . . anyway, he was there. This lad's mother has been all over the bridge, making demands like she's mistress of everything."

"Oleda Burrage," Fae said.

"The one who kidnapped you?" Aric said. "The one with the son you were supposed to marry?"

"It must be," Fae said. Her heart sank. There was only one reason why Oleda would be making demands. "Graylon, her son, must be the conjurer. He must be the new Wailes." And if that was true, they already considered her an enemy.

"But you think Hewitt is the one asking about you," Aric said. "Would he be on our side?"

"Hewitt," Fae said. "He'll be on his own side. As always. But we might be able to use him." She tapped a finger against the journal's whaleskin binding. "I should meet him and find out what he wants."

"No!" Aric said. "It's too dangerous."

Fae sighed. "Not knowing what's happening on the bridge is also dangerous." She met Aric's worried gaze. "You can feel that, can't you?"

He nodded and looked away. "Yes. Doing nothing feels worse."

"What do you mean?" Pax asked. "How does it feel worse?"

"Shaman senses," Aric said. "I am my mother's son."

"You are a shaman," Pax said. It was a statement, not a question. "Sigrun said she thought so but I wasn't sure if I could believe her." Pax ran a hand across his forehead. "I wish I could tell the folk. Some have been worried since Sigrun died. Never been without a shaman before, and people are uneasy."

"I could tell a few," Rand said. "Some I know I can trust."

"I'd rather you didn't," Aric said. "At least not until after Fae has met with Hewitt."

"So you agree," Fae said. She was . . . not relieved exactly, but grateful that she didn't have to fight him on this. They had to know what Hewitt wanted with her. And why now? She and Aric had been away for weeks, so what had happened?

"I guess," Aric replied. "I don't like it, and you can't go until I know I can help from here."

"Yes." She wanted to be prepared as well, but she knew they didn't have weeks to practice their magic together. If they were lucky they had a few days.

"Where will you meet him?" Pax said. "Conjurer Hewitt? I can get a message to the Bridger through the fishmonger. Maybe you can meet in a boat? Or at the bottom of the stairs?"

"No. I don't want them to know I'm here," Fae said. "I'll go to Waglenn Landing. I know someone who I think will help. I'll have them send the message to Shiv. I'll say I've been upriver this whole time and pretend I'm going to Hewitt of my own accord."

"Will he believe it?" Aric asked.

"If he chooses to," Fae replied. "Enough to be willing to come meet me." She reached for Aric's hand. "And I'll make sure I can handle him no matter what he might be planning."

"That *we* can handle him," Aric said.

THERE WAS A sharp rap on his door, and it rattled when someone tried to open it. Hewitt hurried over to it. He'd been locking his door even when he was home: he didn't trust anyone enough to allow them to simply walk into his home. But that didn't mean there weren't some visitors he didn't want standing out in front of his door for the whole bridge to see.

It was Tadlow. Hewitt stepped aside to let the man enter before he leaned out to check the street. The cobblestones were empty; he closed and re-locked the door. If someone was watching his house, they were well-hidden. So probably not Bridgers. Hiding would reduce the impact of their favourite weapon—fear.

"You have news?" Hewitt asked as he followed Tadlow into his office. The other conjurer sat down heavily, and Hewitt circled his desk to sit facing him.

"The things Meade has been telling me," Tadlow said with a shake of his head. "Of all the conjurers, why did it have to be another Wailes?" He reached into his robe, pulled out a book, and dropped it on the desk.

"Evil tendencies do seem to be a trait, whether they have the blood or are simply bearing the name." Hewitt snatched the book up and shoved it into the back of his bookshelf. This was the third book with whaleskin binding he'd been given.

Hewitt had told Tadlow and his apprentice, Meade, about the conjurer bloodlines—that Meade would die if he attempted to use any of the spells he came across in his work for Burrage. In exchange, he was supplying Kellen spell books. But he hadn't told Tadlow about Faelin. He'd only told Maykin about her.

"This ancient Wailes conjurer was cruel, or insane, or both," Tadlow said. "But Meade says he was a genius as well. The spells are very powerful, and some are broken into two, three, or even four sections in order to magnify the affect." He shook his head. "And the atrocities! Burning people alive feet first so that they feel and see the flames rising towards them: tearing fingers and toes off one by one: suffocating people by slowly collapsing their lungs."

"That last one," Hewitt said. "It sounds like what happens to Rivermen when they step onto land."

"Meade showed that one to Burrage," Tadlow said. "It's not the curse that was used on the Rivermen—that's what Burrage has Meade looking for—but Burrage was delighted with it anyway."

"Is there anything to explain why such destructive spells were created?" Hewitt asked. Conjurers had been noble, hadn't they? The Kellen journal implied that they had been forces for good. Why had this Wailes conjurer done so much harm?

"Not that Meade has found," Tadlow replied. "We have no way of knowing whether any of these terrible spells were used, other than the Riverman curse, but we don't think so."

"Let's hope it stays that way," Hewitt said.

"I'll not wager on that," Tadlow said. "Mistress Burrage has a temper and no patience. And a son who does whatever she asks."

"I'll talk to Burrage again," Hewitt said. "But she has such power over him."

"And he has such power over us."

"For now," Hewitt said. Tadlow raised his brows, but Hewitt shook his head. He still had no idea where Faelin was, or if she would help. He glanced at his bookcase. But he was ready. Although he was starting to worry that she wouldn't be a match for Burrage and his book of terrible Wailes spells: not if she had to rely on these stolen spells.

"You should tell at least one of us," Tadlow said. "If not me then someone else. In case something were to happen to you."

"I will think on it," Hewitt said. He couldn't very well tell Tadlow that he'd already chosen Maykin to confide in. But it was good to know that Maykin had kept his knowledge of Faelin to himself.

Conjurers had to become great and powerful again. That was the only thing that would make his life—his sacrifice to the pathetic Hewitt spells—have any meaning.

Hewitt would be willing to work with Burrage but he wasn't sure he could manage or trust his mother. Unfortunately, Oleda was willing to use her son's power—ruin her son's potential to be great—in order to exact revenge against those who she felt had slighted her. And so far, Graylon had shown a willingness to satisfy his mother. He would demean his conjurer legacy and waste his great power on pettiness and spite.

It was time to set another plan in place.

"Can you ask Meade to do me a favour?" Hewitt asked. "If it's possible, I would like him to add a spell—one from a whaleskin bound book—to this Wailes book of curses. He must be careful to match the writing, of course. And make the name of the spell compelling."

"Ah, Hewitt, clever man." Tadlow clapped his hands together. "We wondered what these other spell books were for. I'll ask Meade to come up with a spell name that Burrage won't be able to resist trying out. Then we'll be rid of him."

"Not yet," Wailes said. "There is no immediate threat."

"All right," Tadlow said. "If you think it best to wait."

"Yes. Wailes still clings to life. I would prefer to see which way the wind blows when he dies. Will Burrage and his mother force their way to power or will they allow us to elect our own leader?"

"You think they will allow us to do that?"

"No," Hewitt replied. "But if we have elected a leader and Burrage seizes that role for himself, the rest of the bridge will know the truth."

"He will simply rule through fear," Tadlow said. "The same as Wailes."

"But Wailes had our backing before he had the Bridgers," Hewitt said. "And he did nothing to antagonize the merchants. From all accounts, Oleda Burrage has made enemies of everyone."

Tadlow left and Hewitt remained sitting in the dark. If Burrage was a lost cause, was there a chance to preserve the bloodline? Would he be able to talk Oleda into accepting any of the young women of the bridge as her daughter-in-law? Would any of the most suitable women want anything to do with Oleda and her son? Perhaps he could get rid of Oleda and manage Burrage himself? He sighed.

There was no way to know what Burrage would do if his mother died from anything other than a natural death. He had a book full of the most terrifying spells known. Hewitt couldn't risk that he would use them to find out who had caused his mother's death. To find *him*. And then kill him in a terrible, horrifying way.

Chapter Three

ARIC CLOSED HIS eyes and concentrated on Fae. She was close—neither one of them had been off of Rand's boat since they'd arrived—but she'd left him in the bedroom a few minutes ago. Now he was attempting to figure out where she was by contacting her through the magic.

He got an impression of a dark, enclosed space. Not the closet. Mentally he pulled back, trying to feel through her hands. Wood, and rope and . . . the smell of fish. He smiled. He knew where she was. He pictured the locker on deck, where Rand kept his extra nets. There was a short burst of magic from Fae, telling him that he was right.

The boat rocked slightly in response to Fae moving on deck.

"That was the first time I smelled anything," Aric said when he met her in the main cabin. "Fish, of course."

"Are you sure it was from where I was?" Fae asked. "Everything smells of fish around here."

"Not that strong," Aric said. He looped an arm around Fae and kissed her. She sighed and leaned into him. "And not in the bedroom."

"Thankfully," Fae said.

For the past few days, Rand had returned in the evening with dinner—usually fresh fish and seaweed or clams and cattails from the marshes. After eating with them he'd leave them alone on the dark boat. He didn't seem to mind staying with his brother, and Aric felt bad about taking over the man's boat, but he was grateful for the privacy. And not just so that they could enjoy their relationship: it seemed that the closer he and Fae were emotionally, the less they needed to be in physical contact in order to reach each other through magic. Which meant he'd be able to help keep her safe when she went to meet with Hewitt.

They still both had to be concentrating on reaching out in order to make a connection, but their skills were improving quickly. A few more days of this and they'd be ready . . . he shivered, and he lost his train of thought. He felt as though he was hovering above the two of them. It was another premonition, and this time he was aware that he was having it.

He and Fae had been practicing so much with magic that he instinctively tried to take control of it. He saw flashes of images and heard snatches of conversations but he couldn't quite make them come into focus. He turned to Fae and almost lost his hold on the magic when he saw the shadow that overlaid her worried expression.

Frightened for her, he focussed on one thing—how to keep her safe. He saw another flashing image, but this one was clearer: a man walking on cobblestones, just his feet visible. But he knew who it was from those oversized feet.

"Hewitt," Aric gasped. The vision cleared, and he gulped in a breath. Fae leaned over him, worried.

"What about Hewitt?" she asked.

"You need to see him." As soon as he said the words he realized the urgency. "Now."

"Is tomorrow soon enough?"

Aric closed his eyes and tried to feel if Fae's question meant more danger. He didn't think so. "Yes," he replied. "But if it's later than tomorrow it may not matter."

"Why not?" Fae asked. "Why won't it matter?"

Aric tried to remember what he'd felt during his premonition, why he'd said that. He shook his head. "I don't know. Sorry."

"That's all right," Fae replied. She touched her forehead to his, and he felt their connection solidify. "I'll leave before dawn."

"Yes," Aric said and sighed. "Did I say anything else? In my premonition?"

"No," Fae said. "You stopped talking and your eyes didn't

focus. Then you said Hewitt's name."

"I tried to take hold of the premonition," he said. "It was magic, just like what we've been using to contact each other. But most of it wasn't clear." He rubbed a hand across his forehead. "I guess I shouldn't do that again. I might have stopped myself from saying something important."

"Maybe only try that when no one is around to hear you," Fae replied. "You did get something."

"Yes, but was it the important part?" Aric shook his head. There was no way to know. Maybe even the most skilled shamans from the past—like Zevach—had never known. "You should leave the journal here," he said to Fae.

"Is that from your premonition?"

"No," Aric replied. "I just think it might be better to not let Hewitt know how much we know."

"I need to let him know something," Fae said. "I'll tell him I have a copy, that I made it using my father's spell."

Aric closed his eyes. "Yes, that seems right. He needs to know you have potential, not that you are a fully trained conjurer."

"He might have guessed," Fae said. "If I admit that I have the journal he'll know I've read it. That I know I have Kellen blood."

"But even if you triggered the lessons on how to create spells in the book he has, only you can read them," Aric replied. Even with his shaman skills, Aric couldn't read the hidden writing. "If he knew you could create spells he might see you as a threat to him and his plans. I want you to come back to me."

"I do too," Fae agreed. "I'll pretend I don't know how to create spells. But I will find out what Burrage is up to and if possible, what skills he has."

THE SUN HAD risen by the time she looked out on half a dozen small houses made of weathered wood. A few chickens pecked at the ground, and a goat cropped grass at the side of the road. A light was on in one of the houses, and Fae kept her head down as she hurried past it.

She paused before stepping into the square. A few market stands near the bridge gates seemed to be open this early, but she wasn't planning on getting close enough to the bridge to be recognized.

She walked along the perimeter of the square, past a few of the large houses that lined it. They were the finest houses she'd seen so far—an important man like the head of the council would live in one of them, wouldn't he?

Halfway back to her starting point she noticed a woman hurrying towards the bridge gate. Had she been recognized? Was the woman going to fetch Bridgers? Without pausing, Fae climbed the stairs to the nearest house. Keeping an eye on the woman by the bridge, she knocked.

After a few moments, the door swung open.

"Can I help you?" a woman asked. Middle-aged, she wore a dressing gown and a frown.

"I'm sorry to disturb you," Fae said. "But I was told Councilman Larwood lives here."

"Who told you that? The councilman lives three houses that way." She pointed in the direction Fae had come from. "The house with the green door."

"Thank you," Fae said. The door closed, and Fae headed back down the stairs. She looked across the square and blew out a breath. The woman she'd thought might be reporting her to Bridgers was at a stall near the bridge gates, her head down as she searched the goods on the table in front of her.

Fae calmly walked towards the house the woman had indicated.

Another knock, another woman opening a door, this time a green one.

"I'm looking for Councilman Larwood," Fae said.

"Are you?" the woman asked. "He's not expecting anyone."

"No," Fae said. "But I hope he will see me. My name is Faelin Keetley, and he and I have met."

The woman blinked once, then stepped aside to allow Fae room to enter the house. "It's early, but he's in his office." She closed the door and headed down a hallway.

Fae followed her to an open door. After a quiet conversation, the woman gestured for Fae to enter the room.

"Councilman Larwood," Fae said once she stepped into his office. "I hope you remember me."

Larwood got to his feet. "Don't let anyone else in," he said to the woman. She arched her brows but backed out, closing the door behind her. "My wife told me the name you gave her but I wasn't certain it really was you," Larwood said. He came to stand in front of Fae. "Bookbinder's daughter, I trust your friend is well?"

Fae met the man's eyes. Should she trust him? He'd helped her and Aric once—would he help again? She nodded. She and Aric had already had this conversation. She wouldn't be here if Aric hadn't felt that they could trust the councilman.

"Yes," she said. "He's fine. Although he is not able to leave the river."

"Terrible thing. So much hate for someone to do that to generations of people," Larwood said. He gestured to a chair. "Please sit."

Fae sat and surveyed the room while Larwood returned to his own chair. Based on the outside of the house, she supposed this might be considered a small room, although it was almost as large as her old workroom in the book bindery.

She sighed. She hadn't thought of her workroom in weeks. The books lined up on the shelves here reminded her of it—of the work she'd done in it. A window behind Larwood looked out at a white wooden fence, and a cool breeze blew in, rustling some of the papers on the desk. Larwood quickly stacked the papers and set a glass paperweight on top.

"Many people are interested in you," Larwood said.

"People have asked you about me?" Fae asked. "From the bridge?" Larwood nodded and Fae leaned forward. "I hope we didn't get you into trouble with Head Conjurer Wailes and his Bridgers."

"Not really," Larwood said. "Wailes was angrier at my refusal to hand him young men who could read. And for that I thank you." Larwood shook his head. "Durnham was not so lucky. Besides, it wasn't Wailes who came here asking about you. It was Conjurer Hewitt."

"Hewitt came here?" Fae was shocked. Conjurers rarely left the bridge. "Asking about me? When was that?"

"A few weeks ago now. He was asking about the Riverman as well."

"I see," Fae said. She did a calculation. He was probably here just after Sigrun was killed. The question was, why? "What did you tell him?" Had Hewitt somehow known that she was downriver?

"That I helped you get upriver."

"Thank you," Fae said. "Can you get word to Conjurer Hewitt? And if I could impose, could you have him come here again? To meet with me?" If Hewitt had been willing to come here once, he might again.

Larwood scowled. "It would have to be important to the safety of Waglenn Landing for me to ask him back here," he said. "When he was in town, he invited a lad to visit him on the bridge. The boy went one day and hasn't been seen since."

"You think the boy is dead," she said. Had Hewitt become a killer? Would it change what she needed to do? No. She already didn't trust Hewitt but she needed him. Knowing that he might have had a part in a boy's death didn't change that.

"Yes," Larwood said. "The same thing happened to four Durnham lads. Went to the bridge and never came back. No explanation given, no compensation to the families. It's despicable."

"One of them is still alive," Fae said. "Graylon Burrage."

"How did you know that?" Larwood asked. "I only found out because his mother has been to the market out by the gate, lording it over everyone."

"I've met Oleda," Fae said. "She was married to my mother's cousin, but she's a widow now."

"Faelin Keetley," Larwood said. "Everything circles back to you."

"Unfortunately," Fae agreed. "Which is why I need to speak to Conjurer Hewitt. I believe that everyone's safety—in the towns, on the river, and on the bridge—depends on this meeting."

"I see," Larwood said. "I will insist that you tell me everything, you know. Then I will decide if this is in the best interests of Waglenn Landing."

"Yes," Fae replied without a pause. "I will tell you everything." Except about her and Aric.

"Good. I'd like my wife to hear as well."

COUNCILMAN LARWOOD AND his wife listened for half an hour before sending a note asking Conjurer Hewitt to come visit.

Once that was done, Fae decided that it was time to tell them the truth about conjurers.

"Graylon Burrage carries Wailes blood," she said. "That's why he's not dead. Conjurers are born before they are made. I learned that from a journal that I found along with all of the spell books. A conjurer must carry the blood of one of the ten families but not everyone of the blood has the talent to become a conjurer."

"One of ten?" Larwood asked. "I thought there were only seven conjurers."

"There are only seven now," Fae said. "Three of the families let their name die out when they stopped having sons."

"But this Graylon Burrage has the blood of one of the conjurer families?" Larwood said. "That makes him the most powerful man on the bridge."

"Or off it," Mistress Larwood added. "That's why his mother was so self-important when she was at the market. She thinks no one can stop her son."

"And no one can," Fae said. "Except me. I also carry the blood of one of the Ten. And I have an advantage. The journal I spoke of was more than one man's musings. There was a spell that had some sort of trigger, and once I activated it, I found that it contained instructions on how to create spells: on how to become a conjurer."

"So, you," Larwood said, "are a conjurer? I thought you said Hewitt had the journal, so how did you activate it?"

"He has it," Fae replied. "At least he has a copy. I copied it using the spell my father told me as he was dying. And that was the trigger. Me using Kellen magic is what triggered the spell on the journal that let me read the rest."

"You can do magic?" Larwood asked. "Hewitt told me he'd asked you to be his apprentice. Does he know you can do magic? Is that why he asked you?"

"No," Fae said. "He knows my father left me the spell—he was there—but he doesn't know I've learned how to do magic. But I need to see him. I need to understand what skills Burrage has acquired; what spells he can do and whether he can create new ones or only recite existing ones. And I need to know if he's been through all of the books and found the rest of the curse." She leaned forward. "Burrage is a Wailes conjurer. That means he can complete the curse on the Rivermen."

"Complete the curse?" Mistress Larwood asked. "You mean they were supposed to be worse off than they are? What kind of man would want to do that?"

"That's what I need to know," Fae said. "I've met both Graylon

Burrage and his mother, and I think he is exactly the type of man who would complete the curse. And if he is, then he must be stopped."

SOMEONE WAS HITTING the side of the boat. No, wait. Aric cocked his head. The thumping restarted, and this time he recognized the pattern. The signal!

He jumped up and the book he was reading dropped to the floor. He scooped it up along with the other two, lifted the table, and shoved them into the space below. He'd made this hiding hole to match the one in his mother's boat—just in case. Which was the same reason why he and Rand had worked out the distress signal Rand was currently drumming on the side of the boat.

Aric hurried past the stove, touching it briefly. It was cool; thank Berhalla, so Rand wouldn't have to explain why the stove on his boat had been used recently when he'd been out fishing since dawn.

At the top of the steps, he knelt and eased the door open a crack. He caught sight of Rand on deck, taking his time tying up his dory. Rand gestured with his chin even while he raised a hand in greeting to whoever was heading his way. Aric darted out the door and to the far side of the boat.

He slipped over the edge of the deck and, with his hands on the gunwales, gently lowered himself into the river, sucking in a breath when the cold water reached his chest. He didn't hear any shouts: there were no sounds of people running across the boat towards him. With a worried glance at the boat deck above, he swam to the prow, away from Rand and his mysterious visitor.

He treaded water for a few minutes, staring out at the riverbank. Then he took a deep breath and submerged, skimming along the bottom of the river as he swam. His lungs were burning when he finally surfaced below an overhanging willow. He drew in air slowly, trying not to gasp, and hung onto a branch until his breathing steadied.

He peered back out at the river. He'd have to get higher if he was going to see what was happening on the deck of Rand's boat. He pulled himself along the tree branch until he reached a wider section. Moving slowly, he hauled himself up until he straddled the limb. His feet dangled in the water as he leaned over and peered out through the waving fronds.

It wasn't a Riverman. A Bridger faced Rand on his boat deck, and even from this far away, Aric could see that he wasn't happy.

"I don't have to do anything," Rand said, his voice raised. "You don't run things here."

Curtains twitched on the windows of a few boats close by, and a couple of men stepped onto the nearest dock, fishing gaffs in hand.

"You know the girl," the Bridger said. "You helped her. I want to know where she is."

"I plucked her from the sea," Rand said. "Saved her from drowning. Other than that, I don't know her or where she is."

"Then what about the shaman's son? I hear they are close," the Bridger said. "And don't tell me you don't know *him*."

Aric shivered. Who was looking for him? Was it Wailes? Or maybe Hewitt? It couldn't be Burrage—he didn't even know Aric existed, did he?

"Shaman's son is upriver," Rand said. "Has been for weeks. Don't even know if the lad knows his mother's dead." He spat towards the Bridger's feet. "Your Conjurer Wailes killed her. Scum."

"Watch your mouth," the Bridger growled.

"What, you gonna kill me too? That's the worst you can do. And then the rest of them'll kill you." Rand gestured to the now sizable group of Rivermen who had gathered to watch.

"The Head Conjurer will finish the curse," the Bridger said.

"That threat don't work," Rand replied. "None of your conjurers has the magic to do that."

"Our new one does. The girl, where is she?"

"I'll say it again, I don't know."

"I need to search your boat."

"What! No, you will not." Rand blocked the Bridger when he tried to step onto the boat but the Bridger shoved Rand to his knees. He was through the door before Rand could regain his feet. Rand scowled as he got up but he waved the angry Rivermen off before they stepped onto his boat. A few minutes later, the Bridger came back out onto the deck.

"No one's there," he said.

"Course not," Rand replied. He wiped a hand across his face. "I already told you I don't know where the girl is."

"You better not be lying," the Bridger said. He looked around, and for a moment, Aric worried that he'd been spotted, but the Bridger turned to glare at the group of watching Rivermen before marching away.

"How'd he even get over here?" one of the men said as he approached Rand.

"Dunno, but I'm gonna find out," Rand said. "We better not have another traitor."

"Someone should tell Pax," the other Riverman said. "I'll go. You need to look at that cut lip."

"Thanks," Rand said. "But this Bridger attacked me and searched my boat. I'll talk to Pax."

Once the others had gone, Rand looked towards Aric's hiding spot and shook his head. Aric took that to mean he should stay where he was for a while. He would have done that anyway. Someone with a boat had brought that Bridger here.

A moment later, Rand stepped off his boat. Aric lost sight of him after he crossed a dock heading towards the centre of the village.

"WE NEED TO figure out what to do about Burrage," Maykin said. "Wailes will be dead soon and I want nothing more than to live in peace."

Hewitt looked from Maykin to Tadlow to Sherston before settling his gaze on Yaldon. The other four conjurers had been waiting for him when he'd returned from a fruitless visit to Burrage. Not that he'd actually seen Burrage; instead he'd been forced to spend half an hour simpering over the mother.

"Keep your voice down," Hewitt said. "We don't have a legitimate reason for all of you to visit me at the same time, and Burrage and his mother are suspicious of everyone."

"I have one," Tadlow said. "A legitimate reason for being here. We are discussing the election of a new Head Conjurer."

"Wailes isn't dead." Hewitt glanced at the door, worried that any moment Shiv would burst through with his knife drawn. All the time he'd spent convincing Burrage and his mother that he was on their side could amount to nothing because of this one meeting.

"Not yet," Tadlow said. "But he will be soon. Even the Bridgers realize that."

"Yes, but we need to be careful," Hewitt said. He wished he'd never told any of them anything. Would it result in his death?

"Not about this," Tadlow continued. "You said you wanted to wait for Wailes to die so you could know what Burrage would do. The rest of us talked about it, and we want our selection known before Wailes dies."

"Why?"

"So we can force Burrage's hand," Maykin replied. "And so that all of the bridge knows our choice. It will make it more difficult for him to stand against us."

"He doesn't care about the people of the bridge," Hewitt said. "And the Bridgers will do anything—even kill all the rest of us—in order to stay on the bridge." He met each set of eyes except for Sherston, who still wore bandages. He settled on Maykin, who nodded slightly.

Hewitt sighed. It was done already. Burrage could know about this meeting any time now, and the conjurers fighting amongst themselves would only weaken them.

"We choose a new head conjurer then," he said. "We'll say it's temporary, just until Wailes has recovered."

"He won't recover," Sherston said. "Isn't that what we just talked about?"

"We can't make it permanent," Hewitt said. "Oleda Burrage will hate this enough as it is. I'll have to convince her that we are not taking anything away from her son, but rather that we are preparing a mentor for the lad."

"You think it should be you?" Tadlow asked. "Have you set yourself up to be the new Head Conjurer?"

"Not at all," Hewitt said. He *already* was a mentor to the mother and son but it was getting increasingly difficult to keep the Burrages' trust. And he wasn't certain he ever wanted to be named Head Conjurer while they were alive. He feared that whoever they selected today would not live very long.

"Unfortunately, I think neither Sherston nor Yaldon can be Head Conjurer," he finished.

"I don't want it," Sherston said.

"What's wrong with me?" Yaldon asked. "I have more seniority than the rest of you."

"Be sensible," Maykin said. "You smell like rotting cheese. Oleda Burrage will not allow you within ten feet of her. I think it should be Tadlow. After all, his apprentice is already proving to be very helpful to Burrage. Don't you agree, Hewitt?"

"Excellent choice," Hewitt replied. He nodded and smiled at Tadlow, who sat up straighter. The self-important fool had no idea how dangerous this would be for him.

But all Hewitt needed Tadlow to do was outlive Wailes. A few days, maybe a week. And if he lasted longer than that, Hewitt planned to *find* the Kellen spell embedded in one of the Wailes books, tell Burrage about it, and blame Tadlow and Meade—that would remove both of them in one action. Oleda Burrage wouldn't give anyone who threatened her son a chance to talk so there was little chance of blame landing back on him.

"Is anyone opposed?" Hewitt asked. "There we have it. Acting Head Conjurer Tadlow, I expect you will need to make an official announcement at Conjurers Hall."

Tadlow, Sherston, and Yaldon left, and only Maykin remained seated.

Hewitt wrinkled his nose. "I'll need to open all the windows in order to get Yaldon's stink out of here."

"Yes," Maykin said. "I visited his home once. Ten minutes was all I could stand. I feel sorry for him, but it's not pleasant to be around him."

There was a knock on the door, and Hewitt looked up, startled. He gestured to Maykin, who got up and hid behind the door. Hewitt didn't get farther than the hallway before his front door opened.

"Shiv, what a pleasant surprise." Had Burrage already heard about the meeting and decided he could no longer trust Hewitt?

"Surprise, yes," Shiv said. "Not sure about pleasant." He shoved a piece of paper at him. "This came for you."

"When?" Hewitt grabbed the paper and unfolded it. Waglenn Landing. Faelin Keetley was alive and wanted to see him! "Did anyone read this?"

"No," Shiv said. "I know what it's about though. Consider this to be me fulfilling my part of our bargain. My men have searched, and now the girl has been found. She's not been harmed, and I haven't told Burrage about her. Now you owe me."

"Yes," Hewitt agreed. Faelin was alive and wanted to meet with him right now—today! He couldn't believe his good fortune.

"I have to tell Burrage about your meeting," Shiv said.

"I suspect he's hearing all about it from Acting Head Conjurer Tadlow."

Shiv smiled at that, and Hewitt's grin slipped. Would Tadlow even live to see tomorrow? He had to see the girl right away. She was the only one who could stop Graylon Burrage.

Shiv left, and Hewitt went back to his office. Maykin stepped out from behind the door and closed it.

"The bookbinder's daughter?" Maykin asked.

"Yes. I must meet with her immediately."

"Of course." Maykin opened the door but turned back. "I wouldn't want to owe the Bridgers anything."

"Nor do I," Hewitt replied. "But for now, I have something they want. A guarantee that if I live, they can stay on the bridge."

"Will you honour that?"

"They might kill me if I don't," Hewitt said. "So yes. If you'll excuse me, I have another appointment."

Chapter Four

ARIC FELT FAE in the magic—she was faint but he could tell that she was calm, which meant she was safe. And she was trying to tell him something. Magic burst through their connection and startled, Aric lost his grip and almost slipped out of the tree. Instinctively he reached into the spell and twisted it, forcing it away from him and Fae. Abruptly it changed from focused power to indistinct magic that drifted away.

The spell had not completed—he'd changed it before it could do whatever it was supposed to do. He didn't think he'd destroyed it: he could still feel it.

He concentrated on feeling the magic, on figuring out the intent of the spell, trying to find any trace of the person who had performed it. It had to have been Burrage—no one else had magic this strong, but even knowing that, he wasn't able to trace it back to him. He searched for Fae. She was there, but very faint and . . . was she hurt? No, she was frightened, and then her panic transferred to him. Just as quickly he felt her relief when she realized he was unharmed.

He sighed and relaxed: Fae was safe, and so was he. But he still couldn't track Burrage.

"ARE YOU ALL right?" Larwood asked.

"Yes, fine," Fae replied. She smiled, trying to feign calm. Aric was safe, she'd felt him through their connection, and he wasn't hurt. She searched for him again and relaxed when she felt his presence. She sighed and rubbed her hands along the armrests of the chair. Larwood watched her from the other side of his desk.

"I'm a little nervous," she said.

"Understandably," Larwood said. A knock sounded on the door. "Ah, that must be him,"

Fae heard Mistress Larwood's voice outside the office door, and then Hewitt was there.

"Faelin," Hewitt said. "I am so very glad to see you. You are well?"

"Yes, Conjurer Hewitt," Fae replied. She settled back into her chair, ignoring his outstretched hand. "As well as can be expected for someone who is being hunted." She didn't trust Hewitt and would use magic on him if he threatened her in any way.

"Yes," Hewitt said. "I have not been able to do anything about that. Not yet."

"You have tried?" Larwood asked.

"Of course, I've tried," Hewitt said. "But I am not in control."

"Graylon Burrage is," Fae said.

Hewitt looked surprised. "You know about Burrage?"

"It's all over town," Larwood said. "There's a new conjurer on the bridge. And he's from Durnham."

"He and his mother locked me up," Fae said. "I was trying to help them, warn them, and they locked me up. I managed to escape."

"Oleda told me you warned her," Hewitt said. "And that she didn't listen. Instead she imprisoned you and was willing to hand you over to Wailes. So, you know the type of people they are. You know I need to be careful."

"Who controls the Bridgers?" Fae asked. "Does Quillan Wailes still live?"

"Yes," Hewitt said. "Wailes is alive but cannot function. Shiv takes orders from Burrage but he is not very happy doing it. I don't think he trusts him."

Fae snorted. "Smarter than I thought." She paused. "Why are you looking for me? You came to see Councilman Larwood, looking for me. Why?"

Hewitt leaned closer. "I read the journal," he said. "The one Graylon Burrage and his mother got from you."

"The one they stole from me," Fae corrected. "When they locked me in their cold room."

"Yes," Hewitt said. "And thankfully Graylon didn't read it. He gave it to Wailes, who gave it to me. And I know who you are. I know *what* you are."

"Which is?"

"A conjurer. A Kellen conjurer. Just as Burrage is a Wailes conjurer."

"Why do you care?" Fae asked. "What does it have to do with you?" Would he answer her truthfully? Would she know if he lied?

"I still want you as my apprentice," Hewitt said. "You know I've wanted that for years." He leaned back in his chair, and Fae knew he had told her the truth. Just not all of it.

"So you can use me? So you can control my power; control the bridge through me? Why would I let that happen?"

"It would keep you safe," Hewitt said. "As my apprentice, Burrage would have no influence over you. And when you've had a chance to learn how to use your power he wouldn't be the only true conjurer."

"Who will teach me how to use magic?" Fae asked. "You?"

Hewitt stared at her for a moment before reaching down and slipping off one of his oversized shoes. "They never search here," he said. He pulled out a folded piece of paper and slipped his shoe back on. "Kellen spells," he said. "I've made copies of some spells that I thought looked useful. I plan to get other books and copy other spells. You should be able to recite these. If you truly are a Kellen." He held the paper out to her.

Fae unfolded the paper, her eyes scanning the faded script. "I am a Kellen," she said. "I read the journal as well."

"I thought you must have!" Hewitt beamed. "Otherwise why would you have had it with you when you went to Durnham? I could try to bring it to you next time we meet."

"I have a copy," Fae said. "I used my father's spell to make a copy."

"You . . ." Hewitt paused. "You can do magic! Just like your father."

"Yes," Fae agreed. "I can do magic." *Far better than my father*, she thought. "Do you require proof?"

"It would make my decision easier if I knew for certain,"

Hewitt said. "That you could do magic. And maybe something other than the copy spell?"

"All right," Fae said. She studied the spells, ignoring Hewitt for a moment. The words were archaic but the first spell was a simple fire spell. She wouldn't read it—she wasn't about to trust her life to Hewitt. If he wanted to kill her what better way than to have her read a non-Kellen spell? But she *would* perform magic. She didn't trust him—he'd said he had a decision to make so that meant he still could side with Burrage. But if he did, she wanted him to decide knowing that she was a conjurer.

"Councilman, can you hand me that lamp?" She pointed to the small, unlit lamp that sat on the bookcase behind him. She carefully took it and placed in on the desk in front of her.

"The fire spell," Hewitt said. "A good choice."

Fae stared at the words on the paper before turning her back on Hewitt and concentrating on the lamp. She mumbled some nonsense words, trying to make it look like she was reading them, before she whispered the words *light lamp*. The wick of the lamp flared to life, and she sat back and watched Hewitt's response.

"You did it!" Hewitt said. "I knew I was right, I knew the journal was right."

Fae smiled at him. "I did do it." He seemed genuinely pleased. So, it had been a true Kellen spell. She lifted the paper. "Can I keep these? To practice with?"

"Of course," Hewitt said. "The spells are of no use to anyone else. You will not return to the bridge with me?"

"Don't you think it would be better for me to get used to my abilities?" Fae asked. "To spend some time practicing and maybe get a few more useful spells that I could use—just in case?" She didn't think Hewitt could keep her safe on the bridge, even if she was his apprentice. Quillan Wailes might have honoured the conjurers' rule about apprentices but she doubted Burrage would care. And his mother certainly wouldn't. Hewitt said that Oleda wished she'd listened to Fae and not gone to the bridge, but Fae didn't believe she'd regret that for long. The woman and her son now had power. And neither of them liked Fae.

"Yes," Hewitt said. "I think you're right, it would be best if you had time to become familiar with your abilities. I'll bring more spells." He looked past her to Larwood. "Will you be staying here?"

"Fae is more than welcome to stay as long as she likes," Larwood said.

"Excellent." Hewitt suddenly grinned. "Faelin Keetley, you are making the right choice. Your father would be very proud."

Fae kept a smile plastered on her face while Hewitt said his goodbyes. As soon as the door closed behind him, she let out a breath.

"I take it your father would not be proud?" Larwood asked.

"Not if I apprenticed to Hewitt," Fae replied. "He refused him that more than once."

"But you let him think you would be his apprentice."

"I also let him think I read that spell," she said. "So, I have to wonder what he promised me that *he's* lying about." She looked out the window. It was starting to get dark. She'd wait until the moon rose before heading back to Aric.

Hewitt stepped onto the bridge. The Bridgers manning the gate nodded to him as he walked past them. He breathed in deeply, appreciating the familiarity of the bridge: smooth cobbles underfoot, the stone houses on either side, the way the buildings were set tight against each other.

Larwood's home was pleasant enough—it was certainly larger than any dwelling on the bridge—but it had seemed too quiet and dull. There was no wind whistling past, no gulls diving just outside the windows. He much preferred the bridge. And now that Faelin had agreed to be his apprentice, he would have the very best the bridge could offer.

He strode along the cobbles towards his home. Should he tell Maykin that he'd met with Faelin? That he'd seen her do magic? A true conjurer! And she seemed strong. She'd said the spell and the lamp had lit. There had been no ill effects—not like Burrage had experienced a few times after he'd recited a spell. She hadn't fallen or stumbled or cried out in pain.

True, it might be a smaller spell than what Burrage insisted on reciting, and perhaps the malicious intent of the spells was what caused his discomfort. It would make sense that a killing spell would be dangerous to the one reciting it. He shook his head. No, Faelin was stronger. She had to be.

"Conjurer Hewitt, so nice to see you."

He turned towards the voice. "Oleda my dear," he said. "I hope all is well with you and your son?"

"Yes," she replied. "But I cannot say the same for poor Conjurer Wailes. He died this afternoon."

"Ah, I see," Hewitt said. "We knew it wouldn't be long." He nodded. "I should go. There are things that must be attended to."

"That other one is there," Oleda said with a frown. "That Tadlow fellow who said he was Acting Head Conjurer."

"Yes, he was appointed because Wailes could not fulfill his duties," Hewitt said. "We will need to elect a new Head Conjurer now, of course."

"Ah." Oleda smiled. "So he is just temporary."

"Yes," Hewitt agreed, thinking that Tadlow was temporary whether he agreed or not. "That was always my understanding." Oleda wasn't about to let her son be overlooked. All Hewitt could do was make sure he wasn't in her way. Especially not now that he knew Faelin was a true conjurer and she'd finally agreed to be his apprentice.

"I imagine all of the conjurers are gathering," Hewitt continued. "It is our custom." He waited until she nodded, giving him permission to leave. He smiled at her and turned, the smile sliding from his face. When Faelin was stronger Oleda Burrage would take direction from him. But right now, he had to check Wailes' belongings for more Kellen spell books.

TADLOW WAS THERE when he arrived at Wailes' room. Tymm sat by the bed, rubbing a hand across Wailes' curved shoulder.

"He won't leave," Tadlow said. "We'll need to get the Bridgers to drag him out."

"In time," Hewitt said. "Do the others know?"

"I sent Meade," Tadlow said.

Hewitt paced around the room, scanning for spell books, but he didn't see any. He peered down at Wailes' body. Small and twisted, just like the mind that had inhabited it.

"I need to find something to weigh him down with," Tadlow said. "For the ceremony."

"Perhaps it should be that giant standing over him."

Hewitt turned to find Burrage standing in the doorway.

"He's of no use to me," Burrage continued. "And he's threatened my mother."

"Tymm doesn't know when he's doing something wrong,"

Tadlow said.

"He's dangerous," Burrage said. "I don't want him on the bridge."

"That's not your decision to make," Tadlow said. He stood up straighter.

"You think it's yours?" Burrage said. "Because you call yourself the Acting Head Conjurer?"

"He was voted that by the rest of us, Graylon," Hewitt interjected. "Although it was only until Wailes recovered." He tried to catch Tadlow's eye, but the man was glaring at Burrage. "There will be another vote now that Wailes is dead." He walked over and stopped between Burrage and Tadlow.

"You will name me," Burrage said. "I will be your new Head Conjurer."

Before Tadlow could say anything, Hewitt put a hand on the other conjurer's arm.

"We need to complete the ceremony before any decisions are made," Hewitt said. "But you can certainly make your wishes known to all of us."

"I will do that," Burrage said. "And then you will name me." He turned and left.

Hewitt caught Tadlow's eye and shook his head. He pulled him away from the door to the far side of the room.

"I will not name him," Tadlow said. "He isn't even a conjurer."

"He's more of a conjurer than the rest of us. He can do real magic," Hewitt said. "Powerful magic. And he won't hesitate to use it on anyone who gets in his way." He looked at poor Tymm, who was rocking back and forth as he hovered above Wailes. "And he has a point about Tymm. Now that Wailes is dead, who will be able to manage him?"

"You can't mean to let him ban Tymm," Tadlow said. "He'll die if he's sent off the bridge."

"He might die if he's not," Hewitt replied. He would sacrifice Tymm if he had to. He would not allow Wailes' servant to cause a rift between him and the Burrages. He couldn't afford that, not now that he had Faelin's promise; not when all he needed was more time for her to master her magic.

Aric treaded water and watched the light bob as it was carried away from Rand's boat. He'd been about to drag himself onto the deck when someone had emerged from the shadows of a neighbouring boat. The other person had lifted his lamp high and scanned Rand's deserted boat for a few moments before turning and leaving. He'd kept a hat pulled low on his head so Aric hadn't gotten a good look at him, but he walked like a man born on the river.

Aric didn't like that he couldn't trust his own people and hated that his mother had been betrayed by one of her own. He'd assumed someone would be willing to betray him as well, but that didn't mean he was happy that it looked like he was right.

After a few moments of quiet, he carefully pulled himself up and out of the river and onto the deck of Rand's boat. He crab-walked into a shadow and made his way to the door. He opened it and crawled inside.

Once he was below deck, he searched for dry clothing in the dark. He was tired, hungry, and cold, but he didn't dare light the stove or a lamp.

He tried to reach Fae, felt her presence for a moment, and then she was gone. He sighed. They'd agreed to try to contact each other at midnight and that was still a few hours away. He'd hoped she would be back at the boat before then, but perhaps Hewitt hadn't been able to visit her today.

THE BOAT SHIFTED as someone boarded and footsteps sounded overhead. Aric dove into the bedroom just as the door from the deck to the cabin opened.

"I'll light the lamp." Rand's voice drifted down to him. There was a mumbled response, and then someone clumped down the short set of stairs and into the main room of the cabin.

"Aric?" a voice called. "You in here?"

Aric cracked the door open and peered out, squinting against the glare. Rand swung the lamp and set it on the table, illuminating Pax Oldham's worried face.

"Rand, Pax," Aric said as he opened the door.

"Aric, good," Rand said. "I was hoping you were back on board."

"Someone was watching," Aric said. He joined the men by the table, grabbed a pitcher of water, and poured himself a mug.

"Who?" Pax asked. "Not one of us again?" He frowned and shook his head. "Didn't Fiske's example teach them anything? If you'd betray your own, conjurers and Bridgers aren't about to trust you."

"I didn't get a good look," Aric said. "But it was someone born to the water. What about Fiske's family? Is there anyone who would be angry about what happened to him? Someone who might blame anyone but Fiske?"

"Yes," Pax said. "A cousin came from upriver a few days ago, asking how Fiske died. Must be him."

"How'd he get past the bridge?" Aric asked. "Bridgers don't usually let us pass so easily."

"Said he paid," Pax replied. "That Bridgers are unsettled and are keen to earn coin."

"Probably true enough," Rand said. "But maybe Bridgers wanted more than coin from him. Maybe they also told him to watch my boat, looking for Fae. And then had him bring that Bridger here."

"Must be," Aric said, grateful that both he and Fae had stayed in hiding. "They must have lied to him. Wailes and his Bridgers are responsible for Fiske's death."

"After he handed them your mother!" Pax said.

"Yes. That Bridger had someone with a boat bring him here," Aric said. "And if Fiske's cousin did help the Bridger, then he knows you lied to him, Rand. You told the Bridger I was upriver. Fiske's cousin knows I'm not."

"So the Bridger knows too," Pax said.

"Will it matter?" Rand asked. "If he knows I lied?"

"I'm not sure," Aric replied. He didn't get a sense of danger, at least not about that specifically. "But he might assume you're also lying about Fae."

"Bridger still needs a Riverman to get to me here," Rand said. "Pax can make Fiske's cousin leave. For spying on his own people after his cousin brought shame to their family."

"It might be better to find out what he's doing," Aric said. He turned to Pax. "Can he leave if you don't allow it?"

"We've never restricted Rivermen from going upriver," Pax said. "But I can forbid it. It wouldn't stop him from trying to leave in the middle of the night."

"But it might stop someone from helping him, even innocently," Aric said. "He's from upriver; he's probably not that familiar with the tides."

"You think he might need someone to help him time them in order to get past the bridge," Rand said.

"Yes," Aric agreed. "Even if a Bridger raises a grate to let him through, the river has to be at the right level."

"I'll make sure everyone knows I don't want him to leave," Pax said.

"Good," Aric said. He looked up. It must be midnight by now, time to contact Fae.

He closed his eyes, shutting out the others and the small room, concentrating on Fae. There. He tried to feel what she was feeling, and suddenly he shivered, feeling damp bark beneath his hands.

"Fae's here," Aric said. "Waiting in the trees on shore."

"I'll get her," Rand said. He quickly left, and Aric sighed in relief.

"Another premonition?" Pax asked. "Sigrun never had so many."

"It's because I'm a male shaman, according to what I read in my mother's old books," Aric said. It wasn't a lie, not precisely, but it was also because he and Fae were so close and Fae was a conjurer. But it made him wonder why he didn't feel he could trust Pax with that information. Or was he getting used to not trusting anyone enough to ever tell them the whole truth? Had his mother felt this way about him?

A few moments later, the boat rocked as Rand returned. Aric held his breath until he saw Fae come down the stairs. He hugged her tight, ignoring the chill of her damp clothes.

"Good to see you back safe," Pax said. "Rand, put some tea on. I think we need to warm Fae up before she tells us what happened."

"I could use something to eat as well," Fae said.

"Me too," Aric agreed. He edged aside so Fae could get past him. "I left some dry clothes on the bed."

She gave him a grateful look before she disappeared into the bedroom.

FAE CUPPED THE mug and said a single word to rewarm her tea. Aric was speaking to Pax and Rand but he paused and sent her a smile, acknowledging her use of magic.

She pulled out the sheet of spells Hewitt had given her and

held them up. Aric took the page from her.

"From Hewitt?" he asked.

"Yes. He wanted me to prove that I was a Kellen."

"You didn't read one of these, did you?"

"No," she said. "I said my own fire spell. I'm not about to trust him when being wrong means my death."

"He wanted you to prove that you were a conjurer," Pax said. "What else did he want from you?"

"What he's always wanted," Fae replied. "For me to become his apprentice. But this time I think there's more to it. He gave me those spells so I could prove I was a Kellen—he said it would help him make a decision. And then he agreed to let me practice them before I join him."

"So he would choose you if you had magic," Aric said. "Now he wants to pit you against Burrage."

"That's what I think," Fae replied. "Hewitt will side with whoever wins."

"Whoever's left alive," Aric said.

The tone of his voice had changed, and she looked up at him, startled. Pax and Rand glanced at her, and she whispered, "Premonition."

"Two conjurers will meet," Aric said. "Only one will survive." He slumped over and looked up at her. "I *felt* that one," he said. He held out his hand. It was shaking. "You can't go, Fae. We can go back to my mother's boat and sail far away. You can't set foot on the bridge."

"What about the curse?" Fae asked. "You can't leave and let everyone else suffer. Besides, it will find you wherever we go. And you know Burrage *will* recite it. You've felt how destructive and dangerous his spells are, like the spell he tried to kill with: the one you were able to change, but that almost killed you. And I have no intention of doing anything Hewitt wants me to do."

Aric closed his eyes for a moment. When he opened them, he met hers. "That didn't trigger anything, so we stay."

"That was interesting," Pax said. "Can you feel for danger whenever you want?"

"Not yet," Aric said. "I mean I can try, but it doesn't always work. But I am getting better." He shrugged. "And as for premonitions, that time I didn't hear what I said, exactly, but I felt the danger."

"Hmm," Pax said. "Interesting. I think I'd like to ask the elders about that, see if anyone has heard any stories about your shaman talents, but not yet. We'll let you two get some rest. It's been a busy day."

"I got fish to catch," Rand said. "Best keep the light off once we're gone."

Fae sat in the dark listening to Aric's breathing. The boat swayed for a few moments after Rand and Pax left; then it calmed.

"Hewitt said he'd bring more Kellen spells to me at Councilman Larwood's," Fae said. "So I have to go back."

"I don't like it," Aric said. "But I don't feel any danger. When?"

"The day after tomorrow, I think," she said. "And I may have to stay there for a few days. It would look too suspicious for Hewitt to come every day. He says he's not in charge, and neither is Wailes."

"Do you believe that?"

"Yes," Fae replied. "I know Oleda and Graylon. I don't believe either one of them would do Hewitt's bidding, not when Graylon is the one with magic."

"Hewitt will be eager," Aric said. "Now that he thinks he's getting you."

"True, but he hasn't lasted this long by acting rashly." She'd known Horace Hewitt for a long time—known him as a friend of her father's. And she had to admit he'd acted the same for all the years she'd known him, it just hadn't affected her. Not like now. Because Hewitt *always* did what was best for Hewitt.

ARIC CLOSED HIS eyes and looked for Fae. She cast a small spell— he smiled, she was freezing water again—and he could feel her even more clearly. If he could sense her, would he be able to sense Burrage?

He tried to look for the conjurer but he couldn't locate him, not through the magic. Was it because he'd never met the man? Fae had: could he use her connection to him? He tried to send her a message to think about Burrage but all he felt from her was confusion.

He stepped out of the bedroom to find her in the main cabin, sipping water.

"What were you doing?" she asked. "At the end?"

"I was trying to contact you," Aric replied. "To make you think of something specific."

"It didn't work," Fae said.

"No, but this might." Aric took her hands and stood facing her. "Think about Burrage. I want to try to locate him."

"All right," Fae said. She closed her eyes, and Aric copied her.

With their hands joined, Aric could almost hear Fae's thoughts. He caught a flash of someone's face—was that Burrage? He tried to grasp hold of the image and follow it to where the flesh and blood man was, but it slipped away.

"Nothing," Aric said. He opened his eye. "Maybe it's not something that can be done."

"Why would you want to look for him?" Fae asked. "He might be able to feel you searching and then he'd know someone with magic was out here. And knew about him."

"He might think it was one of the other conjurers," Aric said. "And I'd like to know if he ever leaves the bridge."

"Why would he leave?"

"Why did Hewitt leave?" Aric asked softly.

"To find me," she replied.

"Yes. And I'd like to be able to warn you about Burrage if he heads to Waglenn Landing."

"You don't trust Hewitt not to tell him where I am," Fae said. "I don't either, but I have to go. It's the only way to keep him from coming here to find me." She paused. "Besides, he still wants me as his apprentice."

"Only if he thinks he can control you," Aric said. "Because it sounds like he *knows* he can't control Burrage. He did say Burrage was in charge."

"Yes," Fae said. "And that because they had locked me up I knew the type of people he and his mother are."

"I'm not sure Hewitt knows who to trust himself," Aric said.

"I think it's more that he's not sure who will benefit him the most," Fae said. "Which one of us he should align with in order to get what he wants."

Aric's shaman senses shuddered. "That's crucial," he said. "What does Hewitt want? We need to find out and try to help him get it."

Chapter Five

HEWITT STEPPED BACK and let Tadlow leave the Hall first. He followed, carrying the small bag of ashes that used to be Quillan Wailes. A small rock was also in his hands, along with a paperweight, something Hewitt had plucked from Wailes' desk. He had no idea if it had held any special value to Wailes, but all it had to do was help his remains sink to the bottom of the river and stay there.

Burrage and his mother glared at Tadlow from the cobblestones in front of the square. Hewitt nodded to them as he passed, meeting first Oleda's eyes and then her son's. The woman's pursed lips gentled slightly when she returned his nod.

Hewitt trailed Tadlow to the edge of the square as the rest of the conjurers lined up alongside him.

He stared upriver while Tadlow spoke. The docks for the two towns were empty, and the willow trees that lined the riverbank rustled in the stiff breeze, their branches trailing into the water.

He looked at the small group that had assembled to bid farewell to Wailes. The conjurers, the Burrages, a few merchants, and the Bridgers: nowhere near the crowd that had gathered for Lachlan Keetley. But that had been before the books had been found, before so many deaths and disappearances.

Shiv caught his eye, and Hewitt nodded at him. The other man scowled, crossed his arms, and took a half step sideways towards Burrage.

So, Shiv and his Bridgers had already chosen a side. Hewitt turned his attention to Tadlow, hiding a small smile. They had no idea he had his own conjurer, one who even now was learning to recite her family spells. He'd visit Faelin tomorrow, after he'd had a chance to look through the most recent book of Kellen spells that Meade had sent him.

Tadlow finished speaking and looked at him. Hewitt handed him the bag of ashes.

"Quillan Wailes was of the bridge," Tadlow said. He fumbled when he opened the bag, and the wind caught it and snatched it from his grasp. He grabbed for it and ashes spewed out. In horror, Hewitt watched as Burrage and his mother were covered in greyish powder.

"How dare you?" Oleda said.

"I didn't . . ." Tadlow sputtered.

Hewitt stepped forward before Burrage had time to come to his mother's defense. "This truly is a horrendous accident," he said. "But it *was* an accident." He placed a hand on Burrage's arm, wary of the anger in him. "My dear," Hewitt said to Oleda. "Conjurer Tadlow will make amends for this terrible accident, I promise, but we are in the midst of honouring one of our own. Are you well enough for us to continue?"

Oleda brushed a hand across her sleeve. It came away sooty. "Conjurer Tadlow will pay for this insult," she said. She glared at Tadlow but nodded curtly to Hewitt.

"Thank you," was all he said in reply, all he dared say. Oleda Burrage was furious enough to want someone dead. If he wasn't careful it would be him.

Hewitt turned back to Tadlow, who gripped the small bag tightly in one ash-covered hand. He leaned towards him and handed him the small stone and the paperweight.

"Make this quick," Hewitt said into Tadlow's ear.

Tadlow nodded and moved to the railing of the bridge. Without saying a word, he held up the stone and the paperweight before adding them to the bag. He closed the bag and tied it shut with twine before throwing it over the side.

"Conjurer Wailes has left the bridge for the final time," Tadlow said when he turned back to the group. He nodded once at Hewitt before hurrying past Burrage and his mother, heading back to Conjurers Hall. Maykin, Sherston, and Yaldon followed him more slowly. Meade Tadlow remained where he was, trying, Hewitt thought, not to be noticed.

Oleda glared at the crowd before turning and stomping away, her son following. Meade and the few others still remaining scurried off once the Burrages were gone.

Hewitt walked over to the railing and peered over it at the river below. There, bobbing along the surface, despite the rock and paperweight, was the bag that held the remains of Quillan Wailes.

"Disaster," he muttered. Folklore said that when the dead floated, it was a sign of bad things to come. Hewitt shook his head. He didn't need any superstitious portent to tell him that bad things were about to happen. Right now, Tadlow's life was looking very short. He had to make sure that his life wasn't forfeit as well.

He stepped away from the railing and turned to find Shiv staring at him. Hewitt suppressed a shudder. He had to be careful. Shiv could not know the real reason he had been looking for the bookbinder's daughter. And the best way to preserve that secret was to get Faelin to move back onto the bridge as his apprentice. He walked past the Bridger.

"Shiv," he said. He'd meant it both as a greeting and a goodbye so when Shiv fell into step beside him, fear clutched his belly.

"She's taken the bookbindery," Shiv said. "Mistress Burrage."

"He was her cousin by marriage," Hewitt said carefully.

"That's what I hear," Shiv said. "And the daughter's never been found, as far as most people know. Although I am wondering why that's such a secret?" He chuckled and walked past Hewitt, who had slowed at the mention of Faelin.

He hadn't told Burrage about Faelin, had he? Or had he already been to Councilman Larwood's and killed Faelin on Burrage's orders?

Hewitt was still worrying about Shiv's last comment when the Bridger turned around and called out, "The simpleton? He sank like a stone."

Shaken, Hewitt hurried to his home, closed the door, and locked it. He'd never even noticed that Tymm wasn't at the ceremony, hadn't really spared him much thought. But the poor man hadn't deserved to be tossed off the bridge. Had it been last night? Had the poor soul been alive when he went over? He'd been thinking that Oleda was the worst Burrage, but this was Graylon's doing. He was the one who'd threatened Tymm.

He stood in the middle of his study. If Burrage had instructed Shiv to do that, then Tadlow was in immediate danger. He started to pace. What would help *him* the most?

Tadlow was as good as dead; it would not serve him to try to intervene on his behalf. But Burrage wanted to be seen as a legitimate conjurer, didn't he? At the very least he wanted to be Head Conjurer, and that wouldn't mean anything if the rest of them were dead, would it?

He unlocked the door and headed back down the bridge to the Hall. He heard raised voices the moment he stepped through the door, and nervously, he followed the voices to Burrage's office.

"You are not a true conjurer!" Tadlow said. He was standing in front of the desk. Burrage was in the chair across from him. "You aren't even a real apprentice."

"I'm the only true conjurer," Burrage replied. He noticed Hewitt and gestured him into the room. "Is that not correct, Conjurer Hewitt?"

"You are the only one with powerful magic," Hewitt said. "That is true."

"See, even Hewitt thinks I should be the next Head Conjurer," Burrage said.

"That's not what he said," Tadlow replied. "Is it?"

Hewitt looked from Tadlow to Burrage before he walked over and sat down in front of the desk. "We are typically governed by the most powerful among us," Hewitt said carefully. "But there is usually a vote."

"Usually," Tadlow repeated. "We've *always* had a vote; there's never *not* been a vote." He turned to Burrage. "And I will never vote for you."

"Do it!"

Hewitt turned to find Oleda Burrage standing in the doorway. "Do it," she repeated.

"Mother," Burrage said. "We talked about this."

"He's in the way," Oleda said. "And he spilled that . . . that . . . horrible little man all over me. You promised he would pay." She turned to Hewitt. "My son will be the new Head Conjurer."

"Yes," Hewitt said.

"Then do it," Oleda told her son. "Or I'll ask Shiv to."

Hewitt schooled his features. Perhaps Oleda had given the order to kill Tymm? If she had, she'd enjoyed the power she'd felt by ordering his death. Should he be relieved that it hadn't been Graylon?

"What are you going to do?" Tadlow asked, and Hewitt shook his head again. The man only now seemed to recognize the danger he was in, only now realized that he was not going to leave this room alive. "Hewitt? What are they going to do to me?"

"I believe that's what they are discussing right now," Hewitt replied calmly. He met Burrage's eyes.

"You'll help us?" Burrage asked.

"Of course," Hewitt replied. Any other answer and he would share in Tadlow's fate.

"All right, Mother," Burrage said. "Could you please close the door?"

Oleda Burrage shut the door and leaned against it, her eyes avidly watching as her son recited a spell. Tadlow choked and clutched his throat, but although his mouth was open, it seemed he couldn't take a breath. His eyes bulged and his face started to turn blue. He fell to the floor, heaving, and his limbs started to twitch. Hewitt looked away. And saw Oleda. Her face was feverish, and her mouth was open in a grin. Hewitt thought she might even clap her hands together. Her eyes darted between Tadlow's shuddering body and her son's face the whole time it took Tadlow to die.

There was one final paroxysm and then Tadlow lay still. Oleda went to her son and hugged him.

Hewitt stood up, keeping his eyes averted from Tadlow's body.

"I'll ask Shiv to come," Hewitt said and left the room. He didn't dare arrange a ceremony for Tadlow, not after Oleda Burrage's exhilaration at his death. And who would perform it anyway? Burrage—the new Head Conjurer—the man who had just killed Tadlow?

ARIC SPRAWLED BACKWARDS, collapsing against the side of the boat. He wiped his hair from his face and took a deep shuddering breath. He'd felt a man die, and worse, he'd felt Burrage's satisfaction as the spell he'd recited slowly took that man's life.

"Aric?" Fae's voice was a whisper but he heard the worry in it. "Are you all right?"

"Fine," Aric replied. "I'm coming back in." Keeping to the shadows, he crawled along the side of the cabin until he reached the door. After a quick check to make sure no one was watching, he slipped inside, groped his way through the dark to the bench and slid in behind the table. Fae placed a warm mug in front of him, and he gratefully wrapped his hands around it. She whispered a word and magic flared; the lamp lit, giving off a dim light.

"Burrage killed with a spell," Aric said. "And I felt *everything* he felt."

"Did *he* feel you?"

"No," he replied. "He was too busy enjoying himself." He shivered and reached for her hand. "He liked it, he liked killing." He met her gaze.

"So he'll do it again," Fae replied. "It wasn't Hewitt, was it? The one he killed?"

Aric closed his eyes and recalled the feelings that had emanated from Burrage, and the spell he'd recited. He didn't think it had been Hewitt but there was something familiar about the man who'd died.

"Not Hewitt but another conjurer, I think," he said. He placed his hand flat on the table in front of him. It was steady, which surprised him since the rest of him felt shaky.

"You went looking for him again." It was more of an accusation than a question.

"Yes," he replied. "We need to know what sort of man he is."

"It's dangerous!" Fae said. "He might find out about you."

"Meeting Hewitt is dangerous," Aric said. "But necessary. So is this." And it was something he could do.

"You're right," Fae said. She sighed and covered his hands with her own.

Aric gripped her hands in his and took a deep breath. "You have to create a killing spell," he said. "Because Burrage will not hesitate to use one on you."

"No! I won't."

"Then we really should get my mother's boat and sail away," Aric replied. "No matter what might happen to me when he completes the curse." At least Fae would be far away, and safe, even if he turned into something other than a man.

"No," Fae repeated. "We already talked about that. I refuse to live my life waiting for something horrible to happen to you."

"That's how I feel about you," Aric said. "That's why you need to be prepared in case Burrage decides he wants you dead. That's why you need a killing spell. Before you go to Waglenn Landing."

"I don't want to kill anyone," Fae said.

"I don't want you to die."

"Is that a premonition?" Fae asked.

"Would you do this if I said it was?"

He stared at her until finally she sighed and leaned against the back rest.

"All right," Fae said. "I'll create a spell. Two spells: one to immobilise and another one to kill. But I won't use the killing spell unless I absolutely need to."

Aric closed his eyes and tried to feel danger in this decision, but there was nothing. Did that mean the spells weren't required or that they would be enough to keep Fae safe? He opened his eyes and met hers.

"Thank you," he said. "But we won't have any more time to practice contacting each other over distances."

"You weren't doing that anyway," Fae said. "You were looking for Burrage."

"I was doing both," Aric replied. And he had been. And *because* he'd been doing both, he'd missed the beginning of the killing spell—he'd missed the chance to change it. And someone had died. But he wasn't going to tell Fae that. And when she was in Waglenn Landing? He wouldn't split his attention like that. Not when it might be Fae's life that was at risk.

"I need the cabin," Fae said. She stared at him until he nodded and slid out from behind the table.

She was angry with him for making her create a killing spell— he could live with that as long as she stayed alive. He headed to the stairs. He'd keep an eye on the boat he'd seen the man come from last night. By now, Pax should have told Fiske's cousin not to leave, so maybe he'd try to sneak away now that it was dark.

Then he'd check the lines he'd set out earlier. If he'd caught them some dinner Fae might forget to be angry.

FAE STARED AT the three fish that circled the bucket. "You want me to do what?" she said to Aric, who stood between her and the door to the cabin. She wasn't sure if he was planning on blocking her escape or making his own.

"Test out your spells," Aric said. "On the fish."

"I . . ." She was about to say she wouldn't but it was actually a good idea. She had created the spells—one to immobilize and one to kill—but she hadn't tested them. Hadn't *wanted* to test them. Although she had a mind to test the immobilize spell on Aric right now. But that was dangerous—what if it worked too well? What if it paralysed him so that he couldn't breathe? And what if she couldn't reverse it?

"Please?" Aric asked. "I need to know you're prepared. I need you to be safe."

Fae blew out a breath and frowned. "All right," she said. "But only because it's a good idea."

"Are you admitting that I'm right?" Aric asked. He took a step towards her but when she looked at him, he stopped.

"No," Fae said. "I don't want to kill using magic. It makes me like *him*." She paused. "But now that I have them I need to make sure they work." *And don't do something even worse*, she thought.

Aric wisely stayed back while she peered into the bucket. She singled out the smallest fish and muttered the words to the spell under her breath. The fish stopped moving and sank to the bottom of the bucket. She whispered a spell to reverse it, and the fish thrashed for a moment before it began to swim again. Then she did the same to all three fish at once. When they were all back to circling the bucket, she took a deep breath.

The killing spell had been surprisingly easy to create. One word, that was all, directed in the right way. That had made her appreciate Aric's insistence that she prepare one. Burrage was still working from old spells, as far as they knew, but if he realized how easy they were to create, no one would be safe.

"Die," she whispered to the smallest fish. Immediately, it stopped moving and sank to the bottom of the bucket. She shivered. The spell left a bad . . . almost an aftertaste, in her mind.

Aric plucked the dead fish from the bucket. "Quick and painless," he said. "The opposite of Burrage's spell. Do you want me to kill these two, now that we know it works?"

"No," Fae replied. "I need to do this again. They were always going to be dinner anyway." She muttered the word again, and the other two fish stopped swimming.

Aric grabbed the bucket. "Thank you," he said as he stepped past her. "I'll clean these and then you can cook them."

"I'll be outside," Fae replied. She headed up the stairs and out the door, careful not to let any light spill out onto the deck of the boat.

She'd felt it, when the fish had died. Tiny sparks of life snuffed out. Would she be able to do that to a person? Even if they threatened her life? Or it was a man who took joy in killing others?

Aric's premonition had said that two conjurers would meet and that only one would survive. He'd assumed it was about her and Burrage, but what if it was about Hewitt and Burrage?

Then Burrage would be the one who survived, and Aric and his people would still be in danger from the curse.

She stared out towards the centre of the river. Lights flickered on many of the boats of the village, and shadowed figures moved in the distance. If the curse was completed what would happen to those people? To Aric? She sighed.

What she should do is kill Burrage right now, before he even knew she existed. But she couldn't, not until she knew for sure what he intended to do. Hewitt would have answers, he *had* to have answers. Because despite Aric's premonitions, she couldn't simply kill a man without being certain he planned to do terrible things.

But what she could do was create protection spells—for her and Aric—so that if Burrage struck first—either by magic or through Shiv—she and Aric would survive. If she was attacked— if *Aric* was attacked—she wouldn't hesitate to kill. It took some time to decide what she wanted the protection spells to do, and she wouldn't have a chance to test these spells out, but in a few moments, she was ready.

Fae kept to the shadows as she made her way back to the door. In a few hours, she'd have to leave for Waglenn Landing. She didn't want Aric to think she was angry with him. She *was* angry, but at the positions they were being forced into, at the actions they had to contemplate taking, not at him for telling the truth.

She tiptoed down the stairs. His back was to her, and she

snuck over and wrapped an arm around his waist, slipping her hand under his shirt to rest on his heart.

"Hey!" He turned into her embrace and she leaned into him with a kiss. He wrapped his arms around her and pulled her closer.

"I'm not mad at you," she whispered into his ear. Now both her hands were beneath his shirt, skimming across his chest. His chest rose and fell when he sighed.

"I just want you safe." Aric leaned his head against hers. "And back here in one piece."

"I know." She pulled her hands out from under his shirt and fumbled with the top buttons of her shirt. Once it was loose enough, Aric's hands pushed the fabric down past her shoulders, baring her breasts. She shrugged her arms out of the shirt, and it dropped to the floor. She stepped out of it, kicking it away and moved back into his embrace.

Aric's head bent and his lips touched one nipple, and she gasped as heat spread throughout her body.

She tugged on Aric's shirt, and he raised his head and arms to allow her to pull it off. With a sigh, she leaned into him, relishing the feel of her bare skin against his. She breathed in his scent—he smelled of wind and salt air—before meeting his lips with her own.

She groaned—or maybe he did —as she pushed into him, the urgency building.

Fumbling with her trousers, Aric walked her backwards towards the door to the bedroom. By the time he manoeuvred her to the bed, her trousers were at her knees. She pulled them off and tossed them away as she knelt on the bed, her hands at his waistband. His lips trailed hot kisses along her shoulder as she pushed the cloth away from his arousal. She grabbed him and he tensed before pushing her down onto the bed, her hand still on him, leading him towards her.

And then he was on her, in her, thrusting, meeting her need, her desire with his own. Fae wrapped herself around him, urging him closer, deeper with every push, every thrust. Aric's lips were on hers and her tongue invaded him as he invaded her. Her breath was ragged as her need climbed. Their tempo increased and then it crested. She strained against him, pulling him into her, as close to her as possible. He stiffened for a moment, then relaxed and dropped onto her, his breath hot on her cooling skin. Aric gathered her to him and rolled over, cradling her head on his shoulder as their heartbeats slowed.

Chapter Six

HEWITT STEPPED OFF the bridge and looked around at the bustling market. It was early but apparently not too early for the market vendors. He glanced back at the Bridger who stood behind the now closed gate. The man didn't acknowledge him but Hewitt knew he was watching.

He set off through the stalls, heading towards Councilman Larwood's house.

"Conjurer!"

Hewitt froze. Had the Bridger changed his mind about letting him off the bridge?

"Conjurer!"

The voice was closer now, but female. Hewitt plastered a smile on his face and turned to the direction the voice was coming from. It was the woman who'd found the boy for him, the one he'd hoped was a Kellen.

"Mistress . . ." Hewitt paused. "Bleddyn, I think?"

"Yes, Conjurer," the woman replied, beaming. "So good of you to remember me."

Hewitt relaxed. "What can I do for you, Mistress?"

"Oh." She seemed caught off guard. "Nothing. I mean, I saw you and thought I would give greetings."

"I see," Hewitt replied. He smiled. "How kind of you."

"Yes, and well. We heard about poor Collen," Mistress

Bleddyn said. "Poor lad."

"Yes," Hewitt replied. "Terrible to go missing like that. And right after he'd been to see me. He was so excited during his visit."

"Just so," Mistress Bleddyn agreed.

"If you'll excuse me, I am late for an appointment," Hewitt lied. He didn't actually have an appointment to see Faelin, just a promise that he would return as soon as possible. Mistress Bleddyn made no move to depart so Hewitt bowed his head slightly. His meetings weren't exactly secret, not with the Bridgers marking his every move, but he didn't need the town's biggest busybody taking note of where he went. Unlike Burrage and his Bridgers, Mistress Bleddyn knew who was up to what on this side of the river.

"Oh, of course," the woman finally said. She waited for another few moments before she nodded and turned back towards the vendors.

Hewitt watched her hurry away before he turned and walked towards the far side of the square. He angled left, away from Councilman Larwood's house. Once he reached the edge of the square he looked back.

He could no longer see the busybody so he headed past half a dozen lawns and up the front steps of Larwood's house. A quick rap on the door and Mistress Larwood opened it.

"Conjurer Hewitt," she said. "Come in. My husband is in his study."

"Thank you," Hewitt replied. He stepped into the hallway. "And the girl? Is the bookbinder's daughter with him?"

"Oh, no. She's still upstairs in her room. I'll let her know that you're here and have her join the two of you."

"Thank you," Hewitt said. Until now he hadn't realized how worried he was that Faelin had run away, that she'd decided to refuse his offer, again. He blew out a breath as he watched Mistress Larwood climb the stairs. Then he headed down the hallway that led to the Councilman's office.

Hewitt knocked on the closed door. A muffled voice urged him to enter and he opened the door.

Larwood sat behind his desk, a pile of papers in front of him.

"Conjurer Hewitt." The other man bowed his head. "Come in. Please, have a seat." Larwood gestured and Hewitt took a chair across the desk from him.

"I hope I am not disturbing you," Hewitt said. "I know how busy you must be."

"Do you?" Larwood said. He smiled. "It so happens that you can help me." The smile slid off his face and he leaned across the desk. "I hear such news from the bridge, yet I have no way to know what is true."

Hewitt leaned back in his chair. The Councilman's job probably did require knowledge of the bridge—and *everyone* should worry about Burrage—but Hewitt had to be careful what he told him.

"Councilman, Conjurer Hewitt."

Hewitt turned to see Faelin at the door to the room.

"Faelin, so nice to see you again," Hewitt said. Faelin slid into the chair beside him before he could rise to greet her. "I hope all is well with you?"

"Yes," Faelin said. "I am doing very well."

Hewitt followed her eyes to the sheet of paper clutched in her hand. He smiled. She'd been practicing the Kellen spells! And it sounded as though she'd been able to master them.

"Excellent," he said. "I have brought more spells for you." He wouldn't give them to her now, not when it meant removing his shoe—focussing attention on his grossly oversized feet—in front of Faelin and Councilman Larwood again. It was humiliating. And sneaking spells out in his shoe made it apparent that he had very little control on the bridge.

"I was just about to ask Conjurer Hewitt about some troubling news from the bridge," Larwood said. "You know the people as well, Fae, perhaps you can help me understand what this means for Waglenn Landing."

"I'll do my best," Faelin replied. "I know many of the people, but am less certain of the politics."

"Then I shall rely on Conjurer Hewitt for those insights," Larwood said. He turned to Hewitt. "I hear that Head Conjurer Wailes has died."

"I am afraid so," Hewitt said. "I cannot say that it was unexpected. He was old, and quite frail."

"Yes, confined to a chair," Larwood said. "An attendant had to help him get around."

"Yes. We had his ceremony just yesterday," Hewitt replied. "We have not yet named a successor."

"I understand that your ranks are quite depleted," Larwood said. "The conjurer named to lead you temporarily is also dead."

Hewitt schooled his features. "Where did you hear that?"

"I have many sources," Larwood said. "Which one was it?"

Hewitt stared at the Councilman. Did he know? Was this a test? He glanced over at Faelin. She sat straight, staring ahead. If he was caught lying she might never trust him. And he needed her.

"Tadlow," Hewitt said. "Tadlow was named Acting Head Conjurer while Quillan Wailes was incapacitated. And you are correct, he, too, is dead."

"Who's left?" Faelin asked. "How many Conjurers are still alive?"

Hewitt met her gaze and looked away, quickly.

"My family brought all of this onto the bridge," Faelin said. "Because of the books they copied. I need to know who remains."

Hewitt sighed. "Very few of us, I'm afraid. Yaldon, Maykin, Sherston, Meade Tadlow, and myself."

"That's it? Half of your number dead in a few months?" Faelin asked.

"I'm afraid so," Hewitt replied. "But Wailes is dead now."

"Are you saying that Quillan Wailes was responsible for these deaths?" Larwood asked.

"Yes," Hewitt lied. He wasn't going to tell them that Burrage was a worse tyrant than Wailes. Faelin might not agree to be his apprentice if she knew that. "He became obsessed with the books Faelin referred to and made some of us read from them. They are very dangerous books."

"Who's in charge of the conjurers now?" Larwood asked. "Is it Burrage?"

"No one," Hewitt said. "Until we select a new Head Conjurer. And Graylon Burrage is new to the bridge. It's uncertain whether he would be selected."

"When will the vote take place?" Larwood asked.

"Soon," Hewitt replied. "We can't be leaderless for long." Not that the head conjurer did anything now, other than preside over the far-too-many final ceremonies.

"Could it be you?" Faelin asked. "Could you be selected as Head Conjurer?"

"Were you hoping for that?" Hewitt asked. What if she didn't want to apprentice to him unless he was Head Conjurer? "We who are left will vote for the one we feel will best serve us. If that is me, then of course I will accept."

"That is good to hear," Larwood said.

Hewitt sat back as they exchanged a few pleasantries. Eventually Larwood pleaded work he must get back to, and Hewitt followed Faelin out of the office and into a front sitting room.

While she stepped away to get them some tea, he pulled the sheet of paper from his shoe and smoothed it out. When Faelin returned, he laid it on the table beside the tray she brought.

"For you," Hewitt said. "More Kellen spells."

Faelin picked it up and scanned the sheet. Her eyes widened. "This seems very powerful," she said. "Are you certain I will be able to recite it?"

"I have full faith in you," Hewitt said, pleased that she'd understood the most important spell he'd brought. Meade had done well when he'd found this page with an eradication spell.

Faelin folded the paper and tucked it into the waistband of her trousers. "All the same, I will test the other spells first."

"Of course." He took the cup of tea she offered but he set it down without touching it. "Faelin, I hope that hearing how many conjurers have fallen does not sway you from our course of action. You will still agree to be my apprentice."

"It's a shock, Conjurer Hewitt," Faelin replied. "But I know first-hand how obsessed Conjurer Wailes became when he found my father's books."

"Indeed," Hewitt agreed. "His mind must have become as unstable as his body, at the end."

"That must be it," Faelin said. She looked at him. "Now that he's dead, can I return home?"

"Not yet, child," Hewitt said. "A new Head Conjurer must be decided on. Then it should be safe for you to come home. And you must master your talent before you come." She would need to pry Oleda Burrage from the bookbindery, and she'd only be able to do that if Burrage was dead, but he wasn't going to tell her that. Instead he smiled and sipped his tea.

It was time to go. Hewitt took his leave, again encouraging Faelin to practice the spells he'd given her. Would it be enough? Would she be able to defeat Burrage? He had to hope so. But in case, he would ask Meade to try to emphasize the non-Wailes spell he'd hidden in one of Burrage's books.

Faelin was willing to apprentice to him so it might be time for Burrage to die. His hope of having two true conjurers alive on the bridge was gone. Now he must do everything he could to make sure that the one who survived was the one willing to work with him.

FAE HEARD THE front door close and she let out a deep breath. She smoothed out the sheet of paper Hewitt had given her and shook her head. Did he really hope she could defeat Burrage with these small spells? One *was* an eradication spell—but her ancestor had created it to rid the bridge of moss that grew on the stones that were submerged in high tide. It was no match for the killing spell Burrage had used on poor Tadlow—or the one Aric had insisted she create.

"So, our conjurer did give you something," Larwood said as he entered the sitting room, followed by his wife. "It's safe. He is truly gone. I saw him step through the gate a moment ago."

"Simple spells," Fae said. "Useful enough for household tasks."

"But no use against a powerful conjurer," Larwood finished for her. "He does seem to be quite relaxed for a man who's seen half his contemporaries die in the last few weeks."

"He's playing us off against each other," Fae said. "Me and Burrage. He probably did the same with the rest of the conjurers. That could even be why so many of them are dead. At least I know what he's doing."

"Do you think he's sincere?" Mistress Larwood asked. "About taking you on as his apprentice?"

Fae laughed. "Yes, but only as long as it benefits him. If Burrage promises Hewitt what he wants, I'm certain I will no longer matter. Except as a threat to Burrage and by extension, Hewitt."

"Is that a possibility?" Larwood asked. "That Burrage would promise Hewitt something?"

Fae paused. She wished she could ask Aric—he might be able to *sense* how likely it was—while she had to rely on her own knowledge of Conjurer Hewitt. "I think so," she said. "As you said, Hewitt is relaxed for someone whose fellow conjurers are dying. He might already have an agreement with Burrage."

"Or with his mother," Mistress Larwood said.

Both the councilman and Fae looked at her, and she shrugged.

"I've done my own asking around," Mistress Larwood said. "From what I hear, Oleda Burrage influences her son. And not in a good way."

"No," Fae agreed. "Not in my experience."

"Ah, right, you've met her," Mistress Larwood said.

"She was married to my mother's cousin," Fae replied. "Although Graylon is not a blood relative. Wailes brought her to my home after my father died. She assumed she and her son would inherit."

"But Conjurer Wailes said no?" Mistress Larwood asked. "That's probably one of the reasons why he's dead. Apparently, she is quick to hate anyone she feels keeps her—and her son—from getting what they deserve."

"And she would kill for that?" Fae asked. "Has she killed before?" It wasn't that she didn't think Oleda Burrage capable—she'd imprisoned Fae after all—but Durnham had laws against murder.

"I've heard rumours," Mistress Larwood said. "About her husband's death. Nothing definite, but I am trying to get more information. One opinion is that her terrible temper and fondness for revenge has only been hampered by a lack of power."

"Which she has now," Fae said. "Through her son. I wonder what the rest of them did to anger her. And is that how Hewitt is managing the Burrages? By being nice to that horrid woman."

"He would need to fawn over her." Mistress Larwood frowned. "And even that might not last."

"That sounds exactly like Hewitt," Fae said. "He also might see me as the better option because Oleda *is* unpredictable." She sighed and glanced out the window. It was early afternoon. Should she travel back to the Riverman village or should she stay overnight?

She sighed again. "I should stay the night, if you don't mind," she said. She would rather see Aric—he might be able to sense the right course of action, but as Mistress Larwood was so ably demonstrating, there were no secrets in Waglenn Landing. She was supposed to be the Larwoods' houseguest; she should attempt to make it true.

"Of course, Fae," Councilman Larwood said. "It's probably for the best. But you'll have to excuse me. I have meetings to attend."

"Then it will be just us for the afternoon." Mistress Larwood beamed at her. "I think we should spend some time in the garden, and maybe later we should go to the market. I do think it wise to have you seen. People will have noticed you and they'll talk—I think they should talk about seeing you with me, doing things any guest would do."

"Thank you," Fae said. "And I agree I should be seen." For a woman who'd lamented not being able to practice her father's trade because she was female, she'd given very little thought to the Councilman's wife. But she seemed as formidable as her husband in her own way. She met Larwood's smiling face.

"You see why I have kept my position for so many years," he said with a chuckle.

"I am beginning to," Fae said. She followed Mistress Larwood out of the office, shaking her head.

Fae watched Mistress Larwood slip back into the house, taking the tray with her. She glanced up at the hedge that separated the Larwoods' yard from their neighbours. Her hostess had assured her that she was being watched—or at least had been noticed—by her neighbour. It was only a matter of hours, she said, before those living in the other homes that lined the square knew about the Larwoods' guest. And that was even before going to the market.

Fae smiled. She was supposedly from Durnham—the daughter of an old friend who was looking for a little time away after a failed romance. Conjurer Hewitt had been contacted because rumour said that he had a spell to help heal her broken heart.

Because if people would talk about Fae, they would definitely talk about a conjurer visiting the Larwoods: they needed a plausible story to mask the truth.

Fae had no idea people gossiped so much, but Mistress Larwood assured her that for some it was how they spent most of their days. On the bridge, she had rarely heard people talking about their neighbours. Although she'd been in a unique position. Her father had been in the confidence of Horace Hewitt. She'd heard the news that mattered—or so she'd thought at the time—directly from a conjurer.

A bird twittered from the top of the hedge, and she peered up at it. Suddenly, fear clutched at her, and she almost fell off her chair. Aric! Fae sucked in a shaky breath.

Something had happened to Aric! She closed her eyes and tried to find him, tried to connect. He was there, far away, but there. He seemed confused and worried, but not afraid, not in danger. She sighed in relief and tried to project calm to him. She thought she felt a small frisson of relief, and then he was gone.

She opened her eyes to the sunny afternoon and shuddered, suddenly chilled. She shook her head. Aric was fine, she was fine; there was nothing to worry about. She'd spend a restful night with the Larwoods, would wait to see if Hewitt came back tomorrow, then she'd return to the boat, and Aric.

ARIC RUBBED HIS shaking hand across his face. Fae was safe, that was the important thing. He'd felt her, when his dream—his *nightmare*—had shocked him awake from a nap.

He sat up, bumping his shoulder against the edge of the table, and slid off the bench. At the counter, he grabbed the jug and gulped water directly from it. He wiped his mouth with the back of his hand and carefully set the jug back down.

Fae was fine, he repeated to himself. But the intense sense of impending doom wouldn't let him believe it.

It hadn't been a nightmare: it was a *premonition*. One that was important—maybe even critical—to Fae's safety.

Why did he have to have a talent that required another person as a witness? He sat back down and dropped his head onto the tabletop. He needed to know what his premonition meant, what it was trying to tell him.

He sat up and purposely thought about Fae returning to the boat. Nothing about that felt ominous. Would it matter if she returned tonight or tomorrow? Still no change in what he felt.

He took a few deep, slow breaths and concentrated on the gentle movement of the boat and the shadows that darkened the nooks and crannies of the unlit cabin. When his mind was clear and his heart was no longer racing, he let one thought enter his head. How to keep Fae safe.

He closed his eyes, trying to *not* look for answers, trying to let the answer come to him. A minute passed, then two. Gently, almost imperceptibly an image began to form in his mind. It was a view of the bridge from below.

He could see the stairs as they trailed up towards the book bindery. A cloud seemed to linger at the top of the stairs, and Aric peered upwards. Was there someone there? Were they the key to Fae's safety? The moment he tried to force an answer, the bridge disappeared, and he was left with only his sense of approaching disaster.

He tried to clear his mind again, but the same image of the stairs and a vague shadow at the top crept back into his head. Was whatever lay at the top of the stairs the answer or was he now simply obsessed with this image?

He didn't know, and it was frustrating. He sighed. He was too anxious, too worried to be able to force a solution. He'd have to calm down before he tried again. So, he set about trying to empty his mind in order to allow his shaman senses to find the answer.

He was still sitting in the dark hours later when Rand stepped on board.

"Aric, you here?" Rand called from the stairs.

"Yes," Aric replied. He stretched his arms, straightening out the kinks from the past few hours. "Fae's not, though."

"So she's still in Waglenn Landing," Rand said. He lit a lamp, and Aric squinted against the flare of light. "Brought dinner." Rand dropped a couple of fish onto the counter and grabbed a flint to light the stove.

"Yes," Aric said. "She's meeting Conjurer Hewitt." He felt for Fae and relaxed when he found her. She was composed and unworried. "She's probably staying the night."

"Pax said he's coming by later," Rand said. "With news."

Aric nodded. It was too much to hope that the news was good.

He and Rand ate in silence. Aric cleared up afterwards, and then they sat at the table across from each other.

"If I have another premonition," Aric said. "Take note of what I say."

"You already had one?"

"A big one. One I need to know about," Aric said. "But I can't force it. I don't know how. When I try too hard everything just slips away." But now that Rand had lit the lamps he might be able to find something in his mother's books.

He slid off the bench and went to the bedroom, returning with the books. He flipped one open. He'd been through them all countless times, but there was still a chance an answer was there, something that he would recognize only because now it was a problem. He feared that Fae's life depended on him figuring this out. Urgency stabbed at him at that thought. Whatever he needed to do, he must do soon.

HEWITT DIDN'T RISK pausing in the street—instead he swiftly opened the door and entered. He'd be furious if anyone did this to him, but he didn't dare let Burrage or his mother see him. He'd had a hard enough time explaining his second trip to Waglenn Landing—he'd been making sure that the Councilman who had interfered with bridge business understood that there would be no second chance once Burrage was Head Conjurer, he'd said. But he couldn't afford to raise Burrage's suspicions with his visit to a dead conjurer's apprentice.

And his visit to Meade Tadlow would look very suspicious.

"Meade," he called out in a low voice. "Sorry to intrude but I couldn't chance being seen waiting at your door."

The hallway was dark, as were all the rooms that led off it, but he heard a shuffling step from one of them.

"Come with me," a voice said.

"Sherston." Hewitt followed the voice until an arm gripped him.

He was towed along the hallway to the back. A door opened and dim light spilled out: Meade's wan face peered at him. Hewitt slipped through the door, and Meade shut it, leaning over to stuff rags along the floor underneath the door.

"Hewitt."

He turned to see Maykin staring at him. He wrinkled his nose—Yaldon was here as well, his stench making the small room seem even smaller.

"We weren't sure you were coming back," Maykin said. "From seeing the girl."

Hewitt felt the colour drain from his face. "Burrage doesn't know, does he?" He looked around at the grim faces but there was only wariness and fear. No looks of satisfaction or smugness, which he'd expect if someone had told Burrage his secret in order to gain a favour.

"Not from us," Meade said. "But when I told Maykin that you'd asked for more spells and then you went to town, he told me about the bookbinder's daughter. A true conjurer. Is it true?"

"Yes," he replied. "I've seen her do more powerful magic than any of us in this room have ever managed." He paused. "And without any affliction."

"Like Burrage," Maykin said. "Is she on our side?"

"She's of the bridge," Yaldon said. "She has to be on our side."

"She's afraid," Hewitt said. "And none of us stepped in to help her when her father died."

"But she can't want Burrage to rule the bridge," Mead said. "Not if she knows what he's doing."

"It doesn't matter what she wants," Maykin said. "Not unless she can defeat Burrage with magic. Can she?"

"I think she is willing to help," Hewitt said. "At least she seems willing to learn to use magic, but will she be able to defeat Burrage as soon as we need her to? I'm not sure. That's actually why I came to see Meade." He turned to the younger man. "I asked Tadlow to have you add a spell to a book. Did you do it?"

"What spell?" Maykin asked.

"A spell that Burrage will not be able to recite," Hewitt replied. "And live."

"That came from you?" Meade asked. "I was very impressed with that. Tadlow never said it was your idea, but it's done."

"Can you entice Burrage to recite that spell?" Hewitt asked. If Burrage was dead there would be no reason for Faelin to not take her rightful place on the bridge as his apprentice.

"Probably," Meade said. "He's been studying a few other books but they don't have spells nearly as powerful—or horrific— in them. He likes the idea of doing terrible things to people so it shouldn't be difficult to get him to look at this book again."

"But it will kill him?" Sherston asked.

"Yes," Hewitt replied. "I suspect it will be much like what happened to Dabel. The spell is from a book with the same binding." A Kellen spell book, but they didn't need to know that.

"Nothing left but ash," Maykin said. "That would be good. Then we'd just need to get rid of the mother."

"And the Bridgers," Sherston added.

"Don't worry about the Bridgers," Hewitt said. "Shiv will follow whoever wins. He's already been hedging his bets with me." And he also knew about Faelin. Hewitt looked around the room, a knot forming in his stomach. Too many people knew about Faelin: he wouldn't be able to keep her a secret much longer. But what to do?

"Well, that's something," Maykin said. "Meade, you have to get Burrage to recite that spell. It may be our only hope."

Hewitt watched Meade's face as he prepared to refuse, then came to the conclusion that he had to try.

"I'll do my best," Meade said. "But if he catches me he'll kill me." Meade glared at the rest of them.

Maykin ducked his head and Yaldon looked away.

Hewitt met his gaze and snorted. "He'll kill *me* if he learns I've kept news of Faelin Keetley from him," he said. "He'll kill all of us sooner than later. I'd rather die trying to fight him than let him and his mother kill us off one by one, whenever they feel they've been insulted or shown disrespect or one of us just made a mistake, like Tadlow. And that could be today, tomorrow, or years from now, but it will happen, because in my opinion, there is nothing on the bridge that can *ever* make Oleda Burrage content with her position. She must always find someone to conquer, someone she must prove she's better than, and someone to pay for whatever trivial affront they chanced to give her. And she's doing that by having her son kill them."

"What if we killed her?" Maykin asked. "She's in the bookbindery. Someone could take the stairs from the bakery and kill her in her sleep."

"You better make sure it looks natural," Hewitt said. "And that Burrage doesn't have a spell that can reveal the difference. There's no telling what he would do if his mother was murdered. Probably raze the whole bridge."

"That would take enormous power," Sherston scoffed.

"Who do you think built this bridge?" Hewitt asked. "Conjurers—true conjurers."

"He could do it," Meade said quietly. "He *would* do it. He doesn't care about anyone on the bridge other than his mother. He'd simply move to one of the towns and start terrorizing them."

Hewitt would have found the play of emotions across the faces of the others comical if their situation hadn't been so grave. Meade was right. Burrage would destroy the bridge—and everyone on it—if he thought he would be killing his mother's murderer.

"He's that powerful?" Maykin finally asked.

"Yes," Hewitt said. "He's a true conjurer. With the spell book of the man who cursed the Rivermen."

"I know you said that before," Maykin said. "But I didn't realize what it meant. Untold power. And the ill will to use it against anyone."

"And everyone, if he feels like it," Hewitt said, glad that Maykin finally understood the seriousness of the situation.

"I'll try to get him to read the other spell," Meade said. "Maybe this will be over soon."

"And Hewitt, you need to convince the Keetley girl to work with us," Maykin said. "We can't risk her falling into Burrage's hands."

"No, we can't," Hewitt replied. Could he manage another visit to Faelin tomorrow? Should he tell her about . . . everything? Would she be willing to help? When her father had died, all she'd wanted was to stay on the bridge, stay in her home. Was that enough? Did she even still want that? "I'll try to slip away tomorrow for another visit. But it is a risk."

"We're all taking risks," Meade replied.

Hewitt met his gaze and nodded. Some more than others, but Meade was right, they were all taking risks.

Hewitt left the dark house, taking care to make sure no one was on the street watching him. He made his way to his own dark home and entered, re-locking the door once he was inside.

He leaned against the wall. Had he truly made his decision? Was he fully committed to destroying Burrage even if it meant his own death?

He sighed. Despite what he'd said to the others, he still wasn't certain of his own path. He had some influence with Burrage and his mother. He could keep that for a very long time. But he knew that eventually Oleda would see him as an enemy—he could not see another way for it to end. Not unless Burrage had reason to mistrust his mother.

Hewitt slowly trudged to his bedroom. He pulled his oversized shoes off and sat on the bed, staring into the dark. His stomach rumbled—he'd hardly eaten anything today, and the stress he was feeling clutched at his bowels.

He'd have to think about undermining Burrage's faith in his mother—but how? He sighed. That was a worry for another day, right now he needed sleep. He had to be sharp in the morning, in order to come up with a reason to visit Waglenn Landing again— to see Faelin.

Chapter Seven

FAE STRETCHED AND groggily eyed the door. There, another soft knock.

"Yes?" she called out. Her whisper seemed loud in the pre-dawn. She could hear birds chirping outside of the bedroom window, but only a faint light filtered through the curtains.

"A visitor, Faelin," Mistress Larwood said when she poked her head into the room. "Same one as yesterday."

"Oh." Fae threw the bedding off and set her feet on the floor. "Tell him I'll be down in a moment."

Mistress Larwood nodded and gently closed the door.

Fae scrambled into her clothes and ran a hand through her tangled hair. What was Hewitt doing here so early?

Had something happened on the bridge? Anxiously she tried to feel for Aric. And relaxed. He was fine, he was just barely awake. Afraid she'd caused him to panic she tried to project her own sense of being safe to him. She shook her head in frustration, wishing they could do better than send vague feelings to each other. At least she knew he was well, at least they could communicate that much.

She hurried out and down the stairs. She'd be home tonight—hopefully then they would have a chance to come up with a better way to convey information to each other.

Mistress Larwood stood up when Fae entered the small sitting room.

"I'll just get the tea going," she said and left.

"Conjurer Hewitt," Fae said. "Is something wrong?"

"Of course, there is," Hewitt replied. He was sitting on a small settee, one leg crossed over the other, his large shoe dangling in the air. "And I need your help."

Fae ignored the shoe and sat down opposite him, in the chair just vacated by Mistress Larwood.

"My help," Fae repeated. "For what?"

"To save the bridge," Hewitt said. "I fear that it and everyone on it are in great danger."

"Why should I?" Fae asked. "No one helped me when my father died."

"I tried," Hewitt said. "If you had become my apprentice you would have been safe."

"Would I?" Fae asked. "As safe as the other conjurers? So many have died—how can you say I would have been safe from Wailes?"

"You're right." Hewitt sighed. "I can't be sure. And now, the others—the ones left alive—asked me to come. It's very dangerous, but we have few options. You know you are not the only true conjurer."

"And you're all afraid of him," Fae said.

"We have reason to be," Hewitt replied. "Conjurers are dead because of Wailes, that's true enough. But it was because he was trying to find someone who could recite the spells in the books your father left. But Burrage? He killed Tadlow because the man accidentally offended his mother."

"Graylon Burrage," Fae said. "Wailes would have married me to him."

"And I offered you a way out of that," Hewitt said. "By becoming my apprentice."

"A choice my father said no to even when he was dying," Fae said. "He and you were friends for many years—he knew you as well as any man on the bridge did. And yet he kept saying no to that."

"Still, it was a better choice than marrying Burrage," Hewitt said. "And living with that mother of his."

"Neither choice was pleasant," Fae said. "Or anything I ever wanted. But you're telling me that Graylon is cruel and spiteful?"

"Yes," Hewitt said. "And he has access to the most evil spells. He used one to kill Tadlow. It was a slow death."

At a soft knock on the door, Hewitt looked up in fear, his mouth a tight line. Fae thought he was truly afraid.

Mistress Larwood edged into the room carrying a tray.

"Don't mean to interrupt," she said. She set the tray down on the table beside Fae. "Let me know if you need more." And as quickly as she came, she was gone.

"I fear I didn't even apologize for the early intrusion," Hewitt said.

Fae poured two cups of tea and handed one to him.

"Why did you come so early?' Fae asked.

"I met with the other conjurers last night, and we all decided we needed to know if we could count on you." He fixed his gaze on her. "Can we? Not for us, but for all the regular people on the bridge."

"What do you think I can do?"

"You have magic," Hewitt said.

"And only a few spells that you've given me," Fae lied. "Burrage has a spell that will kill, you said so yourself." But it killed slowly, Hewitt had said. Her killing spell was one word—fast—she would have the advantage. "Do you expect me to fight him to the death?" She could see by the look on his face that was exactly what he'd expected. It was what Aric had foretold as well.

"I am sorry," Hewitt said. "It is preposterous—hearing it said out loud makes that clear."

"But you are desperate," Fae replied. "Is there no other way?"

"We have set a plan in motion," Hewitt said. "Even if it succeeds, another conjurer will probably die. If it does not succeed then I fear you are all that stands between those of the bridge and Graylon Burrage."

"What is this plan?" Fae asked. Hewitt hesitated and she frowned. "If I'm to be the fall back, I need to know how likely it is that I will have to act."

Hewitt sighed. "Yes, you are right. The time for secrets is past." He leaned forward. "We have inserted a spell—a non-Wailes spell—into one of the old Wailes spell books. Burrage will be encouraged to recite it."

"And if he does?"

"He will die," Hewitt said.

"I see." It was a better plan than she'd expected. "And who is doing the encouraging?"

"Meade Tadlow," Hewitt said. "He's been helping Burrage catalogue the Wailes spell books." He looked away. "If it does not succeed, Burrage will kill Meade."

"And if it does?"

"I suspect Shiv will kill Meade anyway," Hewitt said.

Fae shivered. Burrage and his mother must be truly horrific if Meade was sacrificing himself in this way. "Let us hope that it succeeds," Fae said. She paused. She'd hoped to have time to discuss everything with Aric, but she had a better understanding of just how dangerous it was for Hewitt to visit her here. "And if it does not, I will do my best to help. That I promise."

"Thank you, my dear," Hewitt said. "That is all I can ask."

Fae nodded. "I know that communication will be difficult," she said. "But perhaps you could try to get a message to Mistress Larwood."

"Mistress Larwood," Hewitt asked. "Not her husband?"

"Not her husband," Fae said. "I'll fetch her and she can give you the details."

"So," Mistress Larwood said. "Will it be easier for you approach Mistress Pullen or shall we work through Charnock?"

"You know both the baker's wife and the fishmonger?" Hewitt asked. He was learning much about how news spread even with the bridge as a barrier.

"Well, I don't know them personally," Mistress Larwood said. "But they both have relatives who live on this side of the bridge. Mistress Pullen is more direct for me. Her sister lives one street over. And she talks to everyone who comes into her shop. The fishmonger is less inclined to gossip, so he has less information."

"The baker's wife," Hewitt said. "Thorpe was her son."

"Terrible thing, what happened to him," Mistress Larwood said. "I hear the poor lad was practically lame when he disappeared." She squinted at him. "Will Mistress Pullen even talk to you?"

"Yes," Hewitt said. "She blames Wailes, not the rest of us."

"She should though," Faelin said. "None of you intervened."

Hewitt sighed. "You're right. My only defense is that we never thought Wailes would use him so recklessly."

"I saw him," Faelin said. "His body. I saw what was left of him."

"How?" Hewitt asked. "We were told he was dead, but Wailes said he had been reduced to ash."

"He was found down river," Faelin said.

"You were there!" Clever girl, making them all believe she'd been upriver all this time.

"Not for very long, but I was there when they found Thorpe. He was too twisted to walk, so there is only one way he ended up in the river."

"He was thrown?" Hewitt asked and sighed. So Wailes had been lying to them all even then. "Wailes told us he'd read a spell and was reduced to ash. Shiv tossed poor Tymm off the bridge as well. But that was at Oleda Burrage's direction."

"Oleda Burrage!" Mistress Larwood said. "I have heard nothing good about that woman. I even hear she killed her husband. She married him because she needed a roof over her head, and once she got it, she didn't need him anymore."

"You think she killed him? I met him once," Faelin said. "He was my mother's cousin."

"What else do you know about Oleda?" Hewitt asked. Was there some tidbit of information that he could use against her with her son? "Or Graylon. How did they support themselves?"

"Hmph." Mistress Larwood pursed her lips. "They lived better once Oleda got her claws into Tadeus. I suspect they lived off what little money he could earn. He was a drunk, I hear, and on his rare sober days made candles."

"Not a trade he passed on to either his adopted son or his wife," Faelin said. "Their house was very rough."

"So they had little to lose," Hewitt said. "And perhaps were desperate." He turned to Mistress Larwood. "Is there anything you know about the Burrages that they would not want to become common knowledge? I'm specifically looking for secrets they've kept from each other."

Mistress Larwood's face crinkled in a smile. "Not yet, Conjurer Hewitt, but I'm doing my best to find out."

"I would especially like to know if she's ever betrayed her son," Hewitt said. "I fear *she* would forgive him anything. I'm less certain he would forgive her." Especially now that he was the one with real power.

"Don't you worry," Mistress Larwood replied. "If there's something, I'll find it."

Hewitt nodded and smiled. He couldn't say he was full of confidence. Apparently, Mistress Larwood was good at searching out secrets, but they had to be there in the first place. At least Faelin had promised to help. That is what he'd come for. He sighed and looked out the window. It was almost midmorning and he had to return to the bridge. If he was lucky, he'd return to find Graylon Burrage already dead.

ARIC CLOSED THE book and stacked it on top of the other two. He hadn't really expected to find anything new—not after he'd already read and reread the shaman books so many times—but there was always hope that something could make sense in a new way. Now that he knew more about . . . everything.

He leaned over and peeked out the window. It was just after midday. Fae wouldn't be back until well after dark, and the hours between now and then seemed endless.

He gently set the curtain back into place trying not to create any movement that might be noticed from outside.

Aric doubted anyone was watching Rand's boat, but still, he had to be careful. He hated that he had to think about it, about spies amongst the Rivermen, but one had been responsible for his mother's death. And if that man's cousin *was* working with the Bridgers, he didn't think he'd be overly concerned with the health of the shaman's son.

He sighed. Watching out for Fiske's cousin wasn't accomplishing much of anything, but it was the only thing he could do until Fae came back. That and look through the books, yet again.

Waiting for her was agonizing when his shaman senses told him that something important—something that put Fae's life in danger—was going to happen.

He slammed his hand against the tabletop. What use was a premonition when he was alone or asleep? Why couldn't he *know* what he saw or said during his premonitions?

He'd had another one last night. A premonition or a bad dream—which could be one and the same for him—that had left him with the same feeling of dread that he'd had yesterday. He'd woken up, his heart racing and fear gripping his belly. He'd spent the rest of the night running scenarios through his head, testing to see which plan would lessen the fear. But try as he might, nothing dulled the sense of urgency around Fae's safety.

Needing to do something, anything, he started to pace. Three steps to the door to the bedroom, three steps to the stairs, then back to the bedroom door.

He reached out, trying to detect Fae. He felt her briefly before he was slammed by magic. A spell. Burrage must be reciting a spell.

Aric closed his eyes and reached into the magic, and frowned, puzzled by what he could sense about it. A small spell with one simple purpose—not the long, multi-faceted spells Burrage had been performing lately. He started to tug on the magic, trying to make it fold in on itself, trying to force it to collapse and lose its focus.

Fae!? She was in the spell. And there was another presence in the magic—the spell caster—it had to be Burrage! But what was Fae doing in this spell? He lost control of the magic, and the spell was completed, the magic twisting away from him.

Aric slumped down on the bench and leaned his head on the table, his breathing ragged. A wave of dread washed over him, leaving him shaking. This was it, this was the event that put Fae in danger.

Because Burrage hadn't recited a Wailes spell—he'd recited a *Kellen* spell. That was why he'd felt Fae so strongly in the spell. But it was *worse*. Burrage must have Kellen blood because he'd recited that spell and *lived*. And he'd been aware that someone else was in the magic with him. Burrage would look for whoever it was, maybe even by using magic. If he found Fae, he'd kill her.

Aric stared at the door that led to the deck. He knew what he had to do in order to stop Burrage from looking for Fae.

Fae slumped in the chair and pressed a hand against her temple.

"Are you all right?" Mistress Larwood asked.

"I'm not sure," Fae replied. "I have a headache." What had happened? She'd felt Aric, and then a spell—Burrage, she'd assumed. But then the magic had somehow pulled her towards it. And just as she'd felt Burrage, she knew he'd felt her. But how? She'd watched Aric manipulate Burrage's spells before. What made this time different?

She closed her eyes and felt for Aric. Yes, he was there. He seemed troubled, but not because he was hurt or in danger. It felt more like he was worried about her.

"I'm fine now." She opened her eyes and met her hostess's worried gaze. "But I must leave as soon as it's dark."

"Of course," Mistress Larwood said. "Then it's a good thing I found out something that might be useful about the Burrages. At least about Oleda Burrage."

"Already? Conjurer Hewitt only just left."

"My network is most active in the morning," Mistress Larwood said. "When the market goods are fresh, so is the gossip. And because she and her son are now living on the bridge, Oleda Burrage has been a topic of conversation for days."

"I don't think I can get this information to Conjurer Hewitt," Fae said. "He'll want to know right away."

"Not to worry, my dear," Mistress Larwood said. "Conjurer Hewitt will know this today if he visits the baker. Now, this came from a very trusted source. It seems young Master Burrage was engaged at one time. A love match, by all accounts."

"Graylon in love? But he's so . . ." Fae tried to picture Graylon Burrage, the man who'd hoped to marry her, in love, but she couldn't. "Hateful," she finished.

"Apparently, he wasn't always," Mistress Larwood said. "He was in love and the young lady loved him back. They were even engaged. Until his mother intervened."

"What did she do?"

Mistress Larwood leaned over the table. "No one can prove anything," she whispered. "But someone saw Oleda Burrage visit the girl in secret one night and a few days later she died of a mysterious illness." She leaned back in her chair. "Graylon was brokenhearted. Everyone thought it such a tragic story until Oleda's husband died two weeks later of a very similar ailment."

"You did say you thought she killed Tadeus," Fae said. "Do you think he knew the truth about what his wife did to the girl?"

"He might have suspected," Mistress Larwood said. "Perhaps he found whatever poison she used. I think Oleda wanted Graylon to be unattached. Whether it's because she had other plans for him or she didn't want to share him with anyone, we may never know."

"Conjurer Wailes would have tried to force me to marry Graylon," Fae said. "After my father died. Oleda seemed to like that idea. Could she have somehow planned this? She seemed eager to live on the bridge." And after seeing their home in Durnham, Fae couldn't blame her.

"Oleda doesn't sound like the type to do anything without some kind of reason or plan," Mistress Larwood said. "How long ago did she marry your mother's cousin?"

"Almost ten years," Fae said. "You think that could be why she married Tadeus in the first place. So she could eventually lay claim to the Bookbindery on the bridge? Although she couldn't have expected my father to die." No one had, including him.

"I think it's more likely she needed a man, and then once she heard about your father's death she saw an opportunity for her son to marry you," Mistress Larwood said. "Although it's possible she'd been looking for just such an opportunity for a long time."

"Her son is the one with magic, with power," Fae said. "Let's hope this information surprises him and makes him angry with his mother." Would it be enough to drive a wedge between Graylon and Oleda? She hoped so.

"I think that's what Conjurer Hewitt is counting on."

HEWITT HURRIED DOWN the hall as fast as his oversized feet would allow. Burrage had sent Shiv for him, and the Bridger had been waiting at the gate when he stepped back onto the bridge. Shiv hadn't said a word, but he'd been in a hurry and he hadn't treated Hewitt as an ally.

Something must have happened. Had Shiv told Burrage about Faelin? Had the Bridger decided that Burrage was the only one who could guarantee the safety of his people?

Was he now hurrying to his own death? Would Burrage believe him if he said he was looking for Faelin to become his apprentice?

"Conjurer Burrage," Hewitt said as he knocked on the door jamb. "It's Hewitt."

"Get in here!"

With a sinking feeling, Hewitt stepped into the room. Burrage stood glaring at Meade, who cowered in the corner. A book lay at his feet and there was a red mark on the poor man's face. Meade looked up at Hewitt with empty eyes.

Not about Faelin, then. Hewitt did his best to look angry and worried, instead of relieved.

"What's going on?" Hewitt asked. "Has something happened?" He knew full well what had happened. Meade had tried to get Burrage to recite the non-Wailes spell. Burrage must have noticed it, somehow. He kept his eyes away from Meade. The man was dead, they both knew it. The only question now was whether Hewitt would die with him.

"Yes, something has happened!" Burrage said. "Shiv."

Hewitt swallowed as the Bridger closed the door and stood in front of it, barring anyone from entering or exiting. The only saving grace was that Oleda Burrage wasn't on this side of the door.

"Meade suggested I recite a spell," Burrage said. "It sounded promising." Burrage walked over to Meade and stared at him. "*Promising*. That was the exact word he used." He turned and looked at Hewitt. "What he meant was that it would kill me." He whirled back to Meade. "But as it turns out I'm not so easy to kill. But you, apprentice, will be very easy for me to kill. Or I could let Shiv spend some time with you. My mother would love to watch that."

Hewitt suppressed a shudder. He didn't need to look at Shiv to know that the Bridger was grinning. He couldn't let Shiv get his hands on Meade. He wouldn't be able to hold out against torture—he'd tell Shiv about the rest of them and they'd all die. *He'd* die.

"Meade singled out a spell?" Hewitt asked, trying to sound angry. "One that would kill you? Thank the Seven you didn't read it."

"The Seven had nothing to do with it," Burrage said. "I *did* read it! It just didn't kill me."

Hewitt covered up his horror with feigned relief. "Then thank the Seven for that." He kept his eyes averted from Meade. He couldn't afford to let Burrage see how wretched he was that the plan had failed—or that Meade would die. "His punishment must be swift," Hewitt said. "As a warning to anyone else who might think to harm you."

Burrage stepped away from the cowering figure of Meade and paced the room. "Mother would agree with you," he said. "If she were here. Unfortunately, she's gone to visit our old neighbours."

Burrage smiled grimly. "She will be sorry to have missed this, but it has to be done." He stopped beside the desk and dragged a book towards him. "Which spell, Meade? You can choose." He raised the book and chuckled. "You catalogued the many ways this book has to kill a man. You must have a favourite. Which one will it be?"

Meade looked up from the floor. Hewitt met his eyes before the other conjurer's gaze swept past him, settling on Burrage.

"Can I?" Meade asked calmly. He grabbed the book at his feet and flipped through it until he found the page he was searching for. "I choose this one," he said and started to read.

"No!" Burrage shouted just as Meade was swallowed in a burst of flame.

The Kellen spell! He'd read the Kellen spell! Hewitt shielded his eyes against the glare and sighed, grieving silently for Meade, the last of the Tadlow conjurers.

It would seem Meade had actually been waiting for his chance to die on his own terms. He would tell the others that Meade had made the bravest of sacrifices.

"Why didn't you stop him?" Burrage shouted.

Hewitt looked up to find Burrage standing in front of Shiv. "You should have stopped him!"

"You asked me to watch the door," Shiv said.

"Don't tell me what I asked you to do!" Burrage said. He turned back to the corner that now held a small pile of ash and the spell book. He stomped over and picked up the book before kicking at the ashes.

"This better be cleaned up before I come back." Burrage swept past Hewitt and through the door quickly opened for him by Shiv.

Hewitt let out a sigh and turned to leave but Shiv blocked his path.

"Did you know about this?" the Bridger asked. For once he didn't smirk as he addressed Hewitt.

"No," Hewitt lied.

"Too bad," Shiv said. He stepped aside and Hewitt left the room, wondering if Shiv regretted that Burrage hadn't died, or that he didn't have a reason to kill Hewitt. Another dead conjurer would have appeased Burrage, Hewitt thought, and directed his anger away from the Bridger. At least there had been no mention of his second trip to Waglenn Landing in as many days.

Hewitt quickly made his way out of Conjurers Hall and onto the cobblestones of the bridge. He hurried to the baker's, not wanting to spend any more time out of doors—exposed—than necessary. He'd ask for information and then head straight home. And hope Burrage would somehow forget he even existed.

ARIC LIFTED HIS face to the sun, enjoying the warmth after being forced to stay inside for so many days.

He didn't think anyone had seen him leave Rand's boat. He'd slipped into the river and let the tide and the current sweep him down to his mother's boat. Now the sails fluttered in the breeze as he steered into the middle of the river in order to pass the village.

He'd be seen by Rivermen but it didn't matter, not now. He wanted to be visible to everyone on or above the river—and especially to Burrage. And if Burrage didn't happen to notice him, he'd make sure he felt his presence. That was the whole point.

He'd been startled by another Kellen spell being cast so soon after the first. And horrified when he'd felt someone die. It hadn't been Fae, thank Berhalla, he'd connected with her in the magic, frantic with worry. Nor had it been Burrage, although whoever had died had been on the bridge.

But Aric had realized that he had to act now, before Burrage did anything that caused harm to Fae.

Now that he'd felt him in the magic, or maybe because he'd recited a Kellen spell, he could track Burrage. He was somewhere ahead of him, on the bridge. Aric squinted and looked upriver. Despite the fear he had for himself, it was good to be sailing on the river again, good to have the bridge in his sights. Good to have the sun on his face.

And good to have the gnawing unease over Fae's safety finally gone. He smiled. No matter what happened to him, she would be safe. And that meant he'd made the right decision.

A few Rivermen stared at him from smaller fishing boats. Aric thought he recognized Rand but he was too far away to be certain—until the figure in the boat hurriedly dragged in all his nets and hoisted his sail. By then Aric was too far ahead for him to catch up.

He felt a twinge of guilt for repaying Rand's generous help by saying nothing about what he planned to do, but he couldn't be talked out of this, and he didn't want anyone else to be put at risk by even knowing his plans.

A few minutes later, the base of the stairs loomed ahead. The tide was out and the footing of the pier was exposed. He looked up the stairs to the bridge high above. He hadn't been up the stairs since Fae's father's ceremony. He looked back at the pier. He had been close to the pier one time since then.

Fae's life had been changed by the death of a parent. As had his.

His mother had died on this exact spot. He'd been too far away to see her clearly, but he'd felt her death—felt when she took her last breath—felt the moment her shaman abilities had passed to him. He'd also felt her peace at her death. Felt that she'd embraced him—finally—that after years of neglect and indifference, she'd realized that he *was* her son and he would inherit her shaman gifts. Had she had some insight at the end? Had she sensed that he would be so much more than what shamans had become over the years? He hoped so.

He sighed. He'd rather remember all the times he'd tied up here to visit Fae. All the times she'd set a lamp out to draw him over to take her fishing, or swimming or to just float on the river, talking.

He jumped out of the boat and onto the slippery rock of the pier. He didn't expect to need the boat again but it had been his mother's—he couldn't just let it drift off to crash into the bridge or run aground. He grabbed the painter and tied the boat to the rusty ring set into the stone.

Maybe someone—Rand perhaps—would take his mother's boat back to the village—and Fae. She might want it, when he was gone.

By the time he'd climbed to the fork in the stairs, his breathing had become laboured. He paused and gulped in a breath before taking the path that led up to the book bindery. He'd need to find Burrage fast—before the curse made it impossible for him to do what he must to keep Fae safe.

Even though he knew where to look to find the opening to the hidden room, he almost missed it. He ran his hand over stones that all ended at a single edge. He leaned away from the wall to get a better look. Now that he knew where to look, he could see the outline of a doorway. He pushed on it, and it sank inward slightly. Aric looked up at the door to Fae's workroom. It would be better to go through Fae's old room and not risk being trapped in the room beneath Lachlan Keetley's workroom.

The door to Fae's workroom wasn't locked, and Aric eased through it. He stared around the room that Fae had spent so much of her time in. Leather was still stacked neatly on the shelves, although there was a layer of dust on everything, including the work table.

Was anyone even living here? He knew Wailes had been accessing the books in the room below, but he didn't know if Burrage was doing the same. Perhaps he'd already taken all the Wailes spell books he needed? Would he be back for the Kellen books now?

He reached out to sense Burrage. He was close, but not in the bindery. Aric tried the door that led into the house. It wasn't locked.

Once out in the hallway, he paused to listen for sounds from the rooms above. The quiet reassured him until he realized that he was quiet as well. Unexpectedly quiet.

He took a deep breath—and then another. His lungs didn't constrict and he had no trouble breathing. The curse didn't seem to be affecting him. Why?

Curious, he stepped back out through Fae's workroom and out to the stone stairs: and struggled to draw a breath. Back inside, he could breathe easily again.

What had happened? Had the curse been transformed by one of the many spells Burrage had recited or one of the ones Aric had changed? Had some magic altered the curse to allow Rivermen to breathe on the bridge but not on the stairs?

He could live here with Fae, was his first thought. Except he didn't expect to live through the next few days. He pushed that thought out of his head and went back to the hallway. Not dealing with the effects of the curse would give him more time and make his task more likely to succeed—that was all.

Half an hour later, Aric stood at the door that led out onto the bridge. He'd checked all the rooms. Someone was living here, although they weren't here at the moment. Lachlan Keetley's bedroom had been used recently and there was half a loaf of bread in the kitchen. At least there used to be. Aric had eaten the bread, along with a cold fish pie he'd found in the larder. As a last meal, it could have been worse.

Burrage was a short distance away, just across the cobblestones, so that's where Aric had to go. He stepped out onto the cobbled streets and bumped into someone.

"Watch . . ." the voice trailed off. "Aric?" Horace Hewitt gaped at him. And then the man shoved him through the door and back into the bindery.

Chapter Eight

Hewitt pushed the door closed and leaned against it, his breath ragged and his heart racing.

"What in the name of the Seven are you doing here?" he asked the Riverman. "Bridgers will kill you if you're caught." He stepped away from the door. He didn't think anyone else was outside—he'd been very careful when he'd left the baker's next door—but that didn't mean someone couldn't walk past the book bindery and hear them.

"Come, get away from the street," Hewitt said and steered Aric towards the kitchen. "They'll kill me too if they find us here." Why was the Riverman here putting him in danger?

"It's still Fae's home," Aric said. "Isn't it?"

"No," Hewitt replied. "It belongs to Oleda Burrage now, and she doesn't share." Not even her son, as he'd just learned from the baker's wife.

Hewitt followed Aric into the kitchen and sat down at the table. Aric stared at him for a few moments before taking the chair opposite.

"Oleda Burrage," Aric said. He smiled. "I ate her supper."

"Aric," Hewitt said. "This is nothing to smile about. She's had men killed for less than that."

"Yes," Aric replied. "I'm sure she has. Fae told me she met with you in Waglenn Landing. And you met again this morning?"

"She . . ." Hewitt trailed off. He'd thought he could trust Faelin, he'd desperately needed to trust her. His shoulders sagged. "She didn't tell me she had spoken to you."

"No. It's so difficult to know who to trust these days," Aric replied. "My own mother was betrayed by one of her people."

"Ah, yes, the Riverman who brought her to Wailes. It didn't end well for him," Hewitt said. "Are you going to see Faelin? I have terrible news about Burrage."

"Does he know?" Aric asked.

"Know what?" Hewitt stared at him, puzzled. "About his mother? That she poisoned the woman he was engaged to? I've only just found that out myself." He paused. "I doubt he knows."

"What?" Aric straightened. "She did that?" Hewitt nodded. "I'm not sure even Graylon Burrage would forgive his mother that. No, I was talking about the spell he cast earlier—the one that wasn't a Wailes spell."

"How do you know about that?" Hewitt whispered, horrified that his secret wasn't secret. His breath caught in his throat. "Does Faelin know?"

"Yes," Aric said. "I'm sure she does. Just as I'm fairly sure Burrage knows there's another magic user out there."

"He knows about Faelin?" Hewitt felt ill. The hidden spell had failed, and now Faelin was the only hope of defeating Burrage. "He'll look for her."

"That's why I'm here," Aric agreed.

"No, you don't understand," Hewitt said. "He'll look for her. And he won't stop until he finds her. And then he'll kill her, just as he's killed the rest of us." He closed his eyes as despair washed over him. He might as well jump off the bridge at low tide—his death was certain—and imminent.

"That's why I'm here," Aric repeated. "I'm going to find him so he won't bother looking for Fae."

"How will that help?"

"My mother's shaman abilities," Aric said. "They passed to me. And in part because I'm a male shaman and in part because Burrage is a Wailes conjurer and we are tied together through the curse—his spells are . . . evident to me. I can tell when he's casting one, and if I'm quick enough I can change it so that it doesn't do what it was intended to do."

"You can . . ." Hewitt stared at Aric, Faelin's childhood Riverman friend. He'd known the boy's mother was shaman, but he'd never really wondered what that meant. "Shamans do magic?"

"So it seems." Aric shook his head. "Women shamans have always had some limited abilities—but it turns out that men wielded magic more closely tied to conjurers." He paused and Hewitt could see that he was trying to decide something.

"You can trust me," Hewitt said. "I would never do anything to harm Faelin. Although I cannot guarantee I wouldn't sacrifice you to save her." There, he'd said it. He would sacrifice anyone—himself included—to help Faelin defeat Burrage.

"Thank you," Aric said. "That's exactly why I'm here. My sacrifice will allow Fae to live."

"You are certain?"

"As certain as my gifts allow," Aric replied. "When Burrage finds me, he will stop looking for anyone else."

"But he doesn't know about Faelin?" Hewitt asked. He didn't think a conjurer had told Burrage his secrets, not when Meade had just been killed for inserting that other spell. Had Shiv told him he'd been looking for her? "You know he recited a non-Wailes spell. How? You said Wailes spells were evident to you. But this wasn't a Wailes spell."

"No," Aric said. "It wasn't. It was a Kellen spell. And both Fae and I were in the magic when he cast it. So, he knows someone is out there."

"Can you convince him that it was you?" Hewitt asked. It didn't sound as though Aric's shaman magic was as nearly as powerful as a conjurer's.

"Yes, although I probably don't have enough magic to kill him. It will be up to Fae to do that."

"Can she?" Hewitt asked. "She has so few spells to work with."

"Your Graylon Burrage is nothing more than a reciter of other conjurers' spells." The Riverman smiled, and Hewitt started to believe Faelin could win.

"Fae creates her own spells," Aric continued. "And she's quick and powerful. She is a true conjurer."

"She creates her own spells?" Hewitt repeated. He felt the despair that had enveloped him for days lift a little. "She creates her own spells!" She had a chance—and therefore he and the rest of the people of the bridge had a chance—to defeat Burrage. Faelin Keetley was even more powerful than he'd hoped. He met Aric's eyes. He would keep her secret at all costs.

"What do you plan to do now?" Hewitt asked.

"I'll wait until you get back to your home and then I will find Graylon Burrage."

"He'll kill you," Hewitt said.

"He'll try," Aric replied. "With magic. And if that doesn't work I suspect he'll want to . . . study me."

"Yes," Hewitt replied. "Shiv will do it." He shuddered. Aric would be tortured, and he knew it. "His mother will want to watch."

"Then that might be a good time for me to divulge that secret you mentioned earlier," Aric said. "I'll need to know the name of the betrothed."

FAE LOOKED OUT from behind a willow tree. It was dusk, and lights were just starting to glow in the windows of the buildings on the bridge. Someone had died there by reciting a Kellen spell, and it hadn't been Burrage. Meade Tadlow, probably, based on what Hewitt had told her. The plan to have Burrage die by reciting a non-Wailes spell had failed because Burrage had Kellen blood. So, Meade was most likely dead. And Burrage was not.

She rubbed a hand across her temple. The headache was fading but she was tired from the pain. And from pretending to the Larwoods that nothing was wrong when she was worried that Burrage was much worse than Hewitt said he was.

Out of habit her eyes found the book bindery. The windows were dark—was Oleda Burrage with her son at Conjurers Hall?

Mistress Larwood's information was proof of the cruelty and ambition of the woman who had married her mother's cousin— the woman who'd been her own potential mother-in-law.

With what she knew, Fae was certain that her own life would not have been long if she'd married Graylon Burrage as Wailes had wanted. After a child or two born and trained in bindery, she would have probably shared the fate of Patia, Graylon's betrothed.

The willow fronds swayed in the breeze, and the base of the arch came into view. Fae stared. Two boats were tied up at the foot of the stairs. A small fishing boat and a larger one . . . her heart skipped a beat. What was Aric's mother's boat—*Aric's boat*—doing at the bridge? It should be far downstream, hidden in the trees that overhung the river.

She automatically felt for him—he was *on* the bridge. Aric! He didn't seem hurt, or angry, or afraid. All she could sense from him was a strong resolve. She tried to get his attention but he was concentrating on something else and didn't notice her.

As she stared out at the bridge, someone climbed onto Aric's boat from the smaller one. Was it him? No, the person didn't move like Aric. It was Pax, she thought, and the other boat looked like Rand's fishing boat. She watched as Pax jumped onto the pier and then got back onto Aric's boat. Then Rand headed downstream, followed a few minutes later by Pax.

She stared at Aric's boat—the boat that had been her home when they'd lived in secret on the sea, discovering what they could about their respective abilities.

Should she follow the boats to the Riverman village? Would either Rand or Pax know why he'd gone to the bridge? Or should she go back to Waglenn Landing and hope that Hewitt sent her news?

She was certain that Aric had gone to the bridge on his own. Just as she was certain he hadn't discussed it with either Rand or Pax. Why else would they have needed to retrieve the boat? Why else wouldn't Aric have had Rand drop him off at the base of the stairs?

It had to do with Burrage being a Kellen conjurer—she didn't need a premonition to tell her that. But why hadn't he waited for her to return?

She stepped away from the river bank and started to retrace her steps back to Waglenn Landing. She hoped the Larwoods would let her stay with them again. Because the only reason Aric would have left before discussing it with her was because he didn't want her to talk him out of whatever it was he planned on doing.

Which meant it was dangerous—and he probably thought he was saving her by sacrificing himself.

She wasn't going to allow him to make that decision for her.

She was halfway back to town when she felt a huge pulse of magic. She caught it, trying to peer into it. Aric was there—and he was alive. Then frighteningly, she could no longer sense him.

Fae turned down a laneway that led to the bridge gates. She stared at the gates for a full two minutes, trying to get a sense of Aric. She *thought* he was there but was she just hoping he was? A moment later she felt him, and she almost dropped to her knees in relief. He didn't respond but he was alive—and in pain. What could she do? How could she help him? She couldn't—*wouldn't*—let him die.

She stepped under a tree and leaned against the trunk, hoping it would hide her at least a little, while she figured out her next step.

Immediately going to Aric's rescue—and using magic to get past the Bridgers—would make Burrage aware of her, and she'd become a target. If Burrage had enough warning, he could find a spell to use against her. She couldn't afford to give away any advantage, not if both she and Aric were to live through this.

She closed her eyes and concentrated on creating a spell. It was one she'd worked on—one Aric had made her create—but now she made it so small that even Aric wouldn't notice. Then she tucked it into a protective spell.

She whispered two words and the spells raced away from her. She followed the magic straight to Aric and felt the spells melt into him. He didn't flinch or try to connect to her so she had to assume he hadn't noticed it. And she knew that he was alive, and conscious.

Fae stepped back onto the lane and hurried towards the Larwoods' house. She needed a plan, a way to get to Aric off the bridge without Burrage knowing she was a conjurer. But how?

HIS HEAD THROBBED and his vision was blurry when he opened his eyes. He closed them and sucked in a breath. Tentatively he reached up and felt his face. A lump was forming on his right temple where Shiv had struck him. He felt magic building nearby and automatically reached into it. This time he tried to siphon a tiny amount into him, before twisting it and sending it away.

"What are you doing?"

Aric opened his eyes to find Graylon Burrage's rage-filled face looming over him.

"How are you changing my spell?" Burrage said. "Stop it!"

Burrage backed away and Shiv's face replaced his. Aric automatically raised his arm to protect his face from a blow. The

Bridger had already hit him hard enough to knock him unconscious once. He couldn't afford to have that happen again—he wouldn't be able to deflect Burrage's killing spells.

"Not yet," Burrage said, and Shiv stepped away.

Aric sat up a little, the floor's smooth tiles beneath his palms. Was the pain subsiding? Was the magic he'd pulled into himself helping him heal, giving him energy?

Burrage leaned down and stared into his eyes. "Who are you? Why can a Riverman do magic?"

"Why can you?" Aric asked. He wasn't about to tell him he couldn't actually do spells—that he could only manipulate existing spells and magic.

"Hewitt said it's because I carry the blood of a Wailes." Burrage straightened and walked over to a chair.

Slowly, Aric got to his feet. He was feeling steadier every moment, and by the time he stood facing Burrage, his head was clear and he could focus.

"Same thing for me," Aric said.

"But you're a Riverman," Burrage said. "There have never been Rivermen conjurers."

"No," Aric replied. "We've always had shamans." He looked at Shiv and then back to Burrage. "Which I became when my mother died at the base of the bridge."

"The old woman?" Burrage asked. "She was your mother? She hardly looked human." He paused and frowned. "That wasn't my doing. That was Wailes. I had no power."

"Not yet," Aric said. "But the Bridger was there, weren't you?"

Shiv nodded. "Following orders."

"Yes," Aric agreed. "But you like it. Just as you liked hitting me. I think you want to hit me again." Aric had to force himself not to react when Shiv's eyes narrowed and his fists clenched. He turned to face Burrage. "You might want to be careful," he said. "This one enjoys his work a little too much for me to be safe around him. You might want to talk to me."

"Shiv will do what he's told," Burrage replied.

Aric was watching Shiv when Burrage spoke. The Bridger's nostrils flared, but there was no other sign that he resented the conjurer's words.

"So, you are a shaman," Burrage said. "What does that mean?"

"I'm not really sure," Aric said. Burrage glared at him and Aric shrugged. "I know what it meant to my mother, but she died before she could tell me what to expect."

"Even these pathetic excuses for conjurers have apprentices," Burrage said. "You expect me to believe your own mother didn't train you at least a little?"

"I wasn't supposed to inherit her gifts," Aric said.

"Because?" Burrage prompted.

"I'm a man. Shamans have always been women," Aric said. "At least as far back as our oral history goes. If there was a male shaman before that, every Riverman has forgotten it." Which was true—he wasn't going to tell Burrage about the books he'd found.

"Was your mother able to tap into spells?" Burrage asked. "That was you the other day, wasn't it? I felt someone in the magic when I was reciting a spell."

"Yes, that was me," Aric replied. He put as much truth into his words as he could—Burrage had to believe he was the only one who'd been in the magic with him. "I felt the magic and just . . . I don't know, looked . . . and that's when I sensed you."

"Is it a shaman ability you inherited from your mother?"

"I don't know." Aric shrugged. "My mother never spoke about being able to feel magic. And as you know, the conjurers who exist now do not have much magic. Perhaps my mother never felt magic because it has to be someone with real power? Maybe shamans can only notice truly powerful spells?"

"Yes, that makes sense," Burrage said. "I am the first true conjurer in generations." He leaned back in his chair. "Why did you come?"

"I felt you in the magic," Aric replied. "I could tell where you were and I thought we should meet. I didn't realize you would assume I was an enemy."

"Aren't you?" Burrage asked. "You're a Riverman and I am a Wailes conjurer. I would think that puts us on opposite sides."

"Maybe I was hoping we were on the same side," Aric said. "You may be a Wailes conjurer but you are only a very distant relative of the one who created the curse. I hoped that the old hatred had died out. Because as a Wailes conjurer you could remove the curse your ancestor laid on my people."

"What's the benefit to me?" Burrage asked.

When Shiv smirked, Aric knew that Burrage was exactly what he and Fae had expected. He had all the power, so he thought, so in his mind there was no reason to show kindness to anyone. Ah well, he'd had to try to reason with the man.

"Peace," Aric said. "And the goodwill of Rivermen."

"Neither of which I care about," Burrage said. "Shiv." He rose and walked past Aric. "Lock him up, but make sure he's alive."

"Unharmed?" the Bridger asked.

"Relatively," Burrage replied. He paused at the door. "But you're not to touch him. He's right, you do like it too much, and I fear you could get carried away. There would be terrible consequences for you, but my pet shaman would still be dead."

Burrage left, and the smile Shiv gave Aric made his heart race. He wouldn't die, not yet, but he might wish he had.

Shiv pushed him out the door and down a hallway. He shoved him towards a short set of stairs. Aric braced his shoulder against the wall as he half stumbled down them.

He had barely gotten his feet back under him when he was thrust around a corner and slammed against the wall. Shiv half dragged him down a short corridor. He paused in one of the doorways and shouted at someone. Then he laughed and heaved Aric into a small room. He stepped inside and Aric backed into a corner.

"My son," Shiv said as he made way for another, younger Bridger to enter the room. "Since Conjurer Burrage told *me* not to touch you. Don't kill him," he said to his son. "But anything short of that is fine with me."

Aric stood upright, using all his will to keep the fear he felt from bubbling to the surface. That would only make them hurt him more than they already planned. Could he somehow use magic to help him survive? Did he even want to survive? Wasn't he here to sacrifice himself so that Burrage didn't look for Fae? He'd done that, hadn't he? He pasted a smile on his face and tried to detect danger for Fae but his intense fear—for her and for himself—was muddling his senses.

"Wipe that smile off his face," Shiv urged his son. He stood back, arms crossed, and his son took a step towards Aric.

Aric met the younger Bridger's eyes as the man raised a fist, drew back, and hit him.

At least he'd planned to hit him, and Aric had fully expected to be hit. Instead, there was a blast of power and a flash of light, and Shiv's son crumpled to the floor.

"What did you do to him?" Shiv shouted. He knelt and felt his son's neck. "He's dead." Shiv stood up, anger burning in his eyes. "And so are you."

"More likely it will be you," Aric said. He didn't know if it was true, didn't know if Fae's spell would protect him again, but Shiv didn't know that either.

The Bridger glared at him for a moment before stooping to pick up the body of his son. He carried him to the door and turned to Aric.

"I can still starve you to death," he said. "It's not a good way to die."

"Then Oleda Burrage's supper truly was my last meal," Aric said. "Thank her for me." He was still hoping for an audience with both Burrage and his mother. Aric wanted to be the one to disclose the murder of the betrothed. Burrage might eventually forgive his mother but he'd consider even a temporary rift between them a success. Anything that distracted Burrage from magic—from using his deadly spells—would help Fae. He hoped.

The door slammed shut and he heard a bar slide across it. He sat down on the narrow cot that was the only furniture in the small cell.

It was time to try to reach Fae. And when had she put that spell on him? The minute it had been triggered he'd known is was her—a Kellen spell, created with subtlety and skill. Despite his circumstances, he couldn't help but be proud of her.

He reached out through the magic: there was no sense of where she was, but he could tell that she was safe.

Aric sighed and lay down. He might as well try to sleep. Burrage would want to see him again soon enough.

"He wants you."

Hewitt looked up from his desk to find Shiv glowering at him. One look at the Bridger's angry face and tense jaw and Hewitt dropped the book he was reading and stood up. He barely had time to shut the door of his house as he hurried to keep up with the other man.

A couple of other Bridgers glanced darkly at him as he followed Shiv into Conjurers Hall. Had Aric already been tortured into giving away all his secrets? Hewitt nervously smoothed a hand along his robe as he waited for Shiv's knock to be answered.

"Get in there," Shiv said. He stepped aside just enough to allow Hewitt to brush past him and into the room.

Hewitt slid to a spot near the back wall as Shiv closed the door and leaned against it.

"He can go."

Confused, Hewitt looked up at Oleda Burrage. But she wasn't looking at him. Instead, her gaze was fixed on Shiv.

"No," Shiv said. "It was my son that died."

Shocked, Hewitt dropped his eyes to the floor. Had Aric killed Shiv's son? No wonder the Bridger looked angry. But that meant the lad must be dead. Shiv wouldn't have let him live after that.

"He can stay, Mother," Burrage said. "He's the only one who was there when it happened." Burrage turned to Hewitt. "What do you know about the Rivermen and their shamans? It seems we've caught one and he can do magic."

"I don't know much about the Rivermen," Hewitt replied. "They have reason to keep their distance from conjurers." It sounded as though Aric was alive. He ventured a glance at Shiv. Had Burrage been able to rein in the Bridger even after his son's death? And did that mean the Bridger had chosen a side?

"Yes, yes, the curse," Burrage said. "But you've never wondered about their shaman? About her abilities?"

"They weren't much, from what I understand," Hewitt said. "Perhaps Conjurer Yaldon knows more. He has spent some time with them."

"Yaldon, which one is that?" Oleda asked.

"The one you want to meet with outdoors," Burrage replied. "Shiv." He nodded and Shiv slipped out of the room. "Yaldon knows about the Rivermen?"

"More than me," Hewitt replied. "As you say, he spends a lot of time outdoors." He glanced around the room. "Which is where we should meet him, unless you want to have to air this room out for a few days."

"I'll stay here," Oleda said. "I have no need to subject myself to that disgusting man."

"Suit yourself." Burrage opened the door and gestured for Hewitt to precede him.

"This shaman," Hewitt said. "You have him?"

"Yes," Burrage said. "Although Shiv's not happy that the

Riverman is still alive."

"I'm surprised," Hewitt said. Shocked was more like it, but he didn't want Burrage to know he doubted his control over Shiv. "If he caused the death of Shiv's son, I would have expected him to be dead."

"Shiv's afraid," Burrage said. "He said the shaman warned him that if he tried to hurt him he'd end up dead too."

"He can do magic?" Hewitt asked. Had Aric lied to him? Did he have his own magical ability? How else could he have killed a Bridger? If Aric could control magic, should he still be allowed to sacrifice himself? He might even be *more* powerful than Faelin.

But he still wasn't a *conjurer,* even if he did have powerful magic. He had the inferior abilities of a Riverman shaman because he didn't carry the blood of a true conjurer. Aric was potentially a tool to be used to help conjurers become great again, nothing more.

"He says he felt me in a spell a recited yesterday," Burrage replied. "But he wasn't sure about anything else." He paused at the door to the street. "I think he's lying, but I won't know unless I can find out more about Rivermen and their shamans."

Burrage stepped out onto the cobblestones and Hewitt followed. He saw Shiv, one hand covering his nose and the other pushing a terrified Yaldon towards them.

"Perhaps we can meet in the square?" Hewitt said. "There should be a breeze to help with the smell, at least. And fewer chances to be overheard." Not that something like this would be a secret for long on the bridge. No doubt more than a few nervous tradespeople were spying at this little gathering. Conjurers were dying: they had to be worried that they would be next.

"Follow us," Burrage called to Shiv. He led the way towards the square, holding a finger up to determine which way the wind was blowing. Once he and Hewitt were positioned upwind, he nodded to Shiv, who pushed Yaldon towards the railing.

The moon cast a silvery glow on the river. Both town docks were dark and empty but a few lights bobbed close to the bend in the river. Rivermen out fishing, Hewitt assumed, but he knew even less about the Rivermen who lived upriver than he did about those who lived down.

It spoke to the arrogance of all the conjurers, not just him, that the *expert* was a man who'd visited the Rivermen no more than half a dozen times. Only Faelin had befriended a Riverman. And because of that, because she'd been able to count them as friends, she was still alive.

"Hewitt tells me you have knowledge of the Rivermen," Burrage said. "Tell me."

"Rivermen?" Yaldon asked, sounding confused. "Yes, I have met with them from time to time. Their leader is Pax Oldham. At least downriver. I'm not sure who's in charge upriver."

"And their shaman," Burrage asked. "What do you know about him?"

"Her," Yaldon corrected. "She's dead." He seemed to realize that one of the people instrumental in her death was standing beside him, because he shut his mouth and took a shuffling step away from Shiv.

"Not her, her son. The new shaman."

Yaldon looked up in surprise. "Her son is now the shaman? I don't think that was expected. Are you certain?"

"At least you are confirming that what he said was true," Burrage said. "No one thought he would become shaman because he's male. He has some magical abilities. I need to know what they are. Did the mother have them as well?"

"I don't think so," Yaldon said. "At least not like the magical abilities we . . . you have."

"Are you sure?" Burrage took a step forward and Yaldon shrank in on himself.

"Perhaps the Rivermen kept this knowledge from Yaldon," Hewitt interjected. "Or perhaps they themselves didn't know."

"Pax Oldham was extremely worried about not having a shaman," Yaldon said. "He did not expect the son to become one."

"You're not much help," Burrage said. "Let me know if you remember anything else."

Yaldon nodded and kept his eyes on the cobbles as Burrage walked away.

Hewitt would have tried to signal to his colleague, but Shiv was watching him, his eyes angry and his body tense. The Bridger wanted to kill someone, and if it couldn't be Aric, Hewitt didn't think it would matter who. He wanted to warn Yaldon to tell the others to stay inside. It was very likely that someone was going to die tonight.

Chapter Nine

Fae sat down on the bed in the Larwoods' spare room. She was grateful that Mistress Larwood had welcomed her back. She'd appeared at the door in her nightclothes, holding a lamp, and had quickly led Fae through to the kitchen.

Just after her hostess went to rouse her husband, Fae felt the spell she'd placed on Aric trigger, and she'd panicked until she sensed him. He was alive. Before she had a chance to cast another protective spell over him, the Larwoods had joined her in the kitchen.

Fae had rushed through her explanation of why she'd returned to Waglenn Landing, keeping track of Aric, ready to intervene, if she had to. Thankfully he remained calm, and eventually she realized that he was asleep.

Mistress Larwood and the Councilman had led her back to this room and then returned to their own bed.

Now, finally, she had a chance to protect Aric.

She took a deep breath, closed her eyes, and found him. He was still calm, still in the same place, still sleeping. She scanned past Aric, searching out even the smallest hint of Kellen magic. Now that Burrage had used it, she thought she'd be able to find him. Yes, he was there, not far from Aric, so very likely they were in the same building.

Could she cast a spell on Burrage without him sensing her? She'd done it with Aric, could she do the same to Burrage? Set a spell on him while he was asleep, one he wouldn't feel, one he wouldn't even know was there?

It was risky—it might make him realize that someone else with magic existed, someone other than Aric. If she could find him, then he could find her. Would knowing that she was out there make Aric safer?

Fae let out a deep breath. That was it—that was why Aric had gone to the bridge. Burrage had felt them in the spell; the Kellen spell that Burrage had recited and lived through. Aric wanted him to think it was only him, wanted to keep Burrage from looking for anyone else. Fae smiled for the first time since she knew that Aric had gone to visit the enemy.

She wouldn't let Burrage know she existed. Instead, she would make him think Aric was more powerful—more dangerous—than he actually was. If Burrage was afraid of him: if she made it so that he was afraid to hurt or try to kill Aric, he'd have a better chance of staying alive.

Her decision made, she recited a small spell and focussed it on Burrage. It was a nothing spell: created to do little more than make Burrage aware of its existence. He grunted and woke up when it settled into him. Then he followed the magical trail Fae had left. And it led him straight to Aric.

Before Burrage had even reached Aric through the magic, Fae had already placed an improved protection spell on him. This one was created to keep him safe even with repeated attacks. And it guarded against both physical and magical attacks.

For safe measure, she added the same protections to herself and the Larwoods. Even if Burrage was looking for magic in Waglenn Landing, he wouldn't be able to do anything to them if he found them, not now.

Aric sat up, gasping for breath, his heart pounding. Fae. He could sense her presence. And she'd done . . . something, but what? He relaxed and lay back down and focused. Ah . . . she'd placed another spell on him, most likely another protective spell.

A noise sounded in the hall outside his cell, and he frowned. Perhaps he'd need that protection sooner than expected.

"Open the door!"

The door flew open and a furious Burrage entered the cell. He loomed over Aric, who sat up with his back to the wall. Shiv hovered in the background, and Aric thought he saw Hewitt's pale face out in the hall.

"What did you do?" Burrage asked. "Just now, what did you do to me?" His arm rose as though to strike him.

Aric shrugged. "Do you really want to hit me?" He glanced at Shiv. "Ask your pet Bridger what happened to his son."

Burrage dropped his arm, but he leaned in and glared.

"I will kill you for this," he said. "I have plenty of spells to choose from. And none of them are pleasant ways to die."

Aric shrugged again. "Are you certain your magic will work on me?" Burrage thought he'd done something to him, but it must have been Fae. He was going to assume that she'd cast a spell that protected him from Burrage's magic, but that didn't tell him what she had done to Burrage.

"Perhaps this terrible spell will backfire and affect you?" Aric continued. He almost wished Burrage would try to kill him, almost. Fae had never wanted to create a killing spell but he was thankful that she was willing to use them to protect him. He hadn't expected to come away from his meeting with Burrage alive. Now—with Fae's help—he thought he could see a way.

He stood up, forcing Burrage to back away from him. "I told you that I didn't assume you were my enemy, but you've made it very clear that I am yours. So." Aric leaned forward to stare into Burrage's eyes. "Unless you want to discover exactly what I am capable of, I suggest we go somewhere more comfortable to talk."

Burrage scowled, but he blinked, and Aric smiled. Burrage would probably eventually defeat him. The man could recite spells, and Aric could only twist ones already created, but Burrage didn't know that.

As he followed Burrage out of the cell, Aric tried to exude more confidence than he felt. He could hear Shiv breathing behind him, and he almost wished the man would try to hurt him, just to get it over with. He was confident Fae's spell would kill the Bridger. He almost stumbled when he realized he was hoping for a death, hoping that Fae's magic killed again. When had it become all right for her to become a killer?

When he'd had a premonition that only one conjurer would

survive, when it had become clear to him that Fae would only live if Burrage was dead. She had to be prepared to kill in order to save herself. But should he expect her to kill again on his behalf?

Burrage stepped through a doorway, and Aric recognized the room where he'd met him. Where the first action the conjurer had taken was to order his Bridger to hit him hard enough to knock him unconscious. *That* was why Fae had to be prepared to kill.

Burrage sat down behind a desk, and Aric settled into a chair across from him. Hewitt stood close to the door, with his back against the wall. He seemed to shrink away from Shiv, who closed the door and stood in front of it, his arms crossed and an angry look on his face.

Smiling, Aric turned to face Burrage.

"You think this is humorous?" Burrage asked. "Shiv's son is dead."

"I've spent my whole life downriver," Aric said. He turned to stare at Shiv. "And I've seen enough bodies to be confident saying that Shiv has killed more than a few sons of other men." He turned back to Burrage. "So forgive me if I don't weep for a man who was going to hurt me. Or the man who gave the order." He stared at Burrage until the other man looked away. "I did tell you he liked hitting me too much."

"Yes, well," Burrage said. "I think we got off to a bad start. I'm willing to correct that."

"What is the benefit to me?" Aric said, repeating Burrage's earlier words.

"I'll let you walk away," Burrage said. "No one from the bridge will bother you or your people."

"What makes you think I need your permission for that?" Aric asked. He paused. "And it's very telling that you didn't offer the one thing I would want—to remove the curse from my people."

"I haven't found the spell yet," Burrage said. "So I can't remove it."

"Once you find it you're simply going to complete it anyway," Aric said. "No matter what you agree to tonight."

"I . . ." Whatever Burrage had planned to say, he stopped talking when there was a knock on the door.

A woman's muffled voice demanded entrance, and Aric glanced at Hewitt. The conjurer tilted his head in a slight nod. So

Oleda Burrage was about to join the conversation.

"Mother," Burrage said when Shiv finally opened the door. "What do you want?"

"I want to see your prisoner," Oleda said. "Where is the Riverman?"

"Here," Aric said. "I've been wondering where you were." He didn't bother to turn to look at her, and it had the expected result.

Graylon Burrage's mother stomped over to him.

"Shiv!" Burrage yelled, and Shiv rushed over.

Aric turned in time to see Oleda Burrage, her hand raised above her head and her legs kicking as Shiv dragged her away from him.

"Let go of me!" she shouted with rage. "Graylon, get him off of me!" The Bridger calmly set her on her feet, but his hands on her shoulders kept her in place.

"You should thank your son for your life," Aric said.

Oleda Burrage glared at him and, with an angry shrug, shook off Shiv's grip and stepped away from him.

"He's right, Mother," Burrage said. "He has some sort of magic that has already killed a man."

Aric watched the fury on Oleda Burrage's face fade to surprise and then fear before he turned back to Burrage.

"How nice to see how much you care for your mother," he said.

"Of course," Burrage replied. "She's always cared for me."

"Perhaps," Aric said. "Or perhaps she's always cared for herself, and she needs you for that."

"Who are you and what do you think you're insinuating?" Oleda asked. She moved up to stand beside Aric and scowled down at him. "And tell me why I shouldn't have Shiv or my son kill you."

With what he'd learned about her, Aric really shouldn't have been surprised, but the woman's willingness to have him murdered was shocking.

"Because they will be dead if they try," he said. "As would you." Oleda's eyes widened, but the fury in them remained. Aric decided that he would not eat or drink while anywhere near Oleda. She'd used poison to kill before—he didn't think she would hesitate to use it again.

"My mother is right about one thing," Burrage said. "We don't really know who you are. You told us you are a shaman, but do you have a name?"

"Rawley," Aric said. "Rand Rawley." The old Wailes might have told Burrage his name—that he'd been searching for both him and Fae. He didn't want Burrage to know about his relationship with Fae—didn't want her to become his target. He needed to keep his attention focussed on *him* for as long as possible.

HEWITT HID HIS surprise when Aric gave a false name. He tried to think back to his own conversation with Burrage. He didn't think he'd called Aric by his name—just the shaman's son.

"Rand Rawley," Burrage said. "You know who I am. And this is my mother, Oleda Burrage, but I think you know that as well." Burrage sat back in his chair, and Oleda perched on the chair beside Aric.

"You sought me out," Burrage continued. "You told me you thought we should meet—because we share magic. What does that have to do with my mother?"

Oleda's head snapped towards her son, but she wisely kept her mouth shut. Hewitt knew what Aric was planning, so he edged ever so slightly along the wall. He wanted to see both Oleda and Graylon's faces when Aric spoke.

"Yes, I sought you out," Aric agreed. "And you assumed I was an enemy. That doesn't mean I didn't search out information about the two of you." Aric looked from mother to son, his face impassive. When his gaze rested on Oleda, Hewitt heard her sharp intake of breath.

"You can't believe anything this Riverman says," Oleda said.

"I haven't said anything yet," Aric replied. "What are you afraid I might say?"

"I'm not afraid," she snapped. "Graylon, kill this man right now."

"I can't, Mother," Graylon said. "His magic protects him." He gestured to Shiv. "The Bridger's son is already dead."

"And I won't be eating or drinking anything *you* prepare," Aric said. "I've heard that can sometimes have harmful . . . consequences." Oleda's face turned red, and her son stared at her.

"What does that mean?" Burrage asked, and Hewitt had to stop himself from taking a step closer.

"Just that I wouldn't want to catch the fever that took your mother's husband." Aric paused. "Or the lovely Patia, just days before you were to wed."

"That's a lie!" Oleda yelled.

"Lie? I simply made a comment," Aric said. "It's well known that the two of them died of the same disease." The Riverman paused, and Hewitt tried to gage Burrage's reaction. He was staring at his mother, but nothing on his face gave away what he was thinking. At least not to Hewitt. "Weeks apart, when no one else contracted that disease, ever. Your neighbours believe your mother poisoned them."

"That is a serious accusation," Burrage said. "What proof do you have?"

"None," Aric said, his voice almost cheerful. "But your mother has either tried to kill me or asked you to kill me twice already. I'd say she's more than capable of murder." Aric leaned across the desk, and Hewitt could no longer see his face. "But you know her better than me." Aric settled back in his chair. "I guess the girl—your betrothed—really wasn't that important to you."

"Get out!" Burrage barked. "Mother, get out."

"Graylon." Oleda reached a hand out to her son.

"I said get out!"

"I assume that means I'm free to leave." Aric stood up. "Because I'm not going back to that cell."

Hewitt hesitated. He wished there was a way to make any of these three attack Aric, because if what he said true was true, they would die. And the deaths of any—*of all*—of them would suit him. Oleda, with one last glance at her son, shrank away from Aric as she headed for the door. Shiv stepped aside but didn't open it for her. The Bridger smiled a mean smile as she struggled to open the door and then left.

When the room had been quiet for a few moments, Hewitt cleared his throat.

"The shaman can stay with me, if he wishes," he said. He would dearly love to talk to Aric. Something had changed since they'd spoken earlier, and he would like to know what.

"Yes," Burrage said. "If he wants."

Aric nodded at Hewitt and sauntered past Shiv and out of the room. Hewitt ducked his head and shuffled past the Bridger, hurrying to catch up to Aric.

"Master Rawley," he called. "Please, my feet are too big for me to walk so quickly."

"Sorry," Aric replied, and Hewitt thought there was genuine remorse in the man's voice. "I should leave the bridge," the Riverman continued. "But I would like to know more about Conjurer Burrage. No offense to the rest of you conjurers but he's the only one who might be able to help me understand my own magic."

"Of course," Hewitt replied. "Please, my home is just a few steps this way."

Hewitt led the way to his door. Once they were both inside, he ushered Aric into the kitchen. It was the room furthest from the street and so the one where they were the least likely to be overheard.

"Will they die if they try to harm you?" he asked.

"I think so," Aric replied. "Fae has set more spells on me. It's a reasonable assumption they're the same as the spell that killed Shiv's son when he tried to strike me."

"Perhaps we can goad Burrage into attacking you," Hewitt replied. This was more proof that Aric's abilities were inferior to Faelin's: her magic was protecting him.

"That was my hope," Aric said. "That's how I thought he would react to my news of his mother."

"But he didn't," Hewitt said. "Even though he was furious."

"No. Nor did he attack his mother, although he was angry. I think he already suspected that his mother killed his betrothed. Although it's a different thing to be confronted with the truth."

Hewitt set the kettle on the stove before shoving some kindling on the spark of flame. The fire caught, and he sat down, gesturing to Aric to take the other chair.

"Why did it have to be him?" Hewitt asked. "Of all people to have not just one but two conjurer bloodlines, why did it have to be that malicious man and his vindictive mother."

Aric shrugged. "If he wasn't a Wailes conjurer he wouldn't be my problem."

"He'd still be Faelin's problem," Hewitt said. "And I think that would make him yours." He wasn't sure how close Aric and Faelin were, but he suspected they were more than just childhood friends. It would suit Hewitt if Aric died helping Faelin defeat Burrage: he didn't want the Riverman complicating Faelin's life once she claimed her position as a true conjurer.

"Maybe," Aric said.

There was a knock on the front door, and Hewitt held up a hand to silence the Riverman.

"I'm not expecting anyone," Hewitt said. "But I'm not surprised either. Stay here." He grabbed the lamp and left the kitchen, closing the door and leaving Aric alone.

The front door rattled as someone tried to open it. Cautiously, Hewitt unlatched it and cracked it open. Maykin. He eased the door open wide enough for the other conjurer to slip inside and took a quick glance at the street before closing and re-latching the door.

"Why did you lock it?" Maykin asked. "It left me exposed."

"Were you followed or watched?"

"I don't think so," Maykin said as he trudged down the hallway. "I spoke to Yaldon." He threw open the door to the kitchen before Hewitt could warn him.

Maykin stepped into the room—then stopped.

"Maykin," Hewitt said from the doorway. "This is Master Rawley. And this is—"

"I know who he is," Aric said. He'd seen all of the conjurers at Lachlan Keetley's ceremony, which seemed so long ago now.

Maykin rocked back on his heels, bumping into Hewitt. "The Riverman shaman. What's he doing here?"

"I'm a guest," Aric said. He sat back down in a chair and crossed his arms over his chest.

"I, I thought you were a prisoner," Maykin stuttered.

"Word does get around," Aric said. "Who told you I'm on the bridge?"

"It was Yaldon," Maykin said.

"Burrage wanted to know more information about shamans," Hewitt said. "Conjurer Yaldon knows the most."

"The one who smells," Aric said. "My mother met him a few times. That's your expert?"

"Yes."

"And he told Burrage everything he knew?" Aric asked.

"Yes," Hewitt said. "He had no choice."

"No, that's good. Because he doesn't know anything, not really. I doubt my mother would have told the truth to a conjurer." Aric tapped his fingers on the table and smiled. "Not that even she had any idea of what my abilities would be. So, everything Burrage knows about shamans he's getting either from me or from Yaldon." He looked from Hewitt to Maykin.

"How much do you know about my abilities?" Aric asked.

"Nothing," Maykin said. "But Hewitt has told me about Faelin."

Aric glared at Hewitt, and he swallowed. "Maykin's the only one I told," Hewitt said. "But the rest of us . . ." He trailed off and took a deep breath. "The conjurers who are left have been trying to find a way to rid the bridge of Burrage."

"How?"

"The Kellen spell," Hewitt said. "We added it to one of his spell books."

"Oh?" Aric looked up in surprise. "I wondered why he would have recited a non-Wailes spell. Could you hide another?"

"No," Maykin replied. "Meade put it there, and he's dead now. There's no one else who could do it: there's so few of us left."

"And maybe even one less," Maykin said. "I went to see Yaldon when I couldn't find Sherston."

"Sherston's missing?" Hewitt asked. "When? How?"

"I don't know," Maykin replied. "I last saw him when we met and decided . . ." He looked away. "When Meade agreed to try to get Burrage to read the other spell. And I noticed that the cloth he put in his window when he's out hasn't changed in hours. He's never gone for that long so I went to his home, in case he forgot to change the cloth. He wasn't there and Yaldon hasn't seen him. I was hoping he was here."

"Would Burrage have imprisoned him?" Aric asked. "I didn't notice anyone else where I was, but that doesn't mean he's not there."

"Sherston's blind," Hewitt replied. "And can't read, so Burrage would have no use for him." His heart sank. Had Sherston been killed because Burrage felt he was useless?

"So, Meade and now Sherston," Maykin said. "I want Burrage dead, so the rest of us—the few that are left—can live in peace."

"And you think there's no way to insert another spell," Aric said. "And have Burrage read it."

"Burrage won't trust any spell we show him," Hewitt said. "Not now." It had been their best chance, and by some odd twist of fate, it had failed.

"I don't think he trusts anyone." Aric frowned. "Except for his mother."

"Yes," Hewitt said. "Although I had hoped her hand in the death of his betrothed would have caused more friction than it did."

"He knew," Aric replied. "Or at least suspected. There were rumours about his stepfather's death that he must have heard. But he knows that she's loyal to him, and now he knows that she's loyal enough to kill to keep him safe. What about Shiv?"

"He's loyal to whoever is in power," Hewitt said. Aric nodded but Maykin scowled.

"We can't trust him," Maykin said. "He's killed more than one of ours."

"No one is suggesting we trust him," Aric said. "But we may be able to use him." He paused. "What about the spell books? Burrage can only recite existing spells. Where does he keep the books?"

"He has a few sets of the more useful ones," Hewitt said. "That was one of Meade's tasks—cataloguing the spells and storing the more important books in Conjurers Hall."

"And the book bindery? Have any been kept there?"

"I don't think so," Hewitt said. "I believe all of the Wailes spell books have been moved. Why?"

"If I can get them to Fae she may be able to . . . I don't know, create counter spells," Aric said. "When he recites a spell I can change it, but it has to be when he's actually working magic. I've only been able to affect the spells that it takes Burrage a few moments to recite. If Fae had the most dangerous spells, and enough time, she might be able to set counter spells so that every time Burrage tried to recite one, it would either not work or the spell would reverse and affect him."

"Reversing the spell and killing Burrage would be best if you want Shiv on our side," Hewitt said. "Especially since you indirectly killed his son."

"Nothing indirect about that," Aric said. "I'm rather sorry it wasn't Shiv." He smiled grimly. "Or Oleda." He stood up. "I'm going. As much as I appreciate your offer of hospitality, I don't plan on being here when the sun rises."

"Probably wise," Hewitt agreed. "Be careful on the bridge," he said. "Shiv is looking for blood tonight."

"He won't dare attack me," Aric said. "He saw what happened

to his son." He opened the kitchen door. "I'll seek him out before I leave and make sure he knows that I left without your consent. That way Burrage won't blame you."

"I would appreciate that," Hewitt said, although he thought Burrage would find a way to blame him anyway. That was what he and his mother did: blame others for . . . well, for everything.

"You can tell him I'll be back," Aric said. "I have to arrange a few things first." He paused. "And I'll ask around about Conjurer Sherston."

Hewitt heard the front door close before he understood what the Riverman meant: that he'd try to find out if Sherston's body had been recovered downstream.

"Fae, wake up."

Her shoulder was being shaken: Fae blinked and opened her eyes. It was dark in her room, and a shadow hovered over her.

"Shhh." It was Mistress Larwood. She lifted her hand from Fae's shoulder. "Someone's downstairs. Inside the house."

Fae slipped out of bed and quickly followed Mistress Larwood's shadow out into the upstairs hallway. Another shadow, Councilman Larwood, stood at the top of the stairs. He pointed, and his wife nodded and grabbed Fae's hand, pulling her towards a wall. She pushed against it and a section swung inward, revealing a dark opening.

Fae scanned the house for magic but she didn't find any, so she knew it wasn't Burrage. The sound of creaking wood floated up the stairs, along with soft footfalls.

Mistress Larwood eased through the opening, gesturing to Fae to follow. Stairs went up, not down as she'd expected. From the outside, the house didn't look as though it went beyond two stories but perhaps there was a secret floor.

She went up three steps and then the path led down a steep, narrow staircase. She held out a hand to steady herself and felt warm stone beneath her palm: the chimney, she guessed.

Magic flared, and she heard a muffled shout of pain. From a few steps below her, Mistress Larwood whimpered.

"A spell," Fae whispered. "I put a protective spell on each of us. The Councilman's has been triggered."

"Is he safe?"

Fae felt through the magic. She didn't have ties to Larwood, not like with Aric, but the spell had done its job. "For now," she said.

Mistress Larwood nodded and took a few hurried steps down. She paused again, and Fae wondered if she'd heard something else. But then Mistress Larwood fumbled at the wall in front of her and a pale light filtered through an opening. It was almost dawn.

"Head across the lawn and just past the apple tree," Mistress Larwood whispered. "If you duck under the blue spruce, there's a path that leads next door." She edged aside so Fae could squeeze past her. "Tell the neighbours to round up the watch and send them here."

"Aren't you coming?" Fae asked.

"No. I'm going to find my husband. We'll pretend that you left already. Hopefully that will hold them until the watch can get here."

"Thank you," Fae replied. She stepped out into the pre-dawn morning, the grass damp with dew under her bare feet. She sprinted across the lawn, ducked under the spruce and . . . something slammed into her head. She felt magic flare and she heard a grunt of pain close by, then she collapsed.

HER HANDS WERE tied behind her back, and she had been propped up in a chair. A comfortable chair. And a cushion had been tucked under her head. Were they trying to show that they didn't want to hurt her?

Faint voices came from somewhere close. There, a voice she recognized. Shiv. Fae searched again for magic but there was no sign of Burrage. Was Shiv here on his own? Footsteps came towards her and stopped.

"I know you're awake," Shiv said from beside her. "I can tell from your breathing."

Fae opened her eyes to find the Bridger looming over her. She was in the Larwoods' living room. "Where are my friends?" she asked.

"They're safe," Shiv said. "And so are my men. Despite whatever magic was used against them." Shiv pulled up a chair and sat, facing her. He stared at her, and she quickly looked away.

She could kill him, she already had the spell on the tip of her tongue. She could kill him and any other Bridgers he'd brought with him. But Burrage wasn't here. Why not?

"What do you want?" she asked.

"I want to know what makes you so special. You and that river rat," Shiv said. He settled back into the chair. "Old Wailes, he had me looking for both of you. He never said why and I didn't ask. But now that river rat shows up on the bridge and he's a shaman—with magic—and says his name is Rand, not Aric. So, I start to wonder. Did old Wailes know something that was lost when he died? Something that it might be wise for me to know?" He paused and leaned forward. "Something you and the shaman are trying to keep secret? And then my men and me get here and don't you and your friends have spells on them. And I'm thinking that's just like how my son died. You are going to tell me why."

"Not if you've hurt my friends," Fae said. So, the spell she'd put on Aric had killed Shiv's son. She'd known it had been triggered, but she hadn't given any thought to what the result had been. She'd been prepared to kill with magic—Aric had made her practice with the fish, after all. Shiv's son had died when he triggered a defensive spell—because he'd attacked Aric. But if she killed Shiv right now it would be deliberate. Was she prepared to do that?

"They're fine," Shiv said. "My men are making them tea." He chuckled. "Good thing I warned them about the spells." He frowned. "I had one throw rocks and knock you out. The magic lashed out all right, but I think you only have one spell and once that's gone, you got nothing."

Fae pretended to study her feet as she tried to feel if Shiv was telling the truth.

"I want to see them," she said.

Shiv laughed, but it wasn't a joyful sound. "You don't get to make any demands, bookbinder. And don't think I've forgotten that you spurned my boy. Not good enough for you, huh? You're gonna regret that. Now tell me why Wailes was looking for you!"

Fae stared at her feet. She could escape any time she wanted, but that would show the Bridger what she was, what she could do. Would that help her and Aric or would it hurt them? And she had to make sure the Larwoods were safe and unhurt. She whispered the words to another protection spell and smiled as she felt it settle around the couple.

"I'll tell you," she said, looking up. "But I need to see my friends first."

"You'll tell me first," Shiv replied. He leaned forward to stare into her eyes.

"No," Fae replied. She stared right back at Shiv, daring him to strike her. It would take the decision about what to tell him out of her hands if he did. "If you don't let me see them, talk to them, I'll assume you've already killed them. If that's the case then you'll need to kill me as well. And Aric," she paused and leaned back, still meeting his eyes, "will avenge my death. I am not saying anything unless I see my friends."

She held her breath as she and Shiv stared at each other. She willed him to give in. She didn't want to kill him but she would do it if the Larwoods' safety depended on it. Shiv seemed to read something in her eyes, because he finally nodded and looked away.

"Don't want no magic user after me," he muttered as he leaned over and worked to untie the ropes on her wrists. Once they were untied, he stepped aside to let her go ahead of him.

The Bridger at the end of the hallway nodded to Shiv as she stepped through the doorway and into the kitchen. Mistress Larwood and the Councilman both lifted their heads. Cups of tea sat on the table in front of them. So Shiv had told the truth about that. Did he think it would make her trust him?

"Are you all right?" she asked. Councilman Larwood shifted his gaze from her to Shiv before nodding.

"As good as can be expected after being accosted in my own home," he said. "Don't think the town will let the bridge get away with this. You have no authority here."

"I have authority where I say I have authority," Shiv replied. "You'll find Conjurer Burrage feels the same."

"You have authority until someone else takes it away," Fae said.

"Is that a threat, bookbinder?" Shiv leaned over her, staring in her eyes.

"An observation," Fae said. She wasn't going to back down even if it meant revealing her abilities. "And where is Graylon Burrage?"

Shiv eyed her for another moment. "Sit down." He nodded to a Bridger who stood near the stove and he poured another cup of tea. "That's my other son, Mert," Shiv said. "The one you was to marry."

Fae sat down but looked up when Mert placed the tea in front of her. He leered at her and licked his lips, and she stared at him, forcing herself to show a calm she didn't feel. "I almost died avoiding that," she said. "And I think I made the right choice." Mert's eyes narrowed and his hands clenched. Fae almost hoped he attacked her. Shiv would have two dead sons by her hand.

Mert's gaze focussed behind her, and he frowned but backed away. So, Shiv had control over his men, at least for the time being. Fae turned to face him. "Besides, even after promising me to one of your sons, Wailes was willing to marry me off to Graylon Burrage," she said. "Where is he?"

"I ask the questions," Shiv said. "I'm the one with the power."

"Really? Burrage and his mother would tell me something different."

"He sent me here," Shiv said. "He's gone after the river rat."

Fae leaned over her tea, pretending to sip it while she looked for Aric. He was out there, he didn't seem to feel he was in any danger, and Shiv was correct—he was not on the bridge. But Burrage was. Why was Shiv lying to her?

"I thought you said Aric showed up on the bridge?" Fae asked.

Shiv scowled at her. "Burrage let him go. After he killed my son."

"Ah, once he found out that Aric has power," Fae said. It was just as likely that Shiv—rightfully worried about another spell— had refused to restrain Aric when Burrage had ordered him to.

"He didn't know," Shiv said. "Burrage didn't know about shamans or that the river rat was one. But Wailes must have. He sent me looking for the both of you. But why you? You said you'd tell me when you saw your friends." Shiv gestured to the Larwoods.

"I did promise," Fae replied. She readied a spell. She would tell Shiv, but she didn't want him telling anyone else. She spoke the words and Mert and Shiv froze. Another word and Shiv blinked.

"What did you do?"

"My secret," Fae said. "Don't worry, your remaining son will be fine—as long as you don't do anything stupid. Here's the truth: I am a conjurer. And a far better one than Graylon Burrage. Now, I'm going to put a small spell on you that will prevent you from telling anyone what I just said. I will have kept my promise, and you now have more information. But you do not get to share this with anyone, especially not Burrage. And you will tell no one that you saw me." She said a few more words. This time the magic seemed to have an almost physical presence as it slowly sank into Shiv and his son.

"If you're better than him, why don't you kill him?" Shiv asked.

"Killing isn't something I ever want to do lightly," Fae said. "That would make me no better than Burrage. Or you."

"Then you're weak and will lose to Burrage," Shiv said. "And I've made the right choice."

"If you think so," Fae said. "I am going to release you and your son from this spell and you are going to leave this house. Now!" She whispered a word, and Mert, looking confused, stared at them.

"Let's go," Shiv said. He turned and left the kitchen, Mert hurrying after him. The front door shut with a bang, and Mistress Larwood dropped her head to the tabletop with a sob.

Because of the spell she'd cast on him, Fae was able to follow Shiv's progress across the square and onto the bridge.

"They're at the gates to the bridge," she said. Would Shiv try to tell Burrage about her? No, he was only halfway to where Burrage was when he stopped. When he didn't move for a few minutes, Fae blew out a big breath.

"I am sorry I brought this on you," she said to her hosts.

"We knew the risks," Mistress Larwood said. "We chose to accept them because it was the right thing to do."

"I have a question," Councilman Larwood said. "Can you kill a man from a distance?"

Fae stared at the councilman and his wife for a few moments before answering. "Yes, I believe I could. But should I?"

"Killing one man might save many lives," Larwood said. "If it's the right man."

"You're not talking about Shiv," Fae said.

"No. Burrage can always find another Shiv," Larwood said. "And Shiv will find another master, but could he find one worse than Burrage?"

Fae met Mistress Larwood's eyes. "You think I should kill him too."

"Yes," she replied. "But it's not me who has to live with it."

Fae closed her eyes. She wished she could talk to Aric about this, ask his opinion, but who knew when she would see him next? And if she was honest with herself, she was pretty sure he would side with the Larwoods.

Fae nodded, her decision made. Keeping her eyes closed she searched for, and found, Burrage. Two words, that was all. She felt the magic race outwards and slam into Burrage. And then it rushed back at her. The protective spell she'd wrapped herself in flared to life, and Fae was thrown out of her chair and crashed painfully to the floor. Larwood huddled over her, helping her sit up.

"Are you all right?"

"I think so." She lifted a hand to her shoulder. She'd landed on it hard, and there would be a bruise, but she didn't think anything was broken.

"What happened?" Mistress Larwood asked. And more tentatively, "Is he dead?"

Fae took a deep breath, bracing herself for what she would find in the magic. The backlash had been intense so the damage must have been considerable. Wait, no . . . Burrage was alive! He seemed weaker than before, but his magic was there and even from a distance she could feel his fury.

"He's alive," Fae said. "I don't know how, but he's alive."

Chapter Ten

ARIC ROCKED BACK on his heels, almost dropping his net. He looked past the sail of his fishing boat. The bridge was a dark shadow in the mist that rose off the river. It was a cool morning, and he'd thought to take advantage of the hour he had before meeting with Pax and some of the elder Rivermen. He was out to catch his breakfast—a simple task he'd not been able to do openly for a long time. Then the early morning calm had been shattered by an intense blast of magic.

What had Fae been trying to do? It was her spell—he could *feel* that—and it had failed, which hadn't happened in weeks. But what was the spell for?

It had been directed at the bridge but Fae wasn't on the bridge—she was still in Waglenn Landing. Had she thought he was still there? But she would know where he was, just as he could always find her. Had something had gone wrong with her abilities? Was that why the spell had failed?

He reached out to her through the magic. She seemed upset and concerned but there was no sense of impending danger. But she was concentrating on something. Aric gently pulled on a thread of Fae's magic and then he was with her, seeing what she saw, feeling as bewildered as she felt.

She was sensing Burrage—a weakened but furious Burrage. Burrage rushed at Fae through the magic and instead of his usual longwinded spell, it was a thought of pure rage. It glanced off Fae and spiralled away, but not before clipping Aric. He was spun out of the magic and tumbled into the bottom of his boat. Chest heaving, he sat up.

He felt Fae's worry and tried to signal to her that he was fine. Then he lost contact with her.

Aric stared at the bridge for a few more moments before pulling his nets in. Something important had happened—he could sense that—but he had no idea what.

He plucked a trout off the net and pulled the last of it into his boat. He stared at the fish as it lay gasping in the bottom of his boat. His shaman senses told him that if he and Fae didn't figure out what had happened, and why, they would not be able to defeat Burrage.

The mist was almost gone from the river. It was time for him to head back to the village. Now that he'd made his presence as shaman known to Burrage, Pax needed him to do the same with the Rivermen.

"Where is the shaman?"

Hewitt opened his door to find Burrage standing in front of it, his face red with anger. A Bridger stood behind him, a stern look on his face.

"He left last night," Hewitt said. "I tried to talk him out of it." He stepped aside as Burrage stomped into his home, followed by the Bridger. He followed them as they stormed from room to room. Eventually they stopped in the kitchen.

"You should have stopped him," Burrage said, glaring at him.

"Conjurer Burrage," Hewitt said. "You yourself had let the man go. I assumed that if you wanted him detained you would have instructed Shiv to not let him leave the bridge. Have you spoken to Shiv?"

"I can't find him," Burrage said. "No one knows where he's gone. Unless that shaman killed him."

"Oh." Hewitt blinked. Aric had said he was going to make sure Shiv saw him leave. Had the Bridger tried to stop him? "Had you instructed Shiv to stop the Riverman?"

"No," Burrage said. "The shaman's too dangerous. I told Shiv not to provoke him."

"Then he wouldn't have," Hewitt said. "And that is exactly why I did not try to force the Riverman to stay. Although, as I said, I did try to persuade him. What do you want with him?"

Burrage slowly turned to face him and Hewitt saw the extent of his fury. "I want to kill him," Burrage said. "Since he tried to kill me this morning." He looked around Hewitt's small kitchen. "He's not here. Let me know if he contacts you." Then he swept out of the kitchen so fast that it took the Bridger a few seconds to realize that he'd gone. He hurried after him, leaving Hewitt to trail behind them, closing doors along the way.

He locked the door to the street and leaned against it. Had Aric tried to kill Burrage? It would have been a good solution, especially if Shiv was also dead after trying to stop Aric from leaving the bridge.

"That went as well as I could hope," Pax said.

The boat rocked slightly as a Riverman stepped from it to the dock. The boat continued to bob from side to side as the rest of them left it. Aric sighed.

"I'm glad you think it went well." To be honest, he didn't really care if the Rivermen acknowledged him as shaman, as long as they supported Fae. But they seemed to need to recognize him as shaman for that to happen.

"Not exactly what I said," Pax replied. "Going as well as I can expect is not the same as going well. But I have hope that they'll come around."

"In a few years, maybe," Aric said. "I need their assurances now."

"You'll get whatever help they can give," Pax said. "They won't want to chance offending you, not until they're sure one way or the other."

"Oh. So it did go well." All he wanted was their willingness to help whenever he—or Fae—might need it. Aric's stomach rumbled. He hadn't had time to cook that trout. He'd just tied up to his mother's . . . *his* boat when Pax had arrived with the other five Rivermen. He grabbed the fish from the bucket of water he'd dropped it into and quickly cleaned it. Soon it was sizzling in a pan.

"Need some breakfast?" he asked Pax.

"Me, no. I ate earlier." Pax sighed. "Gotta smooth over a few ruffled feathers on account of Rand telling everyone he scuttled your boat."

"Coming back from the dead isn't easy," Aric said with a laugh. He flipped the fish over, and the smile slipped from his face. "Something happened on the bridge this morning," he said. "I need to know what. Do you have any way to get word to Fae that I need to see her?"

"I think I can manage that," Pax said. "If it's important."

"Yes, it's important," Aric repeated. "I'd go to her if I could." He grabbed a plate and scooped the fish onto it. He set it down on the table and slid onto the bench seat.

"I know you would," Pax said. He picked up his hat. "All right. I'll go take care of that right now."

"Thanks," Aric said.

"By the way," Pax said, his voice solemn. "That other thing you asked about? Based on your description, someone found Conjurer Sherston this morning. Seemed like one of the more straightforward deaths: drowning, is what I was told. His body was helped out to sea, seeing as no one wants to go near the bridge these days."

"Thank you," Aric said. He'd let Hewitt know, if he had a chance.

He sat staring at the door long after Pax had left. By the time he ate his first forkful of fish, it was cold.

Even if Pax could get a message to Fae, she wouldn't come until dark. That meant he had all day. Plenty of time to pay a visit to the bridge. Hewitt should be told about Sherston. And he also might know what had happened this morning.

And Aric still thought there might be value in the other spell books—Wailes wouldn't have taken all of them and Burrage would only want the Wailes books. That left hundreds, maybe thousands of books no one was paying attention to.

HEWITT SPENT THE rest of the morning contemplating the possibility that Shiv was dead. He smiled, hoping it was true, or that it would be true one day soon.

There was a knock on his door and when he opened it, the smile slid from his face.

"Get in here. Burrage thinks you tried to kill him and now he wants you dead."

Aric brushed past him and into his house, and after peering down the street in each direction, Hewitt shut the door and followed him to the kitchen.

"Burrage said he was attacked?" Aric asked, sitting down at the small table. "Did he say how?"

Shaking, Hewitt slumped into a chair, wondering if anyone had seen Aric arrive. Were Burrage and his Bridgers already on their way back here? If he thought Hewitt had lied to him he would kill him. "How did you get back on the bridge? And why?"

"Same as last time," Aric said. "I took the stairs up from the river. Although I went through the fishmonger's instead of the book bindery. I didn't think Oleda Burrage would appreciate me using her home as a pathway."

"Did anyone else see you?" He could trust the fishmonger, he thought, so maybe no one else had noticed the Riverman arrive. At least no one who would report it to Burrage.

"Not that I saw," Aric said. "Charnock let me out last night too. Loaned me a lamp so I could signal for someone to come and pluck me off the pier. How was Burrage attacked?"

"He didn't say," Hewitt replied. "But he blamed you for attacking him this morning, and he didn't know where you were, so I assumed it was a spell."

"I see," Aric said. "Did he come alone? Was Shiv with him?"

"No," Hewitt said. "Another Bridger was with him. I was hoping that Shiv tried to hurt you last night and . . ." He already knew that Shiv wasn't dead; why else would Aric have asked about him?

"No," Aric said. "Shiv was alive and well when I left him. Angry though." He paused. "I do have news of your missing friend. A body was found this morning."

"My friend . . ." Hewitt stopped. "Sherston. You're talking about Conjurer Sherston. Are you sure it's him?"

"I didn't see him," Aric said. "And these days it's too dangerous to return what's been lost off the bridge, but I was told the description matches. Is anyone else missing?"

No," Hewitt replied. "Not that I've heard, anyway." Not that he would have heard, but it didn't matter: it was Sherston. Another conjurer was dead and there would be no ceremony to mark his passing. And there were now so few left: him, Maykin, and Yaldon.

"I've told you my news," Aric said and got up. "And I found out what I needed to know. I should leave before anyone else sees me."

"What you needed . . ." Hewitt trailed off. "You knew Burrage had been attacked!" He lowered his voice to a whisper. "Was it Faelin?"

"Yes," Aric said. "But since still Burrage lives, I'm not sure what she was trying to do. I really do have to go. Pax is with Charnock—waiting for me so I can return to the village with him." At the door, he turned to face Hewitt. "Feel free to tell Burrage that I was here but that I threatened you with magic if you didn't let me go."

"What would I tell him you were doing here?" Telling Burrage something close to the truth would be the safest thing for Hewitt to do, as long as it seemed plausible. Aric paused and looked around the room.

"Do you have any of the old spell books? You can say I came for them."

"In my study," Hewitt said. He led the way to his study and retrieved the two books from the shelf he'd hidden them on. "I'll tell him Wailes gave them to me when the books were first found. It's close enough to the truth."

Aric tucked the books under his arm, nodded, and left. Hewitt heard the door to the street open and close, and then it was silent.

He would give the Riverman a few minutes head start—and mourn the loss of Sherston—then he would go to Burrage. At this point, he couldn't afford to have Burrage doubt where his loyalties lay.

But no matter what Burrage thought, it hadn't been Aric who'd tried to kill him this morning. And he didn't believe Aric when he said Faelin hadn't been trying to kill Burrage. Hewitt sat down beside his desk, wondering if it was a good sign that she had tried to kill Burrage with magic, or a bad sign that she'd failed.

"I HAVE NEWS."

Mistress Larwood burst into the kitchen, an oiled cloth bundle in one hand. She dropped the package on the counter and sat down across from Fae.

"I heard it at the market," she said. "That the Rivermen from upriver are talking about a new shaman: one they thought was dead. Apparently, they heard it from downriver."

"It's Aric," Fae said. "I'll go see him tonight."

"He's not keeping himself a secret," Mistress Larwood said. "What do you think that means?"

"I don't know," Fae replied. "Except now that Burrage knows he exists, maybe there's no longer a reason to for Aric to hide from his own people. And it could help, having the Rivermen know." At least now Aric wouldn't have to hide out on someone else's boat: he could live on his own, out in the open. Maybe she could too. Who was there to see her in the Riverman village? And what would Burrage do even if he knew about her? Although he wouldn't hesitate to hurt the Larwoods and Shiv knew about them.

"It wasn't even through my network," Mistress Larwood said. "I was simply buying fish for supper."

Fae smiled at Mistress Larwood's disappointment that today the general gossip had better information than her network.

"I'll clean the fish," she offered. "It's the least I can do to thank you for everything you've done for me."

Fae busied herself with the fish while Mistress Larwood headed out to the garden. In a few hours, she would see Aric. She might not even need to come back here, although it had been nice not hiding herself all the time. Hopefully she wouldn't have to on Aric's boat either.

As soon as dusk fell, Fae said her goodbyes to the Larwoods and headed across the empty square to the lane that led south. Birds twittered among the branches of the trees that overhang the lane as she made her way along the cobbles. The lane met the dirt path, and Fae followed it, winding her way downslope, towards the river, where she threaded her way through the gnarled roots and swaying branches of the willows.

Lights from the boats of the village dotted the river. Fae peered out at them and sighed in relief when she spotted a familiar one. Aric's boat was moored in the same place his mother had kept it. There were no lights on it though, so she had to assume that Aric wasn't on board.

Fae took her shoes off and lashed them together with willow twigs. She looped them across her shoulders and walked out into the river.

The water was cool, and the muddy river bottom squished between her toes. She waded out as far as she could but eventually the water reached her chin. She stretched out an arm and kicked with her feet, doing her best to glide quietly. In a few kicks, she was at the dock. She tossed her wet shoes onto it and grabbed the wood.

"I was hoping you would come home tonight," Aric said. He reached down, grasped her hands and pulled her up and into his arms. "I've missed you."

"Me too." Fae nestled her head against his, breathing in his scent. "I'm getting you all wet."

"I live on the river," Aric said. "Getting wet is to be expected. But let's get you inside." He picked up her shoes and grinned. "When are you going to go barefoot?"

"I needed them in town," Fae said. She followed Aric onto his boat, through the door, and down into the living space.

She looked around and smiled. Some of the happiest days of her life had been spent on this boat. "No offense to Rand but this is much better."

"I agree," Aric said. He pulled open the door to the bedroom. "Now get changed and dried off. We have a lot to discuss. Like what the spell that failed this morning was supposed to do to Burrage."

Fae nodded, her happiness at being back on Aric's boat with him tempered with what had happened. She quickly changed, hanging her damp clothes up on pegs behind the door before going back into the main cabin.

Aric was sitting at the table, and she sat down across from him. When she held out her hands, he placed his in hers. She gripped his hands and took a deep breath.

"It was supposed to kill Burrage," she said. "At least that's what I tried to do. What I had *wanted* to do."

"Fae." Aric squeezed her hands. "Are you sure you really want to kill Burrage like that? I thought you didn't want to . . ."

"It *should* have killed him," Fae said. "Even Mistress Larwood agreed that things would be better if Burrage was dead." She met his eyes. "We've talked about killing, and I always thought it would only be in self-defence—like the defensive spell I placed on you. But this . . ."

"But this," Aric repeated. "No matter that everyone might be safer if Burrage was dead, this wasn't self-defence."

"No," Fae replied. "It still should have worked though."

"Maybe there was something you did—without meaning to—that caused it to fail," Aric said. "Now that we're back home we can check the Kellen journal."

"Maybe," Fae said, but she didn't believe it held any answers. She didn't think it said anything about a spell failing if the conjurer didn't like the spell's purpose. Because really, why would you create and recite a spell that you didn't want to work?

"I grabbed a couple of spell books from the bridge when I was there," Aric said. "It's possible there's something about this in one of them."

"You took books from the bridge?" Fae looked up, afraid for Aric all over again. "Where did you get them? Did you go through the bindery? Oleda Burrage is living there." Had Aric needlessly put himself in danger?

"Yes," he replied. "I went through the bindery the first time, but Oleda wasn't there. I left last night through the fishmonger's and went back again this morning the same way. And Hewitt gave me the books. He'd been sneaking Kellen spell books out from under Burrage's nose. For you." He looked at her. "How did you know about Oleda?"

"Mistress Larwood," Fae replied. "Wait—how were you able to breathe on the bridge? What about the curse?"

"I'm not sure." Aric shrugged. "It affected me on the stairs but once I was on the bridge I was fine. Either one of Burrage's spells has changed the curse," he paused. "Or I've been changed by twisting magic. I can't very well ask another Riverman to climb up to the bridge to test it out."

"But you can breathe on the bridge?" Fae asked. Aric nodded and she smiled. "So, we have options once this is all over."

"But for now," Aric grinned and pulled her to her feet. "We should get some rest."

Fae smiled as he led her to the bedroom. Aric didn't have rest in mind, but she wasn't going to complain.

HEWITT TRIED NOT to look surprised when Shiv opened the door, but his face must have given him away because the Bridger smiled.

"Yes, I am alive," Shiv said. "Although I heard rumours that I wasn't."

"I am delighted to see you in good health," Hewitt replied, even as he wondered if Shiv had thrown Sherston off the bridge. He craned his neck and tried to look past the Bridger into Burrage's study but the man blocked the door.

"I came to see if Conjurer Burrage needed me for anything," Hewitt finished.

"I'll let him know," Shiv said. He closed the door, leaving Hewitt standing outside. He took a step back and leaned against the hallway wall. He had to wait now, no matter how long it took. And Shiv would delay. He wouldn't take his time telling Burrage he was here—that would anger Burrage. But if Burrage didn't want to see Hewitt, Shiv could take hours to let Hewitt know he could leave. He sighed and closed his eyes, prepared to wait.

There was a shuffle of feet from down the hallway. Hewitt snapped from his doze and struggled upright. He blinked in time to see Oleda Burrage round a corner. She stopped when she saw him and then, very unlike her, nervously approached him.

"Do you think my son will see me?" Oleda asked. "He hasn't spoken to me since yesterday. Since that Riverman said that I . . ." Her voice trailed off, and Oleda's shoulders sagged.

"It was a shocking thing to say," Hewitt replied. He wasn't going to call her a murderer even though the woman had all but admitted it. "I'm sure your son will come to realize that you only have his best interests at heart." Hewitt was surprised when he saw tears well up in Oleda's eyes.

"I knew you would understand," she said. She placed a hand on his arm. "Thank you. You've been a friend to me—to both of us—from the beginning. I can't tell you how much I appreciate it. As Graylon does, I'm sure."

Hewitt was less sure that Graylon appreciated anything anyone did for him, but he nodded and covered Oleda's hand with his own. And he pretended not to notice when she flinched at his oversized hand and withdrew hers. He needed Oleda to see him as her friend, as someone who was on her side, because if he wasn't, then he was an enemy. And Oleda's enemies tended to end up dead. He didn't think the fight between mother and son would change that.

"Thank you, Oleda," Hewitt said. "I feel the same way about you and your son."

"He will see me, you know," Oleda said. "He will always make time for his mother."

"Of course, he will," Hewitt said. "He's a good son." And in a way he was, but Hewitt couldn't understand why he would still think Oleda a good mother. Unless it really was as Aric said—there was no one else he could trust with his life.

Oleda knocked, and when Shiv opened the door, he simply stepped aside to let her in the room. Hewitt caught a glimpse of Burrage's scowl before the door was shut again.

He had just stepped back to lean against the wall when the door opened again.

"Hewitt," Burrage called. "Get in here."

Burrage stood glaring at his mother, who sat in front of his desk with her head down. Shiv winked as Hewitt stepped past him.

"What can I do for you, Conjurer Burrage?" Hewitt asked.

"What did the shaman say?" Burrage asked. "You were there yesterday. What did he say about my mother?"

"About your mother?" Hewitt asked. He couldn't do anything other than tell the truth—despite the fact that it could make an enemy out of Oleda. "That she caused the death of a young woman you were to marry." Burrage's face contorted with such rage that Hewitt wondered if he would kill *him* in his anger.

"Yes, exactly," Burrage said. "See, Mother? I know what I heard—Hewitt heard it as well. I know you've always been there for me but I thought it was because you were concerned about my safety and happiness. But the shaman said that you killed Patia."

"You know I would never hurt you," Oleda said.

"But if you did this, you have hurt me," Burrage said. "I heard the whispers about Tadeus, and to be honest, I thought he deserved it. But Patia? She didn't do anything to you, and I loved her. My life would have been better if we'd wed. I could have children by now." Burrage sat down across from his mother. He seemed to have forgotten Hewitt.

"I need you to tell me the truth, Mother," Burrage said. He sat back in his chair. "Did you kill her?"

Oleda's back was stiff but her hands trembled. Hewitt hardly dared to breathe, in case Burrage's focus changed from his mother to him. Shiv stood by the door, his usual slouch replaced by a tense stance. What would be better for Oleda, to admit the crime or continue to lie?

Oleda's shoulders dropped. "She wasn't good enough for you," she said in a quiet voice. Her head dropped even lower as her son continued to glare at her.

"Get her out of here," he said, and Shiv moved forward and helped Oleda out of her chair.

She seemed diminished to Hewitt, her haughty air was gone, replaced by regret. But was it regret for killing her son's fiancée or regret that she'd been found out?

Hewitt suspected Oleda would be back in her son's good graces eventually—in part because Burrage had no one else he could trust. And since he'd rather have her as a friend than an enemy, he would try to help.

"Hewitt," Burrage said. "What would do you do to my mother if you were in my place?"

Hewitt shuffled from foot to foot. "She is your mother," Hewitt said. "As a man, and one who is not a father, I cannot judge the actions a mother feels compelled to take in order to help her child."

"You would forgive her?"

Hewitt heard the door close and was grateful that his words would no longer have an audience. "Perhaps not forgive," Hewitt said. "But I would try to understand her reasoning."

"Patia wasn't good enough for me," Burrage said.

"That is what your mother *said*," Hewitt replied.

"You think she lied?"

"To you, to herself," Hewitt said. "Perhaps your mother does not truly know why she was compelled to do such a terrible thing."

"But you think you know," Burrage said. "So, tell me."

"It's a guess, but I think your mother feared losing you," Hewitt said. "And ending up alone."

"She wasn't going to be alone," Burrage said. "She was going to live with us. She was going to leave her drunkard husband and move in with us."

"Yes," Hewitt said. "So a strong woman such as your mother would now be living in another woman's house. What if your bride didn't want her there? What would have happened to your mother then? Would you have been forced to choose between your mother and your bride? She made that choice for herself—and for you."

"Yes, I see," Burrage said. "Thank you, you've been very helpful." He looked up at Hewitt with narrowed eyes. "Why?"

"I want conjurers to return to greatness," Hewitt said. "And you can do that, but conflict with your mother will distract you from that task. Besides, I truly believe she did what she thought was best. We can abhor her methods, but I for one cannot fault her motives." Hewitt held Burrage's gaze. Eventually the other man waved a hand, and Hewitt nodded and left.

He closed the door and took a deep breath and smiled. Now to tell Oleda that he was doing everything in his power to help heal the rift between her and her son, just like the good friend she thought him to be. Restoring Burrage's trust in his mother wouldn't be in Faelin's best interest, but she hadn't yet shown any sign that she could defeat the other conjurer. Until she did, Oleda's trust—and her influence over her son—would keep him alive.

Chapter Eleven

"THERE'S NOTHING NEW here," Aric said. He tossed the book he was reading onto the table and leaned his head back to rest against the hull of the boat. Fae was stretched out on the bench on the other side of the table.

Fae lifted her head from the whaleskin bound spell book she'd been reading. Now that she knew what she was looking at, she could see that at the beginning of the book the spells were simple. They became increasingly complex as the apprentice progressed through their spell creations. She flipped to the last page. A complicated spell to heal a wound, but nothing as intricate as the weather spell contained in the book Aric had just dropped.

"There's a lot here," Fae said. "Just not anything that explains why my spell failed. But I can use any of these Kellen spells."

"As can Burrage," Aric said. "He just doesn't realize it."

"Let's hope it stays that way. From the little I've seen, the Wailes conjurers weren't the most formidable."

"Except for the one who cursed my people," Aric said.

"Yes," Fae replied. "But perhaps it means I am innately stronger than Burrage."

"You can't count on that," Aric said. "Maybe we should try to kill him together? I might be able to see if anything is wrong with your spell. Or twist it to kill him if you lose control of it."

Fae studied Aric for a moment. After her initial shock that her spell had failed, she'd been a little relieved that Burrage had lived. But the reasons for trying to kill him were still there. He was still a danger to Aric and his people, not to mention anyone living on or off the bridge.

She held her hands out across the table and Aric placed his hands in hers. She felt reassured by his grip.

"I'll take it slow," she said. "So you can follow." She closed her eyes and sought out Burrage's magic. There he was; he was stationary—sitting, maybe eating a meal. She paused until she felt Aric's presence in the magic, then she slowly recited the killing spell.

The spell sped away from her, Aric trailing after it as it headed towards Burrage. It almost reached him . . . then suddenly the spell reversed and hurtled back to her, the magic slamming into her. Only it didn't just slam into her. Aric's body was driven back against the seat, and Fae clutched his hands to keep him from sliding onto the floor. His head fell forward and hit their joined hands.

"Aric," Fae said. She shook his shoulders. "Aric!" Panic welled up in her. He'd been *in* the spell—had it killed him? "Aric!" She slipped from her seat and leaned over him, patting his cheeks and shaking his shoulders, trying to rouse him.

He mumbled and Fae almost wept in relief. *Not dead, not dead, not dead*, she repeated in her head as she scrambled for the pitcher of water. A quick spell cooled it down, and she dipped the hem of her shirt into it and dabbed Aric's face.

He sucked in a breath and then slowly opened his eyes.

"Aric," Fae said. "Can you hear me?"

"Yeah," Aric said. He reached a hand to his head and lifted it away, staring at it as if he expected blood. "What happened?"

"The spell rebounded when you were in it," Fae said. "And there was backlash."

"Yes," Aric closed his eyes and took a deep breath. When he opened them, he met her gaze and smiled weakly.

Fae held the pitcher out to him, and he pulled it towards him, lowering it so he could gulp water directly from it. He let the ceramic rest against his head. "It wasn't doing what it was supposed to. I could feel that *something* was changing the spell.

I tried to change it back when it recoiled on to you."

"Are you all right?" Fae asked. Shaking, she sat down across from him. She was never going to allow Aric into a spell again, not if her magic could kill him.

"I think so," Aric said. "Except for a headache." He moved the pitcher to the other temple.

Without thinking, Fae cooled it with a spell.

"Thanks," Aric said. "That helps." He sighed. "I don't think you should try to kill Burrage like that again."

"I won't," Fae said. She placed her shaking hands flat on the table. Aric raised a brow. "We can't tell Hewitt. He won't help us if he knows I can't kill Burrage with magic."

"And we still need his help," Aric said. "Maybe more than ever now. It's too bad he couldn't hide another spell. A non-Wailes, non-Kellen spell."

"It's possible Burrage has other bloodlines," Fae said. "We need another way."

"I'll try to see a way," Aric said. He closed his eyes and winced. "Not right now. My shaman abilities are . . . not damaged, but stunned, if that makes sense."

"Don't push yourself," Fae said, worried. "We have time. Hewitt will wait. He will have to wait."

Aric shuffled to the bedroom, and Fae stared at the water pitcher. What if she couldn't defeat Burrage? What if Aric couldn't sense another way?

She felt a wave of furious magic slip past her. Burrage was looking for her! She drew in a breath and tried to smother her magic. Then she sensed him near Aric—Burrage had found him! As carefully as she could, she placed a spell around Aric to safeguard him, but Burrage didn't try to hurt him.

As quickly as it came, she sensed Burrage's magic withdrawing. She rose and opened the door to find Aric sprawled in bed, sleeping peacefully. Fae closed the door, went back to the bench, and sat staring at the pile of books on the table.

If she couldn't use her magic to kill Burrage, how could they defeat him?

HEWITT SHRANK AGAINST the wall as an angry Shiv pushed his way past him and into his house. Burrage followed, even angrier than Shiv.

"That cursed shaman tried to kill me—again!" Burrage said. He whirled to face Hewitt. "It obviously didn't work this time either but now I *will* kill him. I need to know everything you know about him."

"It isn't much, but I've told you everything I know about his shaman abilities," Hewitt said. Had it truly been Aric who had tried to kill Burrage? Or had Faelin tried—and failed? What if she couldn't kill him? What if Burrage was the stronger conjurer? It was good that he hadn't alienated either Burrage or his mother. Or Shiv.

"Yes, yes," Burrage said. "But what about his family, his friends? Does he know anyone other than Rivermen?"

"I'm not sure," Hewitt lied. "Maybe the fishmonger knows? He deals with the Rivermen daily."

"He's been no help," Burrage said. "Doesn't know the new shaman, so he says. Hewitt, you and Shiv go to the Rivermen and tell them they need to hand him over to me. Or bring him in yourself. I want him dead. And Shiv? Lower the plates you told me about. I want the rest of the Rivermen to see what happens when they anger me."

"Yes, Master Conjurer," Shiv said. "My pleasure on both accounts."

Burrage squeezed past him and out the door, leaving Hewitt staring at Shiv.

"What plates is he talking about?" Hewitt asked as he followed the Bridger outside.

Shiv turned and sneered. "The ones that will dam the river," he said. "And make the river rats pay for my son's death."

"Dam the river?" Hewitt asked, but Shiv was already ahead of him, shouting orders at Bridgers as he strode towards the Waglenn Landing gates.

BESIDES HEWITT AND Shiv, another three Bridgers, all carrying menacing-looking knives belted at their waists, were part of the group that had come with him to the banks of the river.

Hewitt grabbed hold of a willow tree as once again his oversized feet got tangled in the tree roots. The two Bridgers behind him snickered, but Hewitt ignored them, concentrating on trying to stay upright.

He could hear the river, although there were too many trees

in the way for him to see it.

He'd waited while Shiv oversaw his Bridgers lowering metal plates to dam the river. How long would it be before the water level was affected? How long before the Rivermen noticed the change? Would the river dry up completely? He knew that the water level rose with the tide but would that be enough to keep the Rivermen's boats afloat?

As he tried to slip past him, Shiv held out a hand to stop Hewitt, and the others went by them.

"Why is the girl important to you?" Shiv said. "And why doesn't Burrage know who she is?"

Hewitt looked down at his feet before meeting the Bridger's eyes. "I told you, I have asked her to be my apprentice."

"So you said," Shiv replied.

"Why didn't you tell Burrage where she was?" Hewitt asked. "Or that you found her on my behalf?" He knew Shiv hadn't said anything to Burrage: he'd be dead if he had.

"I want to know why she's so important," Shiv replied. "And if you know that she's protected by magic."

"She's . . ." There was only one way Shiv would know that Faelin was protected. "Did you hurt her?"

"No," Shiv replied. "Like I said, she's protected by magic. Tell me what you know about her."

"But you did try to hurt her," Hewitt said. "And failed, otherwise you wouldn't be asking me about her." If Shiv couldn't kill Faelin, could Burrage? He did have a book with the most horrific and most powerful killing spells. "I know that she and the shaman have been friends since they were children."

"You know more than that!" Shiv said. "I know she's . . ."

Shiv's voice cut off in a gurgle, and Hewitt looked at him in alarm. The Bridger opened his mouth but no words came out. His eyes bulged and his jaw worked as though he was straining to say something. Hewitt stepped back from him in fear, desperately looking around for Shiv's men. If they saw their leader they would assume Hewitt had done something to him and kill him before asking questions.

Shiv gasped in a breath. "By the Seven," he said. "She told me this would happen. She told me."

"Who told you?" Hewitt asked. "Faelin?"

Shiv nodded, and his breath seemed to constrict again. He

shook his head and sucked in a breath. "You know," Shiv said. "You know."

"I have no idea what you're talking about," Hewitt said. But he thought he did. Somehow Shiv knew that Faelin was a conjurer. "You saw her?"

"Yes," Shiv replied. "She told me . . ." Sounds stopped coming from him even though his mouth was still moving. "She told me . . . I can't say it. I can't tell what she told me."

Faelin must have somehow done something to Shiv—with magic—so that he couldn't talk about her. But why? And when?

"When was this?" Hewitt asked. "When did you see Faelin?"

"Yesterday morning," Shiv replied. "Early. In Waglenn Landing."

The Bridger didn't have any trouble telling him that. Was the spell—because Faelin must have used magic on him—just stopping him from talking about her abilities? Was it to prevent him from telling Burrage about her?

"Yesterday," Hewitt said, almost to himself. "First thing in the morning?" Shiv nodded, and Hewitt closed his eyes.

That would have been right before the first attack on Graylon Burrage. Faelin must have thought Burrage had sent Shiv to attack her, and she'd retaliated by attacking Burrage. And she'd tried again last night.

And had failed both times. It was beginning to look as though Faelin Keetley could not kill Burrage.

This changed everything. This meant that *Burrage* was the future of conjurers—*Burrage* was the one he had to side with. Because Burrage would kill Faelin. But first he would kill Aric.

"Let's find the shaman and get him back to Conjurer Burrage," Hewitt said, for the first time really meaning it.

He followed Shiv towards the river. He had to keep Burrage's trust, and handing Aric over to him would help. All he could do was hope that once the Rivermen were destroyed Graylon Burrage would be able to forget about destruction and focus on becoming a great conjurer.

Shiv held a hand up, and the small group stopped and fell silent. Hewitt peered past the Bridger to the huddle of boats. A couple of Rivermen were on a dock, busy with ropes or nets or sails, and neither of them seemed alarmed by any change in the level of the river.

"Conjurer," Shiv called softly.

Hewitt crept forward until he was just behind Shiv.

"Have someone bring a boat over," the Bridger said to him. "They won't come close if they see the rest of us."

"I'll do my best," Hewitt said. "They might not come for me either."

"You need to remain useful," the Bridger said. "If you don't want to end up in the river." He paused. "Like your friend."

"Sherston," Hewitt whispered. "You threw him off the bridge!"

Shiv crossed his arms and stared at him, his face impassive. "My son was dead. And he got in my way."

"He was blind!" Hewitt said.

"Still in my way," Shiv said. "Now get someone with a boat over here."

Shaken, Hewitt scrambled past him and into the trees.

"Hello!" he called once he was standing on the riverbank. The Riverman closest to him turned to look at him. "I am Conjurer Hewitt, and I need to speak with your shaman. Can you take me to him?"

The man stared at Hewitt for a moment before he dropped his nets. "I'll get him," he said.

"No," Hewitt said. "It will be faster if you just come pick me up in a boat."

"I'm getting the shaman," the Riverman called. "Stay put." He hopped from the dock onto a larger boat, crossed it, and soon was lost to Hewitt as he travelled across the cluster of boats.

Hewitt closed his eyes: it wasn't what Shiv had asked for, but what would he do? The Bridger wouldn't throw him into the river here, not in front of a Riverman who could save him. No, Hewitt would return to the bridge alive, and then Shiv would be risking Burrage's wrath if he killed him. He'd live another day.

"ARIC." SOMEONE POUNDED on the door. "Aric."

It was Fae. Aric lifted his head off the pillow. He was still unsteady from the effects of the spell backlash but at least his headache was gone.

"I'm awake," he said. He sat up and rubbed his eyes. "Mostly."

Fae opened the door a crack. "Rand is here," she said. "Hewitt is on the riverbank. Asking to see you."

"Hewitt?" Aric grabbed his shirt and pulled it on. "He wouldn't come out here unless it was important."

"I don't like it," Fae said. "He said that Burrage didn't know what he was doing in Waglenn Landing, but showing up here? He never once mentioned anything about coming here to me."

He closed his eyes and tried to feel what it meant, then shook his head. "I haven't recovered enough to use foresight," Aric said. "But you're right; it doesn't make sense for him to be here without Burrage's permission."

Aric followed Fae to the main room, where Rand stood awkwardly by the stove.

"I didn't see anyone else," Rand said. "But the one who's there don't look like he could make it here by himself."

"But it's Hewitt?" Aric asked. Rand nodded. "And he's here to see me. Did he say about what?"

"No," Rand said. "He said his name and that he wanted me to take him to the shaman."

"He didn't ask you to bring Aric to him?" Fae asked.

"Not by name," Rand said.

"Good," Aric said. "I told Burrage my name was Rand Rawley. I didn't want him to associate the shaman with you, Fae, and have Burrage track you down."

"I didn't use your name either," Rand said. "But Hewitt seemed out of sorts when I told him I'd fetch the shaman. Wanted me to bring a boat over to him."

"Bridgers," Aric said, "would need a boat in order to get to the village."

"Conjurer Hewitt must not have come alone," Rand said. "I'll go back and keep an eye on him."

"Thanks, Rand," Aric said. "Tell him I'll be there shortly. I have to speak to Pax."

After Rand left, Aric met Fae's eyes.

"If Hewitt is keeping my identity to himself," he said. "He really might be trying to protect you from Burrage."

"But what about Shiv?" Fae asked. "He knows who you are. Why would he keep our relationship a secret from Burrage?"

"Could the spell you put on him stop him from telling Burrage?" Aric asked. "Or maybe it's part of Shiv's own plan? You said he was curious about you, curious why people were looking for both you and me. It didn't sound like it was on behalf of Burrage."

"No, I'm certain it wasn't," Fae said. "What I'm not certain of is why."

"Maybe it doesn't matter," Aric said, hoping that was the case. His head was still aching too much for his shaman senses to tell him anything with any certainty. "But I'll see if Hewitt will tell me anything. After I see Pax."

"Be careful," Fae said. He nodded and kissed her before following Rand out onto the deck.

Aric took the shortest route to Pax's boat across docks and boat decks. Hewitt was here because Burrage had sent him. And Burrage would never have sent the conjurer alone.

"I'VE PUT THE village at risk," Aric said. He was in Pax's boat, sitting across the table from him. "I'll do what I can to fix it, but Burrage may use magic against me—or you in order to hurt me."

"Against us," Pax replied calmly. "We will fight this together."

"I'm the one Burrage wants," Aric said. "He probably will leave the rest of you alone if he has me."

"I doubt that," Pax said. "He'll eventually finish the curse, won't he? He's worse than the old Wailes because he has real magic. Can your Fae do anything about him?"

"That's why he's come now," Aric said. "Fae and I tried to kill him using magic, but we failed. For some reason, the spell won't work against him. I could leave with Fae. Take her out to sea." Aric shook his head and sighed. Pax was right. Nothing he did now would stop Burrage from destroying the Rivermen. All he needed to do was find the curse and recite it. He had dozens of books to look through so it could take time but eventually he would find it. He could sense that.

"I think we're better off with you here," Pax said. "You can protect us a little, can't you?"

"Yes," Aric agreed. "If I notice Burrage's spells in time I can change them so they're not as powerful or destructive. But I'm not good enough at it to guarantee everyone's safety."

"There's never a guarantee," Pax said. "All you can do is your best and hope Berhalla favours you." Pax stood up. "In the meantime, we'll move the village. It won't make it harder for Burrage to attack using magic but at least his Bridgers won't get to us."

"Unless they find someone with a boat," Aric said.

"They could probably figure out how to row one if they get hold of one," Pax said. "Just to be safe, I'll give the order for fishing to be done downstream only. And no selling. No one goes near either the bridge or land."

Aric stepped onto the dock beside Rand and raised a hand in greeting to Hewitt. The conjurer stood up and waved back, peering over at him.

"Can we meet?" Hewitt called. "I have information that might interest you. As shaman."

"Why has Burrage really sent you?" Aric asked. "What does he expect you to do against me? I know how little power you have."

"Burrage didn't send me," Hewitt said. He glanced behind him before continuing. "I'm here to help you understand your powers."

Aric stared past Hewitt, trying to see whoever was behind him. Shiv probably.

"How can you help me?" Aric said. "You know hardly anything about Rivermen and even less about our shamans. It's not like you have a history of caring about us." Could Hewitt have found a book? Generations of Keetley bookbinders had copied books—could Hewitt have found one that had information about Riverman shamans?

Hewitt twitched and looked behind him again.

"Who's there with you, Hewitt?" Aric asked. "I know you didn't come all this way alone."

Shiv stepped into view. He pushed Hewitt, almost causing him to lose his balance.

"Burrage wants you," Shiv said. "He knows you can't kill him using magic. He wants to talk to you before he kills you."

"I'm busy today," Aric said. "I'll try to find time to meet with Burrage another day." The dock rocked, and he turned to find Rivermen scrambling to untie the boats that were moored to it. One nodded to him, threw his painter rope into his boat, and pushed it away towards the middle of the river.

"Pax is moving the village," Aric said quietly to Rand. When he looked back at Shiv, the Bridger was waist deep in water. It would be over his head by the time he was out as far as the dock, but he might be able to swim a few strokes and reach them. Aric grabbed Rand's arm. "Time to go." He turned to Shiv. "Another time, Shiv, Conjurer Hewitt."

Aric and Rand jogged along the now empty dock. A few moments ago, dozens of boats had been tied up here, now only a couple remained.

Aric and Rand jumped onto one boat, ran across it, and then leapt onto the next dock. Aric split off from Rand and headed to his own boat. He untied it and pushed it towards the middle of the river before heading below.

"Fae?"

"Here." She stepped out of the bedroom. "We're moving?"

"The whole village is," Aric said. "And we need to be ready for magical attacks from Burrage. The good news is, once we're in the middle of the river you won't need to hide any longer. No one will be able to see you from shore."

"Good," Fae said. "I take it things didn't go well with Hewitt?"

"No," Aric said. He sighed. "Shiv was there too, as we expected. It looks like we'll have a fight. Shiv said Burrage wants to kill me."

"I won't let him," Fae said. "I'll see if there's anything in the Keetley journal that will help me create better protection spells. I may not be able to hurt Burrage, but I should be able to defend against him."

Aric nodded and slipped back onto the deck. The boat had drifted a little, and he quickly steered towards the middle of the river and the throng of boats gathering there. He looked back— Shiv had made it to the dock, but he had no way of getting closer to the now fleeing village.

Now that no boats were tethered to it, the dock started to drift downriver with the outgoing tide. Aric laughed when Shiv realized this and jumped back into the water and headed towards the riverbank.

THE SOUNDS OF men calling to each other filtered into the cabin. The boat rocked gently as Fae sat down and dragged Keetley Kellen's journal across the table towards her. She didn't have much hope that she would discover some new fact about protection spells in it, but she would look anyway. She found that flipping through the pages grounded her and made her feel connected to her conjurer heritage. She opened to the first page and started to read the familiar words.

Half an hour later she was ready to put the book down. There was nothing here that she didn't already know; her time might be better used creating her own defensive spell. She could do it, she had already created the small spells for her, Aric, and the Larwoods, but she had hoped the journal would give her a starting point for a larger one, maybe tell her how to conserve power so that the spell didn't weaken.

She flipped one more page and stopped. There, around the edges, was that writing new? She peered down at the words she'd never read before.

"*If you are reading this then you have used magic against one of the Ten,*" she read. "*And have activated the spell the council created after Osred Wailes used his terrible powers on them. The Ten can never again inflict harm on each other with magic. I will record what my brother Vandon told me about this. You do not need to defend yourself against one of the Ten, but in order to protect those you care about, your defensive spell should use magic stolen from your enemy. I do not know how this is done, only that it must be.*"

Fae turned the page. That was it, there was no more new writing. She flipped through the rest of the journal but that was all Keetley Kellen had written about using magic against—and defending against—one of the Ten. She reread the note and then pored over the page it had been written on, but there was nothing there that said how to take some of Burrage's magic from him.

She searched for Burrage and found him on the bridge. He was still weak from her and Aric's attack on him, but she could feel that he was recovering his magic. And no matter how hard she tried, she couldn't siphon any of it from him.

Sighing, she closed the book. The boat lurched, and a moment later, Aric opened the door and came inside.

"We've dropped anchors and lashed the boats together in the middle of the river." He shook his head. "I've heard stories of Rivermen doing this but I've never seen it. We've only moved once in my lifetime, and that was from the bank on the other side. And this? This is done only when we're under severe threat."

"And so we are," Fae said. She opened the journal. "I found something." Aric sat across from her and she read it to him. "I can create a defensive spell," she said. "But according to this it may not be very effective. Aric?" He was staring at the book in her hands. "What is it?"

"I can take his magic," he said. "I've done it when he's been reciting a spell." He looked up at her. "I was even able to use a little of it myself, so maybe I can pass it to you?"

"Can we try?" Fae asked. "I tried to take some of his power already but I couldn't figure out how to do it. Let me create a spell to defend the village and then you can try taking Burrage's magic and giving it to me."

"I won't be able to access his power until he creates a spell," Aric said. "But we can try to do the same thing with you—I'll try to take some of your magic. We have an hour; then Pax wants us both at a meeting he's called."

HEWITT TRIED TO read as slowly as possible, stopping often to rub his eyes. They didn't hurt but he did have a headache from listening to Oleda's non-stop complaining.

Burrage had tasked the remaining conjurers—him, Maykin, and Yaldon—with reading through all of the Wailes books searching for the spell that cursed the Rivermen. Burrage wanted to complete it—it wasn't enough to dam the river, whatever destruction that would cause—he wanted to make certain he was rid of not only the shaman, but all of his friends and family.

They were also to look for spells that could be used against the Rivermen until the curse was found. Burrage wanted to hurt them before he changed them, and Hewitt was worried that his capacity to hate—and his desire to inflict pain—wouldn't end with the annihilation of the Rivermen.

They were in Faelin's old workshop in the book bindery, but even with the doors and windows open, the air was thick with Yaldon's stench.

"Can't you do something about that horrible smell?" Oleda called from the open door that led up to the main floor. She held a handkerchief against her face as she stood in the doorway and glared at them. "I can't stand it: I'm closing the door. You'll have plenty of fresh air from outside." She gestured to the open windows and the door that led to the stairs.

Shiv, who was perched outside on the stairs, leaned his head inside. "Door stays open," he said to Oleda. "Security."

Oleda frowned and huffed, but she didn't argue with the Bridger. Hewitt looked over at Yaldon, who had his head bent so far forward that it was almost touching the page in front of him. He was used to being the cause of people's discomfort, Hewitt knew that, but still, it was cruel and thoughtless for Oleda to be so vocal about her displeasure with the smell. None of them would have chosen to be here—including Yaldon. That was Burrage's doing.

He sighed and trailed a finger across a line of script, only partly aware of the words. He stopped reading and tried desperately to hide his shock. Was this it? He reread the last sentence. He had to be certain.

This spell was almost identical to the rest on the page—the ink was the same faded black—but it was written in a slightly different hand. He traced the words with his finger, trying not to cringe at what they were describing—at what the spell was meant to do.

Carefully, Hewitt flipped the page and concentrated on studying it in the exact same way that he'd studied all the pages prior to this one.

He'd found it. He'd found the second part of the Riverman's curse, the exact spell they were all looking for. And from what he could tell, it had actually been *hidden* in this book. He flipped to another page, trying not to hurry, trying not to call attention to himself. None of the other spells in this book were dangerous or harmful—just that one, written by someone other than the conjurer who had penned the rest of the spells.

He took a calming breath. He didn't dare look up, but he knew Shiv hadn't moved from his spot on the stairs, and Yaldon and Maykin continued looking through the books stacked beside them.

He could take this to Burrage—it's what the man wanted—and he would be grateful to Hewitt for finding it. But that gratitude would last such a short time that it wouldn't guarantee that Hewitt would live for more than a few days. The next time Hewitt said something innocuous that offended either Burrage or Oleda, Hewitt's life would be in danger. And he knew that sooner or later, no matter how carefully he chose his words—it would happen. And then Burrage would kill him.

He would much prefer it if Faelin was the only true conjurer but she'd failed to defeat Burrage. He didn't like her dependence on Aric, and his presence once she was the last conjurer would not be welcome, but if the Riverman was needed to help Faelin defeat Burrage, he couldn't afford to compromise him—which the curse would do. Who knew what would become of Aric's magical abilities if the curse was completed? And he could be left with Burrage as his only hope to return conjurers to greatness.

Hewitt steadily progressed through the book to the last page, and then he placed it with the books he'd already searched, noting a scuff mark on the binding, and picked up the next book from his stack.

A few hours later, Shiv banged his fist on the door, almost startling Hewitt into dropping the book he was studying.

"Time to show Conjurer Burrage what you've found," the Bridger said. "And it better be something useful."

He motioned to them, and Hewitt struggled to his feet, grabbing one spell book he'd set aside. Just one, that's all he had—he hadn't found anything destructive in the rest of the books he'd looked through.

Conjurers had done good things; that's what Hewitt had to conclude. Even the Wailes conjurers had used their gifts to help. He'd found the one spell—the curse—that someone had deliberately hidden in amongst the rest, but every other spell had been created to help the people on the bridge, on the river, and in the towns. And Burrage, who had a chance at such greatness, was intent on using the few destructive spells.

Faelin would be different, wouldn't she? She had tried to kill Burrage, but that was necessary. And she'd attempted it in part because Burrage was needlessly intent on completing the Riverman curse.

Faelin was the one who would use her gifts to benefit people, who would act as the conjurers had acted when they had true power. Hewitt didn't just want conjurers to be powerful—he wanted them restored to their original role, their original glory, their original respect.

Burrage wouldn't do that—he would use absolute power to corrupt the current pathetic version of conjurers even further until conjurers became the most hated people ever.

And Hewitt—*all* Hewitts—would be lumped in with Burrage and despised for all time. He could not allow that—would not allow his life—his innocently pathetic, ineffective life to be tarnished like that. He had no real power, but he'd been ignorant of that fact—that didn't mean he deserved to be reviled.

Burrage stepped into the room, followed by his mother, who had covered her face with a cloth. Hewitt sniffed. After so many hours enclosed in the room with Yaldon, he barely even noticed the odour.

Burrage held his hand out to Hewitt, and he placed the book—open to the spell he'd found—in his hand. Burrage scanned the page the book was open to and then lifted narrowed eyes to glare at him.

"This is a constructive spell," he said. "I need the curse, or a spell I can use to destroy the Rivermen."

"Yes, Conjurer Burrage," Hewitt said. "But so far I've only found constructive spells. However, this spell dates from when buildings were erected on the bridge. You see here," he leaned over and pointed an oversized finger. "The way in which the stones were gathered. They were scraped from the riverbed, which at the very least must have caused rough water. I am guessing boats would have a hard time staying afloat."

"I see what you mean," Burrage said. "I could take all the rocks from under the village and the resulting waves could sink them all. Good. Or—once the river is low from being dammed—I could push them up onto the boats. Anything else?"

Hewitt shook his head, and Burrage moved on to Maykin, who'd found a spell that toppled trees into the river. Neither his nor Maykin's finds were direct attacks on the Rivermen, but Burrage seemed satisfied, commenting that he could send the trees down on top of the Riverman village.

"Just slide the book over to me," Burrage said to Yaldon. "I have my mother's delicate sense of smell." Yaldon slid the book over, and Burrage peered at it, reading the spells on the page. "Nothing useful." He looked around the room. "How many books are left?"

"More than one hundred, Conjurer Burrage," Hewitt said. "It is a slow process."

"Then get back to it," Burrage said. "I expect better. And find that curse!" He spun and exited, followed by Oleda.

Chapter Twelve

FAE WATCHED THE lights in the cabins of the boats of the Riverman village light up as the sun set, leaving a shadowy dusk behind. The meeting with Pax and the elders had been going on for hours. She'd gone with Aric, as he'd asked, and he'd introduced her to the elders, but after a few minutes they'd asked her to wait elsewhere. Aric hadn't liked it, but she'd understood. No matter how close she and Aric were, she was an outsider to the Rivermen—a stranger to all but Pax. And worse, she was a conjurer—blanketed with the same blame as the Wailes who'd cursed them generations ago.

She turned her gaze past the village to the bridge. The lights that lined it seemed to stare back at her in an almost menacing way. Was Burrage preparing a spell to attack them? She'd placed a simple protection spell around the village—one that would stop a direct magical attack—but she wanted Aric with her when she tried to create something more complex. She also needed him to get her some of Burrage's power. If the journal was right, the only way they would survive was by using Burrage's own magic to protect against him.

"I'm not sure how Pax makes any decisions," Aric said. He sat down on the deck beside her. "Elders sure have opinions."

"Based on experience," Fae said. "Isn't that the point?"

"I suppose," Aric said. "Sorry they didn't let you stay. I told them you were our best chance at surviving Burrage but they don't trust you yet."

"Because I'm a conjurer," Fae said. "And a woman."

"Oh, it's because you're a conjurer," Aric replied. "Don't forget that before me all shamans were women and they were always part of the council of elders. But a conjurer cursed us in the past and another one threatens us now."

"Wailes conjurers," Fae said. "In both cases. No other conjurer family ever harmed you."

"Sadly, the elders have never differentiated between the Seven," Aric paused. "Or what we now know as the Ten."

Fae sighed. The elders were right—whether the rest of the conjurers were friend or foe didn't really matter, not when the threat was so great. "And now Burrage," she said. "Have the elders accepted you as shaman?"

"Yes. They may not trust you, but they have decided to trust me. And now that we're in the middle of the river there is no more reason for you to hide."

"Thank the Seven." She leaned her head on his shoulder. "I'm so tired of staying inside." And if they didn't win this fight, she wanted her last days with Aric spent in the sun and under the stars.

"ARIC!"

He turned to find Rand waving at them.

"Aric! Pax needs you. Fae too!"

He got to his feet, pulling Fae with him. "I don't know," he said when she turned a questioning gaze his way. "I just left him." Unless the elders had made a decision about Fae that he wouldn't like.

Nervous, he led the way across a couple of boats to where Rand stood.

"Something's not right with the river," Rand said.

"What . . . ?" Aric stared out towards the bank. The river was low—lower than he'd ever seen it. "They've done it." Worried now, he followed Rand to Pax's boat.

"Aric, Fae," Pax called as they stepped onto his boat. "You've seen the river? I've sent someone to be sure."

"What about the river?" Fae whispered as they joined a visibly troubled Pax on his boat.

"It's low," he replied. "Lower than it should be—ever."

"Aye," Pax agreed. "They've dammed the Aberhayle." He stared out towards the bridge. "Berhalla take all Wailes conjurers." He looked from Aric to Fae. "Can you fix it?"

"Damming the river. That's what Councilman Larwood talked about," Fae said. "He said people—including children—died."

"Yes," Aric said, holding in his anger. "He's retaliating—Burrage—for our attempt to use magic on him."

"He doesn't realize that this will affect everyone on the river," Fae said. "The towns, the bridge—everyone will suffer."

"He doesn't care." And it was true. Burrage was so consumed with hate that he wouldn't even notice if people died. "I wish we'd killed him," he said. All traces of regret that they were forced to resort to dealing death was gone. Graylon Burrage was a threat to everyone and everything that depended on the river for life. Aric would trade his own life to remove that threat; to make everyone else safe.

"Rand, take us to the bridge," Aric said. "Fae and I are going to fix this." He met her gaze and she nodded, her chin raised.

"Even if we have to tear down the entire bridge," she said.

IT WAS CALM on the river. Too calm. Aric had sailed or rowed to the bridge to see Fae or take the catch to Charnock too many times to count. And the water had never been this calm.

He turned at the sound of wood hitting rock. Moonlight glistened on a moss-covered rock. Rand shifted the oar and pushed the small boat away from it.

"Tide will cover that up once it comes back in," Rand said. "At least I think it will be high enough to cover it."

"Maybe not," Aric said. He stared at the bridge, searching for Burrage. He was stationary—had he retired for the night? How did someone so obsessed with doing terrible things sleep? Did he toss and turn or was he so oblivious to his own evil that nothing ever troubled his dreams?

"What makes someone do such dreadful things?" Aric whispered.

"His horrible mother, for one," Fae said. She slipped an arm around his waist and leaned into him. "And I suppose some kind of feeling that he's been wronged; that what he deserves has been withheld from him."

"But what makes him think he deserves anything? Why doesn't he feel he needs to work for the things he wants, like the rest of us?"

"I don't have an answer," Fae said. He could hear the sadness in her voice. "His mother must have a reason for being the way she is too, but why her and not everyone else? We all deserve good things, but we don't always get them."

"Yes, but most people don't threaten and blame others for their own failings." He'd learned about Burrage *from* Burrage. He'd had Shiv hit Aric and then imprisoned him before he'd even had a chance to tell him why he was on the bridge. A man like that didn't deserve a second chance—couldn't be *trusted* with a second chance.

"We could probably walk from here," Fae said. "I think it's shallow enough and it might be safer. Boats are more noticeable than people walking through the water."

His heart sank when he realized that Fae was right; they were still half a mile from the bridge, and the river was shallow enough that they didn't need the boat.

"Wait here," he said to Rand. "We need to take a look and see how they did this, before we can figure out how to undo it."

He stepped out of the boat into water that just reached his waist. He grabbed Fae when she leaned over the gunwales, easing her into the water beside him.

It took them longer than he liked to reach the nearest arch. He felt exposed, although Burrage remained in the same place. Bridgers would wake him if they suspected trouble, he thought. They wouldn't risk his anger if they didn't tell him about something that he later determined was a risk. And to Burrage, everything was a risk.

"It's solid," Fae said. She was standing in front of the arch, her hands on the unbroken metal that blocked the river. "I thought perhaps it would have an opening at the top."

He stared up at where the metal met the top of the arch. "Conjurers made these," he said. "I wonder why?"

"Probably for something good," Fae replied. She stepped back from the metal plate. "Let's check the next one."

The next plate was just as sturdy, and he hesitated when Fae suggested they investigate a third plate. The stairs were on the far side of the next arch. He stared at them, but he didn't see anyone watching from the darkened fishmonger's or the bookbindery.

"We need to check them all," Fae said. "And hope we figure out what to do."

"We already know what to do," Aric replied. "We need to remove them." But she was right—if there was a flaw in one then removing it would take less energy. Energy they would need for the fight Burrage was planning. "Let's be quick." He grabbed her hand and pulled her along.

She didn't see any sign of distress on this plate either. Was it ridiculous to hope that the conjurers who had created these had made a mistake? That they had somehow left a flaw in one? No, better to expect that Bridgers had mishandled them over the years; they had been used at least once that she knew of. And Bridgers weren't known for their gentleness.

Fae sighed and reached for Aric's hand. They had another few arches to check.

The pier—*her* pier—was completely uncovered. She waded past it, looking up at the stairs. To where Oleda Burrage slept in her father's house—lived under the roof that had sheltered generations of bookbinders.

She sighed again and then they were past the pier and at the next arch. She trailed a hand across the solid metal of the plate. Her finger snagged on . . .

"Aric, here." She bent closer to the metal. "There's a crack in this one. It's small but . . ." She ran a finger along it down to the bottom of the river and then traced it up as far as she could reach.

"Is it enough?" Aric asked. He stepped back to look up. "I think it goes all the way up." He turned to her. "This will do. Let's go find Rand."

"We only need the one?" Fae asked. "What happens . . . quiet." She ducked into the shadow, pulling Aric with her. She'd heard something familiar.

"What is it?" Aric asked, his head bent to her ear.

She recognized the sound, and her heart sank. "Someone opened the door to the bindery." She knew the sound of that door; knew the squeak it made when it was opened. Footfalls scuffed stone. "Someone's on the stairs."

She edged towards the crack in the metal. This could be their only chance. She placed a hand on each side of the crack and whispered, "Widen," and forced the magic to respond to her.

"Fae, what are you doing?" Aric tried to pull her away from the plate but she leaned into it, her feet planted on the soft river bottom.

"Undamming the river," she said. "In case we don't have another chance." The line was wider now, a little. She repeated the spell and smiled when water started seeping through the crack.

"Who's out there?" someone called from above. A light flared, deepening the shadows that Fae and Aric stood in.

"Fae, come on, we need to leave."

Aric pulled at her but she shook him off. She could feel the gap growing beneath her hands; feel the water pushing to be free. One more spell. She whispered to the crack in front of her—forcing her magic—her power—her *will*—into it, widening it. Water was streaming through it now. Above her, water fountained out, and then a chunk of metal flew off. It landed just beyond her with a splash.

"Fae, now."

This time she let Aric pull her away. The light on the bridge was moving faster, coming down towards them.

"Stop!"

Fae looked over her shoulder. Someone held a lamp aloft, highlighting another figure lower down, just a few steps from the pier.

With Aric in front of her, Fae tried to hurry, the waist deep water dragging at her. She looked back when she heard a splash. Someone was in the river now, chasing them.

Behind them, metal ground on metal and then she heard a loud screech. Water gushed out through the ever-expanding hole in the plate. With one last burst of power, Fae split the metal plate apart.

A wall of water twice her height charged towards her. Something dark—a chunk of the metal plate—slammed into the person following them, pushing him under.

"Hold your breath," Aric said as he grabbed her. Then he jumped, angling them left into the oncoming wave.

Water crashed over them and then she and Aric were spun and

battered by the river. Her hip scraped painfully against rocks, and then the water that engulfed her calmed. She felt Aric's legs kick out as he propelled them up.

Her head breached the surface, and she gasped in air, Aric doing the same beside her.

"The village," she said. "Will they be all right?" She'd cast a protection spell, but she had no idea if it would keep them safe from a wave like this.

"Should be," Aric said. "The wave would have levelled out by the time it reached them. We need to get back, somehow."

"Rand. He was waiting for us." Had what she'd done hurt him?

"He was probably carried downstream," Aric replied. "We'll need to swim to reach him."

They both struck out downriver but it wasn't long before Fae tired. She wasn't the best swimmer to start with and the spell had sapped her energy more than she'd realized.

"Take me to shore," she panted. "And come back for me later."

Aric stared at her—she knew he didn't want to leave her—before he nodded. A few moments later she was able to stand and climb up the riverbank.

"I'll be back as soon as I can," Aric called softly as he waded back out into the river. He dropped down into the water and soon she lost sight of him.

She turned to stare at the bridge. Lights trailed all along the stairs and a few clustered on the pier. She heard shouts as people—most likely Bridgers—searched for one of their own.

They wouldn't find him—not alive. Fae thought he'd been killed by the chunk of metal—the metal that she'd caused to break off from the plate holding the water back.

Would the Rivermen find him downstream or would the huge wave wash him right out to sea?

Magic swept past her, and she shivered. Burrage, awake now and looking for whoever had done this. She felt for Aric—he was still in the water, but he'd felt Burrage too. Quickly Fae reinforced the defensive spells she'd placed on him. Then exhausted, she wrapped her arms around her legs and rested her head on her knees.

HEWITT LOOKED OUT his front door. A couple of Bridgers ran along the cobblestones towards the book bindery. He saw a few merchants peering out of their own windows and doors, but no one was saying what had happened.

And Graylon Burrage, shouting with rage, left the Hall and strode down the street, his hands balled into fists.

The violently shuddering bridge had woken Hewitt up. It had lasted a few seconds, and once it had stopped, he could clearly hear the sound of rushing water. A quick look out his window upriver and he knew the dam had failed. The river was flowing fast through one of the arches. Tree limbs swirled, ramming against the stones of the bridge as all of the water that had been dammed for the last day rushed out.

Initially he thought one of the metal plates had failed naturally, but now, seeing Burrage, he knew it must have been the work of Faelin and Aric.

Were they all right? Had they done this from afar or had they been up close to the bridge? Had the Bridgers caught them? He needed to find out.

Hewitt stepped back inside, threw on some clothes and shoes and headed to the only building with all lights blazing—the book bindery.

A Bridger at the door stepped aside, allowing him to enter. He noted the Bridger near the stairs to the lower level before walking into the small kitchen. Oleda Burrage sat by the stove so he went over to her.

"My dear, are you all right?" he asked. "What a commotion. Let me make you some tea."

"Conjurer Hewitt," Oleda said. "Yes, a cup of tea would help settle me." She frowned. "So much is happening tonight."

Hewitt fed the small fire in the stove before filling a pot with water and putting it on top of the stove. He sat across from Oleda, chafing at the time he must spend placating her even as he knew that she must be fawned over before she would tell him what she knew.

"My window looks upstream," he said to her. "I can see that the river is no longer dammed."

"It was him," Oleda said. "The Riverman shaman. Graylon can tell where he is, and he was here, at the base of the bridge." She sat back, shaking her head. "Bridgers knew something was amiss. They patrol on the stairs, you know. I allow them to come through my home. It makes me feel safe."

"Of course," Hewitt agreed, thinking that most people of the bridge felt that the Bridgers were the ones to cause danger, not save anyone from it. "They saw the shaman?"

"Shiv said he saw him," Oleda leaned closer. "It was his son."

"His son?"

"The one who was swept away. Shiv's son was about to catch the one who did this—the shaman—when the dam gave way and his son was swept away. They're looking for him now." She sat back and sneered. "I hope they find that shaman's body, that's what I hope. But if they don't, my Graylon will destroy him, and all of his friends."

The water was boiling so Hewitt rose to make tea, welcoming the distraction.

He didn't think they'd find any bodies—and certainly not Aric's: he trusted the Riverman to live through anything on the river—but Shiv now had two dead sons.

He poured tea into two mugs and set them on the table.

"Mother, Hewitt." Burrage entered the room and sat down. He grabbed the tea Hewitt had set out for himself and without looking at Hewitt, took a sip.

"I'm sure by now you've seen that the river is no longer dammed," Burrage said. "And Mother has told you that Shiv's son is missing."

"She did," Hewitt replied. "I am sorry for his loss."

"Better save your sympathy for your shaman friend," Burrage said. "As soon as you find the rest of the curse, he and all his kind will no longer be able to threaten me." Burrage took another sip of tea before looking back at Hewitt. "Well, what are you waiting for? Find that curse!"

"Yes, Conjurer Burrage," Hewitt gave an awkward nod and headed to the door that led downstairs. When he got to the book bindery, he did his best to ignore the Bridgers, who were milling around the door that led outside. He picked up a book from the unread pile and headed to the far wall, as far away from the door as possible.

There would be no more sleep for him tonight—maybe no sleep until the curse was delivered to Burrage. Or he destroyed it and told him it didn't exist.

ARIC PUSHED ANOTHER tree branch out of his way and lifted his head to take a breath.

He was having a hard time staying out of the middle of the river, where the current ran faster, carrying the swirling mass of trees and logs that had come through when the dam had been breached. Even here, nearer to the shore, the river was running swifter than usual. He'd only left Fae a few moments ago and already he was well past where they'd jumped in the river to start walking.

When he took his next breath, he saw the light bobbing beneath the trees. Rand, it had to be. He started swimming towards the light. It was him.

"Rand," he called. The light swung towards him and then he was close enough to reach the oar that Rand held out to him.

"Where's Fae?" Rand asked, half of his worried face illuminated by the lamp hanging on a hook.

"Upriver, on shore on this side." Aric grabbed Rand's hand and pulled himself up and over the gunwale. He lay on the bottom of the boat, his chest heaving. "We have to go get her." He struggled to sit up.

"I'll take us." The light bobbed as the oars shifted in the oarlocks. "I'm lucky I'd tied up to a tree when you undammed the river. And I'm glad you were able to get it flowing proper again."

"Fae did it." Aric sat in the prow, staring as far ahead as the light allowed him to see. Anyone on the bridge would be able to see the light—but so would Fae. Besides, Burrage was the only threat to them—no one else could swim or had a boat—and he could find Aric by magic.

Was that tree near where he'd left her? "Fae!" Aric called, trying to pitch his voice so that it didn't carry too far. Burrage could find him with magic but he still didn't want him to know about Fae. "Fae!"

"Here, I'm coming."

He heard a splash, and then he saw her wading towards them. He silently thanked Berhalla as she reached the boat and he helped her climb in.

With her safely wrapped in his arms, he nodded to Rand.

In moments, he had the boat turned around and headed downriver. Rand barely rowed, allowing the current to carry them.

"He'll be more furious than ever," Fae said as she sat on the seat beside him.

He didn't have to wonder who she meant. He could feel Burrage looking for him, poking at him in the magic, but he ignored him.

"He's intent on killing us," Aric said. "He's always been intent on killing us. Nothing has changed that."

"You're right." She tucked her head onto his shoulder and sighed. "At least now they can never dam the river again."

HE'D BEEN WORRIED—he hadn't said anything to Fae—but when the lights of the Riverman village came into view he sighed in relief.

"It looks fine," he said, more to himself than to either Fae or Rand. People lined the boats ahead of him, and he saw Pax in the middle of the crowd. Aric grabbed the lamp and waved it until he saw Pax nod and step back.

Rand pulled up alongside his own boat—berthed at the edge of the village, as usual, and Aric helped Fae climb from the smaller boat to the larger one before hopping out beside her. She pushed her hair out of her eyes and yawned.

"Whatever Pax wants to know, he can hear it from me," Aric said. He put an arm around her shoulder and walked her to the stern. From there he helped her cross a few more boats until they reached his.

"Are you sure I shouldn't stay and talk to Pax?" Fae asked as she stripped out of her wet clothes. Aric took them from her and shook his head.

"You did most of the work tonight," he said. "You need to rest. We're not done yet."

"No, we're not." She pulled on a loose shirt and slipped into bed. Aric took the lamp with him when he left; closing the door gently even though her steady breathing told him she was already asleep.

"Is she all right?" Rand asked. He and Pax stood in the small kitchen.

"She's tired," Aric said. "And she used quite a lot of magic to destroy the metal plate that was damming the river." He sat down at the table and Pax and Rand sat across from him. "Was the village damaged?"

"No," Pax replied. "We were able to ride the wave." He shook his head. "Partly because we weren't tied to any docks fixed to land. But if it had been dammed for a few more days we might have lost some boats." He paused. "A body was spotted but we let it go. I'm not sending anyone to the bridge for any reason, not even to return their dead."

"No," Aric agreed. "Keep everyone close."

"Should we send word upriver?" Rand asked. "Let them know what's going on?"

"They know," Pax replied. "The moment the river was dammed Chart probably took them far upriver. That's what I would have done."

"So, neither the towns nor the bridge will be eating fish any time soon," Aric said. "Councilman Larwood said that the last time the river was dammed and fishing was disrupted that people in Waglenn Landing starved."

"Then let's hope this doesn't last long," Pax said.

"Fae!"

Fae snapped awake. Aric sat on the bed beside her, a worried frown on his face. She sat up, brushing her hair from her eyes. She was exhausted, but at least she'd had a few hours of sleep. Aric hadn't had any.

"Burrage is reciting a spell," he said. "I can't tell the intent yet so I'm not sure if he's attacking but I'll try to siphon off some magic." He looked at her. "We may not get another chance."

Fae gripped his hand, reinforcing their connection. She shook off the last of her sleepiness and concentrated on the magic. Were they prepared enough? She should have worked on the barriers instead of sleeping, but breaking the dam—and the swim in the wild river—had sapped her energy. Besides, according to the journal, they needed Burrage's magic to be truly protected.

She closed her eyes, trying to feel where Aric's power ended and Burrage's started. There. She carefully singled out a tendril of magic and willed it towards her. It resisted for a moment before it yielded and she was able to gather it to her. Once she'd wrapped it in her own magic, making sure it wouldn't be absorbed into her, she opened her eyes.

"It doesn't feel like an attack," she said. "Or a response to us unblocking the river: nothing triggered the protective spell." Careful not to lose control of Burrage's magic, she examined the spell she'd set out around the village. It was intact as far as she could tell—there were no frayed edges, no weakened areas.

"I think he might have been trying to see if he'd recovered from our earlier attack on him," Aric said. "It was a small spell, I think to light a fire. I didn't bother to change it—and he was furious—so hopefully he didn't notice he had company. Or that I took some of his magic."

"So, there's still time to strengthen our defenses," Fae said. "I need you to tell me all the natural dangers the Rivermen and the village face, and I'll try to create defensive spells for them."

In the end, there were more than half a dozen threats Fae created spells to safeguard against—from flooding, to a dry river, to rocks and trees and earth choking the river, and the most feared—fire in the village. She even guarded against giant sea creatures coming upriver with the tide. She agreed with Aric that the last was unlikely, but who knew what terrible spells were contained in the old books?

And into each spell she added a little of Burrage's power. It was almost dawn by the time she was done. She sighed and leaned into Aric.

"Now we wait," she said. "Should we hope it's a long wait or a short one?"

"A short wait," Aric said.

Something in his voice made her lift her head and look at him.

"The attacks will come today," he continued. "Three, although not the completion of the curse." His head slumped forward onto his chest.

"Aric, Aric." Fae shook his shoulders and he stirred.

"What did I say?" he asked.

"You said three attacks would come today," Fae replied. "But not the curse. We have to tell Pax."

"He won't be surprised," Aric said. He got to his feet, grabbed a shirt, and tossed some clothes at Fae.

Chapter Thirteen

HEWITT STOOD IN the doorway of Faelin's old workroom, looking downriver to where dozens of Rivermen boats huddled in the middle of the Aberhayle. Unleashing the river hadn't seemed to cause them any harm.

He'd visited the baker, who'd had word from Mistress Larwood that Faelin was no longer her visitor. Faelin didn't have a lot of people she trusted other than the Larwoods. So, it was reasonable to think that she was with Aric. Which meant Faelin was on one of those boats that Burrage was intent on obliterating if he couldn't find the second part of the curse.

He'd been looking through the spell books: not for the second part of the curse—he already knew where that was, although it was possible it had been secreted into more than one book.

No, he was hoping to find a solution, something that he could use to turn Burrage away from his intent destroy the Rivermen— and thereby destroying Faelin. And Hewitt's chance to restore conjurers to greatness.

And that was his dilemma. Should he tell Burrage about the curse and doom all of the Rivermen but save Faelin? Or should he let Burrage destroy the village and possibly have Faelin die along with the Rivermen?

If Faelin Keetley was dead, Burrage would be the only one left with conjurer blood: Burrage would have to be the founder of a new era of conjurers. Did Hewitt still have hope for him? Hope that he could be as great as the conjurers who had created these spells so long ago?

At one time, even Wailes conjurers had helped people. The spells in the old books proved it. So that goodness was in the blood in spite of the evil.

So many healing spells, so many ways to help ease the struggles of *all* people, not just those who lived on the bridge. He'd found spells to dig gardens and create sails and ropes. At one time, everyone had lived as one community, with the conjurers acting as the bridge did—connecting the towns to each other and upriver to downriver.

And the bridge! It hadn't been built to be this great dividing line between the communities, controlling who could travel where; instead it had been built to act as a conduit through which people connected. It had been built with good will.

He wished he'd been alive when the bridge had served that purpose—when *conjurers* had served that purpose. How the people must have loved them. How revered and respected they would have been. Oh, to have been a part of that greatness!

"Conjurer Burrage wants to see you."

Hewitt turned to find Shiv standing in the doorway between the workroom and the rest of the house. He nodded. Burrage could be ready to attack the Rivermen. Now that the dam had been destroyed, was there any chance to change his mind?

"Removing the dam won't help them," Burrage said as Hewitt joined him at the open window in his office. The view was the same one Hewitt had been staring at from the book bindery: the Riverman village.

"I'm going to reduce them to a pile of ash and splinters." Burrage looked at Hewitt, who suppressed his urge to step away from the hate and anger in the younger man's eyes.

"I'm completely recovered from their attack on me yesterday," Burrage continued. He stepped away from the window. "Did you find the curse?"

"No, Conjurer Burrage, not yet. I still have a dozen or so volumes to search through." Burrage would kill him if he told him he'd found it but hadn't brought it to his attention. "I should be able to get all the way through them by noon, if you want me to return to that task."

"Worry about that later," Burrage said. "I've decided to use the spells that have already been found. I can always curse the survivors afterwards. If there are any." He leaned over his desk and picked up a spell book, flipping it open to a marked page.

In a low voice, Burrage started to intone the spell. All Hewitt could do was watch and keep his face from showing the fear and panic he felt.

Out on the river, the water started to churn. Whitecaps swirled angrily near the collection of boats, but even at this distance Hewitt could see that they were unaffected. The boats sat in the middle of a circle of calm water.

Burrage was shouting the words now, his face contorted in rage. He shouted one last word then slammed the book to the floor.

The river churned furiously and huge waves lashed against the shore but the boats of the village were undisturbed. An enormous swell erupted from the surface and raced towards the village, but when it reached the boats it suddenly lost its power and melted back into to river.

"No!" Burrage yelled. "No!" He whirled on Hewitt. "That river rat interfered with my spell. *How is he doing that*?"

"I'm not sure, Master Conjurer." Hewitt kept his voice low and soothing despite his own anxiety. The river was calm now, and in the distance, he could see a few figures scurrying about on the decks of the boats. Faelin was safe—Aric had saved them all.

Or perhaps it had been Faelin? Was she the one who had interfered with Burrage's spell? Aric had been confident that Faelin was the one who could defeat Burrage, despite the failed attempts to kill him with magic.

"He won't stop me!" Burrage picked up a second book and started reciting. He spoke quickly, and Hewitt watched in horror as huge trees were pulled from both banks of the river. Some trees tumbled down the riverbanks but most of them *catapulted* at the group of boats in the centre of the river. But instead of crashing down onto the boats, the trees skipped over them. Even when trees collided high above the village they seemed to slide off something to splash harmlessly into the water.

Hewitt shrank from Burrage's rage as the tangle of trees swept downriver and away from the village.

"He interferes again!" Furious, Burrage slammed the book down onto the floor. "I will kill him. I will!" He turned to Hewitt. "Find me more spells that I can attack them with. I will wear him down with my power."

Hewitt nodded and scuttled backwards, away from his rage. Aric—or Faelin—was keeping the village safe. He would not deliver the curse to Burrage, not while Faelin was safe, but he would have to give Burrage another spell. There was one he'd marked—he only hoped it was powerful enough to placate the conjurer.

"Shiv," Burrage called.

Hewitt exited the room as the Bridger approached Burrage. He would have liked to hear what was talked about, what orders Shiv was being given, but angering Burrage at this moment could end in his death.

When the second attack started, pain made Aric double over. Uprooted trees flew overhead, and horrified screams and shouts rose up from the boats. Above, trees tangled and started to fall, only to slide off Fae's spell and splash into the river. As with the previous attack, the water roiled menacingly, whitecaps and waves thrashing about, but under the boats the river undulated gently.

"Aric, are you all right?"

Fae leaned over him, and he looked into her worried face.

"Not sure," he replied. His chest constricted, and he winced as he sucked in a breath. His body ached all over, and he could feel his energy being drawn out of him.

"Sit down." Fae helped him settle onto the deck. "I'll get you some water."

She left his side, and his chin dropped to his chest. "It worked," he said when she returned to his side. "The defenses held." With a shaking hand, he took the cup she held out and sipped.

"It worked," Fae agreed. "But why did it affect you? Did Burrage somehow target you?"

"It doesn't feel deliberate," Aric said.

"Aric, Fae," Pax called. He hopped from the next boat to theirs.

"Well done!" The smile on his face faded. "What's wrong?"

"We don't know," Fae said. "It started with the first attack."

"I'll be fine," Aric said. "Just tired." He looked out at the bridge. Burrage had one final attack to carry out, if his premonition was correct. He tried to sense when the attack would come but his shaman abilities had drained away with his strength.

Was that how Burrage had felt when he'd taken his power? He tried to find the conjurer but he was too weak. Wait, a trail of magic led from the defensive spells Fae had created to Burrage. He was on the bridge, of course, stationary.

And there was another trail of magic from the spell, but this one led to *him*. Now that he knew it was there, Aric could feel its gentle pull. His already low stores of energy pulsed along that trail, feeding into the spells.

Aric wiped a hand across his forehead and plastered a smile on his face. "I can't tell for sure, but I think we have a few hours until Burrage strikes again." He wasn't going to tell Fae that the spells were draining him. Removing him and his power from them could render them ineffective. Protecting the village—and Fae—was so much more important than anything else, including him.

"I think I'll get some rest." He slowly got to his feet and headed below. He was aware of the concerned glance that Fae and Pax exchanged, but he didn't have the energy to even acknowledge it.

"WILL HE BE all right?" Pax asked.

Fae sighed. "I hope so." What had happened? Why was Aric so tired? "It seems we're safe for now." She looked past Pax. Tangled trees floated down towards the sea. "At least Burrage didn't do this when the river was dammed or the tide was going out."

"Yes," Pax agreed. "I am grateful that people on the bridge don't have better river sense. If he'd done this at low tide, we'd be in almost as much danger when the tide returned and brought the trees with it." He sighed. "Even so, the river will never be the same again."

"Or the banks," she said. Great swathes of exposed dirt lined the river where trees had been ripped out. Burrage had changed the face of their world today, and all because he was angry.

"Next big rain will cause a lot of that dirt to run into the river," Pax said. "Fishing will be unpredictable for a long time."

"How long?"

"Hard to say," Pax said. "Some fish will like the changes, some won't. My guess is it'll be a couple of years before the fish settle."

"Years," Fae repeated. "Peoples live affected—changed—and Burrage probably doesn't even realize it. Or care. Can it be fixed?"

Pax looked over at her. "You mean by magic? Can you put them trees back in place?"

"Maybe," Fae said. "I could try."

"I don't know anything about planting so I can't tell you if they would live, but I do know that much of the damage has already been done. Fish spawning and feeding grounds that were there are gone now. Hard to say if putting trees back would help those things recover sooner. But it would help keep the earth from sliding into the river."

"That's the most important thing?" Fae asked. "To fix right now?"

"In my opinion," Pax said. "Yes. Earth will be washed down the hillside every time it rains for the next year. Fish won't settle along the banks with that going on. So, no spawning grounds, limited feeding—there will be fewer fish, that's for sure."

"All right," Fae said. "I'll give it some thought. Putting trees back may not be possible but I'll do something." They'd need to be able to fish: if they lived. She tried not to even think about that, but the power and type of damage Burrage had inflicted made it clear he was out to destroy the village and everyone in it.

FAE OPENED THE door to the bedroom. Aric was asleep, but it wasn't a peaceful sleep. She'd heard him muttering from where she'd been sitting at the table. Quietly, she padded across the room. She didn't want to wake him, especially not if he was having a premonition. She sat on the bed, relishing the warmth of him where his side touched her hip.

Aric flung an arm out, just missing her. His eyes opened, but Fae didn't think he actually saw her.

"The key," he whispered. "I am the key." His eyes closed and he shuddered. Fae dropped a hand to his shoulder. Should she wake him? Would he say more if she woke him up?

"Aric." She shook his shoulder. He rolled over to face her and his eyes opened. "You had a premonition. Tell me about the key. You said that you were the key."

"The key." Aric raised himself on one elbow. His forehead furrowed. "I am the key. The key to what?" He shook his head and closed his eyes. "Sorry. It's gone." He dropped back down onto the bed.

"Don't worry," Fae said. "I'm sure it'll come back. Maybe when you're rested." She leaned over and kissed his cheek but he was already asleep.

HEWITT HEFTED THE book. It contained another spell that he could take to Burrage. Maykin had found it—he'd been excited to tell him about it—until Hewitt had reminded him just what it was going to be used for. It was much better than the spell Hewitt had recently shown Burrage. When he'd given that one to him, he'd been so furious that Hewitt had feared for his life.

Maykin and Yaldon had left a while ago—although this room would probably always smell a little of Yaldon—and Hewitt was delaying his trip to Burrage.

He stared out at the Riverman village. The boats bobbed peacefully on the now calm waters of the river, but the banks were scarred where trees had stood this morning. What else would change before the day was out?

Shiv came into the room, followed by half a dozen Bridgers, and none of them looked happy.

"You done?" Shiv asked.

Hewitt nodded, trying not to anger the man. His last son was assumed dead, and today Shiv had a lot less to lose. He might risk Burrage's anger by killing someone—anyone. Hewitt planned on doing his best to make sure that someone wasn't him.

He lifted the book in his hand. "One more to show Conjurer Burrage."

"Take the rest of them out," Shiv said to his men, and they began grabbing the books off the long work table and heading up the stairs.

"Where are you taking everything?" Hewitt asked. A Bridger picked up the book that held the curse and piled it on top of half a dozen other books.

"Conjurer Burrage wants all his spell books close at hand," Shiv replied. He grabbed a stack of books and followed his men up the stairs.

Hewitt clutched the book he held to his chest. He'd waited too long—giving Burrage the curse was no longer an option. He had to hope that Faelin survived the next ordeal and that somehow Burrage could be killed. Could *he* do it? Could he find a spell that would kill Burrage? He would die as well but at least it would be quick. And over.

This constant dread of Burrage or his mother flying into a rage and killing him was becoming unbearable. Dying fast and on his own terms, like Meade Tadlow, might be preferable.

Maybe, but he wouldn't do anything until he knew for certain that Faelin was safe. He would not destroy Burrage if he was the last true conjurer, not even if that conjurer was malicious and cruel. Conjurers restored to greatness—*that* was what he was working towards.

Hewitt stepped onto the cobbled street and shaded his eyes against the glare of the sun. Shiv led his Bridgers past him back into the book bindery. It had taken the three conjurers days to go through all of the Wailes books, but it would only take the Bridgers a few trips to move them.

The door to Conjurers Hall was open and Hewitt stepped inside.

"Thank goodness you got rid of that smelly one." It was Oleda Burrage, speaking from a room along the hall. Hewitt edged up to an open door and peered inside. Oleda stood with her hands on her hips, surveying the room. Spell books littered the floor and the table. A sob escaped someone who was hunched over the table.

"There, there," Oleda said. "No need for you to worry. You don't smell."

"Get to work."

Hewitt hadn't realized Burrage was in the room until he spoke: his voice came from right beside the doorway. Hewitt took little comfort in knowing that his earlier words to Burrage had worked and that he and his mother were on good terms again.

Carefully, Hewitt backed away from the room and returned to the door that led outside.

"You heard my son, Maykin," Oleda said. "Get to work or you'll end up like your smelly friend."

Hewitt stepped out of Conjurers Hall and onto the

cobblestone road. He took a shaky breath. Maykin was going through the books again, which meant that Burrage didn't trust him. And it sounded as though Yaldon was dead!

He steadied himself against the wall of the building. What to do? Maykin would find the curse—he was bound to—and Burrage would know he'd betrayed him.

A few doors down, Shiv stepped out of the bindery, his men behind him burdened with more books. Hewitt pretended that he had just now reached the hall and entered it slowly.

Shiv laughed as he pushed past. "Those big feet move slow," he said. "I'll tell Burrage you're here." His men trailed him along the hall to the room where Maykin was.

A few moments later, Burrage leaned out of the room and looked at him. He stepped into the hallway, closed the door, and waved Hewitt forward.

"I found another spell," Hewitt said. He followed Burrage to his office, trying to ignore the closed door he passed. "It might work in conjunction with one of the others."

ARIC STARED OUT at the bridge. As home to the conjurer who had cursed his people, it had always seemed a little threatening to him, but now its looming presence felt menacing.

He was the key. He could feel the truth in that. But how? How was he the key? What did he have to do?

He felt a tug on his fishing line and automatically started pulling it in. In a few moments, a trout was in his bucket. At least he could provide supper.

He dropped his line back into the water and resumed staring at the bridge. He had to confront Burrage again. And soon. Thanks to Fae's defensive spells, they had weathered the attacks, and unless Burrage found the rest of the curse, they could withstand worse. At least the village could. *He* might not survive many more attacks. His energy could be completely drained away, leaving him unable to confront Burrage—or worse, so weak that he died. And all of his abilities were telling him that if he did not confront Burrage, the Rivermen—and Fae—would die.

"Caught something, did you?" Pax called from the boats beside his.

"Trout," he replied. "At least something's biting after this morning's turmoil."

Pax jumped over from another boat and peered into the bucket. "Good size," he said. "Fish have to eat no matter how much destruction is going on around them. Same as us."

"Yes," Aric said. "Was there any damage to the village?"

"Nope. Not unless you count a couple of skinned knees from folk rushing on deck to see what was happening. Your Fae worked wonders."

"She did," Aric agreed.

"But Burrage won't stop, will he?"

"I don't think so." Aric shifted his line a little.

"He has to be killed," Pax said. "Can you do it?"

"Fae and I tried," Aric said. "First she tried by herself and then the two of us tried together. Magically she can't harm another with the blood of the original conjurers."

"No way around that?" Pax sat down beside him, letting his bare feet dangle off the edge of the boat.

"None that we've found. It's a spell created by the conjurers' council after one of their own attacked them," Aric said. "Fae tried to remove it but that didn't work. Now she's rereading the journal and going through the old spells books to see if there's anything that will help."

"You don't think she'll find anything."

"My shaman abilities tell me she won't find anything," Aric said. "I hope they're wrong."

"Could they be?" Pax asked. "Have they been before?"

"I don't think so," Aric said, answering both questions at once. "But my belief is that if something changes then another possibility opens up."

"Belief or hope?" Pax asked.

"Both I guess." He paused and met Pax's gaze. "It was the same conjurer. The Wailes who cursed us is the same one who attacked the conjurers but their council only protected themselves."

"So, they made sure their descendants were safe but didn't bother with us Rivermen," Pax said.

"We don't know for sure," Aric said. "But we have to assume the curse can be completed." He looked up at the bridge and shivered. "And it's there. The second part of the curse. It's on the bridge."

"Then let's hope they don't find it," Pax said.

Aric stared at the spot where his fishing line entered the water. The curse had already been found. He wasn't going to tell *anyone* that—not Pax nor Fae. It hadn't been found by Burrage—he would have used it already. No, he *felt* that Hewitt had found the spell and that he hadn't destroyed it. It was still a threat to the Rivermen.

He sighed. He would have to leave soon, whether he knew how to defeat Burrage or not. Before it was too late, before he was too weak to defeat the conjurer.

Chapter Fourteen

FAE CLOSED HER eyes and searched for Burrage's magic. He was on the bridge, as usual. The man didn't travel far. She smiled. Neither did she and Aric. They stayed on this boat just as Burrage stayed on the bridge.

She wished she could tell what Burrage was doing, that she could know if he was getting ready to attack again. She concentrated on trying to sense the intent of the magic that surrounded him, but if it was possible, she had neither the knowledge nor skill.

Fae opened her eyes and stared down at the page in front of her. It was one of the books Aric had gotten from Hewitt. She'd been through it already but now she was taking a closer look, studying each spell to see if there was something that would help her understand how to fix the riverbanks.

By ripping the stones from the riverbed and the trees from the banks, Burrage had shown an incredible ignorance about what it took to feed everyone who lived on the river. If the fishing stock was destroyed, people could starve. But he'd already tried to dam the river; he either didn't understand or didn't care how this would hurt everyone who lived on the bridge or in the towns.

If the damage was concentrated downriver Pax didn't think

fishing upriver would be affected, but he was worried that at low tide the uprooted trees would be trapped in the marshy pools. If that happened, and the high tide wasn't strong enough to dislodge them, they would lose the use of the pools to trap fish.

There would be limited access to fish, seaweed, oysters, even the cattails from the marshes: all of it could be gone or severely depleted. The village could face starvation and that meant the bridge would as well. And if the Rivermen upriver didn't feel safe enough to trade, the towns would suffer too.

Or what if Burrage succeeded in completing the curse and all of the Rivermen changed into something not . . . human?

But no one on the bridge—no one who might be able to talk Burrage out of completing the curse—understood what the Rivermen did, how much they all depended on them for fish.

She flipped a page, running her finger down the script and paused. A spell to help things grow. Would it work on the uprooted trees? Could she even get them back into place? Or would it be better to have something else grow on the riverbanks—grass maybe—to stop the earth from washing into the river and simply help the trees get out to sea?

She closed the book and headed up to the deck. Aric was still fishing, and Pax was keeping him company.

"Anything for supper?" she asked.

"Most Rivermen would consider that question an insult," Aric replied, smiling.

"Under usual circumstances I wouldn't ask," Fae said. "Pax, you asked me to try to do something about the damage to the riverbank."

"I did," Pax said. "You have some ideas?"

Fae nodded. "Yes." She joined them and sat down, dangling her bare feet over the edge of the boat. She'd finally decided to stop wearing her shoes. Her feet were white compared to Aric's, and she lacked the webbing between the toes, but overall it was easier to navigate the deck without footwear.

"I found a spell," Fae said. "To make things grow. Should I do that? Encourage grass to grow on the banks? Then I can simply nudge the trees out to sea when the tide is in."

Pax squinted out towards the riverbank. Ragged edges of dirt and trailing tree roots lined the river. He sighed. "Probably the best you can do. A lot of soil came out along with the trees—who knows if there's enough for them to root in even if you could get the trees back in place?"

"That's what I thought," Fae replied. "This won't take much energy so I'll do it tonight, as long as Burrage is quiet."

"Thank you," Pax said. He sighed again. "I hate waiting for Burrage to act again. I'd rather take a fight to him."

"I can't attack him," Fae said. "Aric told you, didn't he? About the spell put in place to prevent any of the ten conjurers from hurting each other? It's too strong for me to break, and I haven't found anything about it in the books." She got to her feet. "There might be some rumblings from shore tonight."

"Burrage will attack before then," Aric said. Startled, Fae looked at him. His eyes were open, but unfocused.

"Aric, can you tell me anything else about Burrage's attack?" Fae asked. She gently touched his shoulder.

"Stay out of the water," Aric said. Then he blinked and met her eyes. "A premonition?"

She nodded. "That Burrage will attack before night. And to stay out of the water."

"I'll let the folk know," Pax said.

A few moments later he was talking to the couple on the neighbouring boat. Fae looked up at the sky. It was late afternoon; they had a few hours at most before Burrage attacked again.

EVERY TIME SHIV opened the door, Hewitt expected Maykin to enter with news that he'd found the rest of the curse. And every time it didn't happen, he had a moment of relief, followed by panic that it would happen next time.

He'd been sitting in front of Burrage for hours while he read from spell books.

This time when he opened the door, Shiv let Oleda into the room.

"Graylon," Oleda said. "I want to watch."

"There's not much to see, Mother," Burrage said from his desk. "But you are more than welcome." He glanced out the window. "I suppose now is as good a time as any."

"Can we watch from the bottom of the stairs?" Oleda asked. "My eyesight isn't as good as it once was."

"Maybe not the bottom," Burrage said as he rose from his

chair. He motioned to Hewitt and he also stood. "It could be a little dangerous, depending on whether the tide is in or out."

He exited the room and Oleda turned to follow. She stopped at Hewitt's side. She didn't touch him, but she smiled.

"Thank you, Conjurer Hewitt," she said. "For what you said to Graylon about that girl." Her face screwed up at the word girl. "And he and I have had a talk and all is forgiven. I won't forget all of your help." She swept out of the room after her son.

Shiv glared at Hewitt, who hurried after the others, trying to keep from tripping over his own feet.

So Oleda wouldn't forget his help. He almost hoped she *would*. Wished he could go away and have her and her son forget all about him.

The three hours that Burrage had forced him to sit and wait had left Hewitt with nothing to do but contemplate what the nature of the old spells said about the conjurers who had written them down. And what it said about Burrage that he would make an old man wait hours for no reason other than he wanted to make it clear who had the power.

The more he knew about the mother, the less he was surprised. Now she wanted to watch the destruction of a whole village—the deaths of men, women, and children who knew little about her and cared even less and had done absolutely nothing to anger her except exist.

He stepped out onto the cobbled streets. It was later in the day than he'd expected. The sun was just starting to lower in the sky, and the breeze had picked up. Burrage and his mother entered the bindery, and Hewitt wondered what they would do if he didn't follow them there.

When he'd given Burrage the spell he'd thought the man could still be redeemed—could still become as great as the conjurers of the past. And he could, from the perspective that he could recite incredibly strong spells. He had no doubt Burrage could wield as much magic as any of them. But he didn't have their capacity for caring, for helping the people who depended on the river. And that capacity for caring, he now realized, was why they'd done the single greatest thing; the thing they would forever be remembered for: building the bridge, an immense act of creation. Burrage kept proving that he was only interested in destruction.

Faelin may not have as much power as Burrage—he had no

way to judge that. She certainly had better knowledge in that she knew how to create her own spells. And he thought she wanted to use her power for good. *That* was what had made the old conjurers great. And that was what was needed in order for them to be great again.

He entered the book bindery and went down the stairs to the work rooms. The door to Faelin's workroom was open, as was the door to the stairs that led to the river. Burrage and his mother huddled in the doorway, looking downriver, talking in low tones.

"Hewitt, there you are," Burrage said. "Now I can get started." He opened one of the books he carried and started to recite the same spell he'd spoken this morning. Oleda handed him a second book, already opened, and Burrage said a few more lines.

"Let's see what we've wrought," Burrage said. He leaned out the door. Oleda squealed and leaned out as well.

"The river is lifting up," Oleda said, her voice tight with excitement. "This should ruin them!"

"Hewitt, come here." Burrage stepped back and Hewitt edged forward. "I think you should witness this."

Just like this morning, rocks and dirt and plants that were scraped from the bottom of the river rose into the air. Then the steam started to rise off the water and even from this distance, he could see that the rocks glowed red with heat. Gouts of smoke and flame dropped down onto the village, where they encountered a barrier and—just like this morning—slid off and fell into the river surrounding the village. Soon a dense mist rose off the water and enveloped the whole village.

"Is it gone?" Oleda asked. "Did you destroy them?"

"No," Burrage said. "But I will have weakened them. I will do this every day until every last fish is dead and the shaman either gives himself up or allows his people to starve."

Hewitt turned away. He wished he'd destroyed the curse. It would be found and Burrage would use it. What would Faelin do when Burrage changed her friend Aric into something other than a man? Would she attack Burrage even though she'd failed before? Would she use magic against the bridge? She and Aric had been able to destroy one of the metal plates and unblock the river. Could she damage the bridge enough to make it fail? What would happen to those caught in the middle of a fight between conjurers—real conjurers with real magic?

ARIC HELD FAE'S hand as rocks and dead fish and clumps of dirt and burning plants slid down the magical barrier and into the river. Water sizzled and steam rose when the heated rocks and earth splashed down. He concentrated on her hand in his and not the energy seeping out of him each time the barrier spell was activated.

"What in Berhalla . . ." Pax jumped onto their boat, followed by half a dozen men and women.

"Burrage's attack," Fae said. "The one Aric predicted."

"This is why he told everyone to stay out of the water," Pax said. "This is horrible."

"This is what he's capable of," Aric said. He looked out. He couldn't see all the way to the bridge because of the steam rising off the river, but on the section of the river that he could see, hundreds of dead fish floated on the surface. "We're lucky he doesn't understand the tides."

"Lucky," someone muttered in back. "This don't look lucky."

"It is though," Aric replied. "This was high tide. More fish died, but there was more water to heat up. If it had been low tide the water could have been hot enough to damage the boats."

Fae grabbed his hand. "I'll try to push the dead fish out to sea with the trees," she said. "At least we won't be stuck smelling them rot."

"He's stupid," Pax said. "Destroying the fish like that."

"He'll get fish from upriver," Aric said. "Or take food out of someone else's mouth. By force if he has to. Burrage won't be among the ones one who will starve."

"He's getting faster," Fae said. "At casting spells. There wasn't much time from start to finish."

"You're right," Aric said. "There was very little time to change the spell." He wasn't going to tell Fae, but he hadn't had the energy to try to change it once the attacked started. "But it's good for everyone to see that the defenses work." He looked around at the Rivermen. Most were heading back across to their own boats, but a few of them stood staring up at the sky. "It should make everyone feel safe enough to sleep at night."

"I suppose so." She paused for a moment. "The defensive spells seem as strong as ever," she said. "The attacks don't seem to take anything away from them."

"That's good," Aric said. So, they only drained *him*. Why? Had Fae somehow tied his energy into the spell? Burrage's magic was supposed to be in it, not his. Could *he* funnel Burrage's energy into the spell during an attack?

ARIC SNAPPED AWAKE. His head had nodded onto his chest, and he lifted it and looked around. The mist was starting to clear. He hadn't meant to nod off, but he was exhausted. He lay down flat on the deck and stretched a hand out and let it hover above the river. He could still feel heat radiating from the water. It was still warm but no longer blisteringly hot.

Fae and Pax were on the downriver side of the boat with their heads bent towards each other, talking. He felt a tug in the magic and it was all he could do to stop himself from pulling at it, dragging the power towards him. It was as though he himself was an empty bucket just waiting for magic to fill him up.

Maybe he *could* take Burrage's power. He might not be able to put it into the defenses, but he might be able to take enough away from the conjurer that he couldn't do any more damage. He had been able to use it to help himself heal when he was Burrage's prisoner.

Aric sucked in a breath. This felt right. He had to take Burrage's power from him, but not just to heal. He had to take enough to render the man unable to cast spells; he might even be able to make it so that he could never cast another spell, ever.

He sighed. Nothing other than taking Burrage's magic felt like a premonition. But he had to be closer to the man to do it. He didn't think he'd be able to siphon off enough power from this great a distance.

He raked a hand through his hair. His shaman senses told him that he was right, that this was what he had to do. Confront Burrage and drain his power. Perhaps that was how he was the key?

Now all he had to do was go to Burrage.

The defensive spells had depleted him—if he left too soon he wouldn't even make it to the bridge—let alone be able to confront Burrage and wrest his magic from him. Early morning, maybe. He'd have to see how he felt.

He got to his feet and headed over to Fae and Pax. If Fae needed his help then his confrontation with Burrage would have to wait.

Fae stared out at the riverbank. Magic had transformed it this morning, and it would again this evening.

She'd prefer to actually stand on the ground, to see the plants that she would use, but it was outside of the protective barrier and she didn't want to spend more time outside of it than she had to. Trusting her life to an old spell created by long dead conjurers wasn't particularly reassuring. She shivered.

The sheer destruction he'd achieved was daunting. Was it because he was so powerful or was it that the spells—the old spells—were crafted so that the conjurer's abilities were amplified? If there was a trick to spell creation, Keetley Kellen either hadn't known it, or hadn't written about it in his journal.

She concentrated on what she could remember of the riverbank. Willow trees swaying, their fronds sweeping across bushes and a carpet of grass. The grass was what she would use.

She nodded to Aric and Pax, and then she started gathering her power, focussing on the grass. "Grow," she whispered. "Grow." She felt the spell flow towards the bank and settle into the earth. For half an hour, she continued to feed the spell, nudging it along the disturbed dirt, coaxing the grass to spread. Once she thought the new growth had encountered existing plants, she stopped.

"It's done," Fae said. "At least on that side. One more side to go."

She crossed the deck of the boat to stare past the Riverman village to the far shore. This would be harder. She'd only been on that side once, when she'd first fled the bridge. It seemed so long ago, and she'd been so afraid and tired and thirsty. All she remembered was tangling in the vegetation—tripping and stumbling her way towards the marshes and pools of low tide.

She closed her eyes. All she could do was her best. She sent another gentle spell out; coaxing whatever grew there to grow across the exposed dirt.

"Something is now growing there," she said after a few more moments. "I hope it's the right thing."

"Not sure it matters for the fish," Pax said. "As long as the earth doesn't slide into the river when it rains."

"I've never seen anyone on that bank," Aric said. "It's rough, and steep. I still can't believe you made it all the way to the marshes."

Fae caught his eye and shrugged. Now it hardly felt real, but at the time she'd been too afraid of what she was escaping from to worry that she was doing the impossible.

"When is the next high tide?" Fae asked.

"Half an hour," Aric said. "After that it'll start to go out. Will you need to be closer?"

Fae looked downriver. She couldn't see the marshes of course; they were too far downstream, behind a bend in the river. And as much as she didn't want to be outside the protection spell, it was important to move everything out to sea: trees, dead fish, and plants from the riverbed that had boiled. Burrage or no, the Rivermen had to be able to fish and the safest place—and least damaged—was closer to the mouth of the Aberhayle.

"I'll take her," Pax said. "Shouldn't have you two out together."

Fae looked at Aric. He frowned, but nodded. He knew as well as she did that what Pax meant was that the Rivermen couldn't afford to have them both die.

"I should be all right," Fae said. "Burrage hasn't done any magic where he can't see it happen."

"You're right," Aric said. He smiled. "And that's based on my shaman sense. You'll be fine. Both of you."

"Then let's go," Pax said. "Can I take your fishing boat, Aric?"

"Sure. I won't be needing it."

In a few minutes, Fae and Pax were in Aric's small boat, heading downriver. The moon was close to new but it still shed enough light to allow Pax to navigate. He didn't put the sail up; instead he let the river move them along slowly. Trees swirled in their path, and Fae used magic to push them downstream ahead of them.

And everywhere dead fish glinted on the surface of the water. They didn't smell, not yet, but they would if they were allowed to linger. With another spell, Fae drew them away from the banks and swept them into the middle of the river, where they tangled in amongst the trees.

And everything slowly churned its way downriver, nudged along every few minutes by a small magical push from Fae.

She glanced back at the village that floated in the middle of the river. Beyond the group of boats, she could sense Burrage and his magic, stationary on the bridge.

Pax swung the tiller hard to the left and then they were heading around the bend, out of sight of Aric and the bridge.

Fae stifled a gasp. She'd seen the damage done to the riverbanks where the trees had been ripped out, but the immense tumble of trees and bushes that were lodged in the mud flats before her was more than she'd expected.

"I couldn't have done this from the village," Fae said. "Not with so much debris."

"Aye," Pax said. "Without your help, this would have stayed here for years, maybe decades. The river would have adapted, in time, but we wouldn't have been able to fish here again in my lifetime." He shook his head. "Thought it was over—Rivermen suffering at the hands of conjurers."

"One conjurer is helping to fix it," Fae said. "I need to be just a little closer." She took a deep breath. And she was a conjurer. Better—more powerful—than any had been in years. And she would use her gifts to help, not destroy, like Burrage.

Pax took out an oar and paddled them towards the slower moving water of the far bank. "Tide's going out," he said. "Now's the best time to clear everything away."

Fae nodded and gripped the gunwales to steady herself. "Away," she said to the tangled mess in front of her. The boat rocked as an undulating wave slipped past them downriver. Half submerged trees rolled and twisted as they were swept along with it.

AN HOUR LATER, Fae stared out across the marshes. The tide was almost out and in the predawn light she could only see two trees still stuck in the middle of the river.

"Leave them," Pax said. "We can pull them out with boats later." He met her eyes and nodded. "You've done enough. Thank you."

"All right," Fae said. She sank down to huddle in the bow of the boat. Even though she'd used the smallest spells she could, she was tired. And now that it was dawn, they should be getting back to the village and the protective barrier.

She gazed up at the brightening sky and searched for Burrage's magic, worried that he was already awake. But he hadn't moved from where he'd been all night so he was most likely still sleeping. She smiled. She didn't think he'd be very happy when he rose and found that much of the destruction he'd caused yesterday had been repaired.

"Sweet Berhalla," Pax said. "Would you look at that?"

Fae followed his gaze to the riverbank. The one she hadn't been familiar enough with to know what to encourage to grow. She smiled. The sun had just hit the top of the ridge, lighting up a carpet of white flowers. *Aric will love this*, she thought.

Chapter Fifteen

HEWITT HELD HIS palm up, and Maykin stopped mid-sentence. They both turned to stare at the door to the street. The knock sounded again and Hewitt had to fight down his panic. Maykin had arrived hours ago, he told himself: if he'd been seen, someone would have come before this.

Hewitt nudged aside the kitchen window curtain. The sky was pink with sunrise so it was just after dawn. Burrage wasn't usually an early riser but would he be impatient to get started on a new day of destruction?

"I'll see who it is," he said to Maykin. "But more than likely I will have to leave. Can you destroy it?" Maykin had told him he'd found the rest of the curse, as he'd expected him to, but the man had surprised him by not immediately letting Burrage know about it. The Seven—no, the Ten, he amended—were on his side. If Burrage was given the curse now, he would know Hewitt had kept it from him

"I will try," Maykin replied softly. "I'll remain here as long as I can but I am expected in Conjurers Hall early."

"Thank you." Hewitt nodded, blew out the lamp, and headed to the door. He looked around to make sure there were no signs that Maykin was hiding in his kitchen before he tugged the door open.

"Shiv, what an unexpected pleasure," he said.

Shiv frowned and gestured with his head for Hewitt to exit. "Next time don't make me wait," the Bridger said. He spun and headed towards Conjurers Hall.

Hewitt closed his front door, pretended to lock it, and followed as quickly as his oversized feet would allow. Burrage had little patience on a good day. If Shiv was out so early, it meant this wasn't a good day.

The door that led to the room where Maykin had been searching the books was closed when he went by. Shiv was a few steps ahead of him, and Hewitt wished he had the nerve to duck into the room and take the book—or at least the page the curse was on—and toss it into the closest fire. Unfortunately, any detour would be noticed by Shiv. He would have to trust Maykin to destroy it.

He trailed the Bridger into Burrage's office and stopped at the look of rage on the conjurer's face.

"I felt magic being used in the night," Burrage said. "Nothing close enough to threaten me, but look." He gestured out the window. "The Riverman mocks me."

Hewitt took a step closer and peered out at the riverbank. The scars left on the land from Burrage's devastating spells the day before were blanketed with white.

"What is it?" Hewitt asked, squinting.

"Flowers!" Burrage said. "He tossed aside the trees and rocks I flung at him and instead of showing the fear he should—he plants flowers! I loathe him." He grabbed a book from a pile on his desk and tossed it onto the floor. "I've been going through all the books myself, looking for a spell to use against him."

Hewitt felt his face go cold. Burrage had been looking through the books from the other room—where the book that contained the curse was.

"Did you find anything useful?" Hewitt asked, trying to keep his voice steady. If Burrage had found the curse he would have used it already—and be gloating about it. And he himself would probably be dead. "I apologize if I missed anything useful to you."

"You didn't." Burrage swept the books off the table. "Such incredible power in these spells, yet they are for the most mundane tasks. Tasks that are beneath conjurers." He stared out the window. "I will not be wasting my time on them, I'll tell you that." He turned back to Hewitt. "Go back to the bindery. There must be another Wailes book that was missed or hidden. That curse exists, I know it."

Hewitt turned to leave.

"And Hewitt, whichever of you finds it—you or Maykin—that's the one who will live."

Hewitt closed his eyes briefly. When he opened them, Shiv was smirking at him. "As you wish, Master Conjurer," Hewitt said.

"Yes," Burrage said. "Exactly."

As soon as Hewitt left, Shiv closed the door, shutting him out of Burrage's study.

Down the hall, Hewitt paused beside the door to the other room—the one that held the rest of the books. He cracked it open and looked in. Maykin was not yet there but the book with the curse was. He glanced at the closed door to Burrage's study before he ducked into the room, grabbed the spell book, and tucked it under his robe. He backed out of the room and gently closed the door.

He straightened his robes to hide the book and sighed. Now that he had the curse, he had some control. He would give it to Burrage if he had to. He wouldn't enjoy sending Maykin to his death, but he was the one who had been in contact with Faelin; the one she knew and trusted. He was the one who could help Faelin claim her place as a true conjurer.

He left Conjurers Hall and in moments was knocking on the door of the bindery. Oleda Burrage eventually opened the door. He stood outside until he convinced her that he was here on orders from her son. She let him in but watched as he descended the stairs to the lower level. Ignoring the bindery, he trudged along the hallway to Lachlan Keetley's workroom.

The table had been upended and placed against the wall, and the trap door had been ripped off its hinges. The hole in the floor gaped black, but a lamp sat on the floor beside it.

Once the lamp was lit, Hewitt made his way down the stairs and into the gloom below.

Shelves stretched the length of the room, most heaped haphazardly with books.

He sighed and extracted the book he'd brought from within

his robe. He didn't expect to find any more Wailes spell books—even Shiv's men could tell one hide from another—so there was no way to suddenly *find* this book—overlooked—amongst the other books that had been left behind. He could maybe discover it behind one of the shelves—at least he could tell Burrage that's what had happened. Would Maykin speak up if Hewitt betrayed him? Would Burrage believe the other conjurer even if he did?

ARIC STOOD, DRIPPING, on the pier. He looked at the stairs that stretched up the side of the bridge.

He was tired; still weak from being drained of energy by the spell that had protected the village. As well, the swim from the village had taken a toll. He brushed water from his eyes and looked over at the shoreline.

He'd been aware of Fae's magic all night—a steady flow until an hour ago. That's when he'd decided to leave—decided that he had to confront Burrage now.

Fae had repaired the damage, and now it was Aric's turn to use his skills against the conjurer. He leaned against the bridge. Like the last time he'd been here, his breathing became shallow on the pier. He stepped onto the stairs, his chest constricting a little more with each step he took upwards. By the time he reached the top, he was struggling to breathe.

The door to Fae's workroom was locked when he tried it. He leaned his head against the wood. Could he break in without rousing Oleda Burrage? Would being caught help him complete his task? No, the risk was that he would be killed by Shiv; being thrown off the bridge might not trigger Fae's defensive spell. He had to get inside another way.

He backtracked to the landing that joined the stairs from the bookbindery and the fishmonger's. Should he try the fishmonger's? Or the hidden exit from the secret room?

He stared at the line where a section of stone blocks ended. He may not be able to climb up into Fae's father's workroom—the trap door in the floor might have been blocked. But at least he wouldn't be outside clinging to the side of the bridge. And he might be close enough to steal Burrage's power, all while being safely hidden.

The sun was almost up and his breathing was ragged by the time he felt the stones swing outward. He had to scramble out of the way as the door swung open, but then he slipped inside and pulled the entrance closed.

And took a deep breath, thankful that the curse was no longer affecting him.

He hadn't been able to close the stone door completely and slivers of daylight spilled in around the cracks. Up ahead, where he thought the stairs that led up were, a faint light glowed. He reached out to a shadowed shelf that was empty of books. He carefully passed the shelf and headed towards the light.

He sensed magic, and when he followed it, he found Burrage. He was close. Aric closed his eyes and concentrated.

Burrage was coming towards him: now he'd stopped just a few yards above him. He must be in the corridor that ran between Fae's and her father's workrooms. Was he coming down to the secret room? Burrage should already be close enough for Aric to steal his power.

"Hewitt," someone called. "Hewitt!"

"Conjurer Burrage?"

Hewitt's reply came from just ahead. Aric peered out into the dimly lit space. A light bobbed into the aisle, and he saw the white hair of Horace Hewitt.

"You have need of me?" Hewitt asked.

"The curse," Burrage said. "Give it to me." He stepped off the stairs and headed towards Hewitt.

"I am sorry, Conjurer Burrage," Hewitt replied. "But I have not yet found it."

"Don't bother lying about it," Burrage said. "Maykin told me."

"He told you what?" The light Hewitt held bobbed backwards.

"He was begging for his life," Burrage said. "He told me that he'd found the curse but that when he looked for the book this morning, it was gone." Burrage took a step towards Hewitt and the other man backed up. "Shiv was very . . . persuasive. Maykin said you had asked him not to tell me he'd found it. Give me the curse!"

The curse had been found, but Burrage didn't have it, not yet. Aric would not let him complete it. He concentrated, and slowly, gently he started to draw magic from the conjurer.

"Where's Maykin?" Hewitt asked.

"Where do you think?" Burrage asked. "He'll never lie to me again. Give me the curse!"

"No," Hewitt said. "I'm dead anyway." He seemed to shrink in on himself. "The last of the Seven—the last conjurer," Hewitt said.

"The last charlatan, you mean," Burrage said. "I am the only true conjurer alive."

A laugh bubbled up from Hewitt, and Aric—worried that Hewitt would lose all hope and tell Burrage about Fae—redoubled his efforts to siphon magic from Burrage. But his fear made him use too much force. He gasped when the flow of magic slammed into him.

"Who's there?" Burrage said, trying to peer past Hewitt.

Hewitt took two quick steps backwards, flinging the lamp at a bookcase. Burrage stared at Hewitt for a moment before he opened a book he held.

Already tied to Burrage's magic, Aric felt the spell as it was being created. Instead of twisting the magic, as he'd done before, he drew the power from the spell to him. It surged into him, and he stumbled into the middle of the aisle. He looked up as Burrage shouted the final words of the spell. Hewitt crouched on the floor, silhouetted by flames.

"Where are you?" Burrage roared. He shouldered Hewitt out of the way and hurried past the now blazing shelf to the back of the room.

Aric grabbed onto a shelf and dragged himself up to face the conjurer. He lifted a hand and reached out to the other man's power, feeling it soak into him, filling him up.

"What are you?" Burrage stopped, fear in his voice. "How are you doing that?" He took a step backwards, almost tripping over Hewitt, who was trying to stand. Both men stared at him, their mouths open in alarm.

And Aric realized that Burrage and Hewitt's faces were lit from the front. He stared at his hand—light shone from his skin, illuminating the previously dark end of the room. The flames up ahead were dim in comparison to the light he himself cast. So much magic, so much power—it was literally leaking from his skin.

Could he use it? Could he tap into that power? He concentrated on Burrage, trying to send the magic back to him; trying to force it to enter him, but it was no use. The power stayed with—*in*—Aric. And it was too much. Without any way to discharge the power—without the ability to create a spell—would it consume him? If it did, Burrage would still be alive and the curse could still be completed. He *would not* allow that.

But how to get rid of all this magic? Aric headed back towards the exit that led to the stairs. He shoved the stone door aside and stepped out into the light of a sunny day.

He was halfway down to the pier when a small stone rattled past him. He looked up. Someone else had exited the book bindery. It was Hewitt, his oversized feet balancing precariously on the steps. Did he have the curse with him?

Aric hurried to the bottom and looked up as Hewitt descended. By the time the conjurer joined him on the pier, Burrage and Shiv stared down at them, smoke billowing out of the opening.

"Can you swim?" Aric asked. Hewitt shook his head. "Jump in anyway," Aric said. "I'll tow you."

"You may not need to," Hewitt said.

Aric followed his gaze to the small boat that was heading their way. Pax and Fae. He hadn't felt her presence in the magic before, but now he could feel her panic.

He glanced up at the bridge. Shiv and Burrage were gone, and the smoke was barely noticeable. They must have put out the fire.

"Do you have the curse?" Aric asked. "Or did you destroy it?" His visit wouldn't be a complete disaster if the curse was gone forever.

"Neither," Hewitt said. "I hid it amongst the other books, but I'm afraid it wasn't on the shelf I set on fire. I am sorry. I should have taken the page out while I had the chance."

"Burrage will find it," Aric said, and he felt the truth of that. Why hadn't Hewitt destroyed the curse? Had he planned to use it against him or Fae? Had he thought it would afford him some measure of leverage with Burrage?

The boat pulled up and without a word, Aric helped Hewitt board before shoving off and hopping on. Then Fae was wrapping her arms around him. He met her eyes, and she sighed and shook her head. She took hold of one of his hands and held it up. It still glowed with Burrage's stolen power.

"What happened?" Fae asked. "Never mind. You can tell me later." She closed her eyes. Her relief in finding Aric alive had been replaced by fear. The power was consuming him.

"I need to help Pax," Aric said.

"No," Fae replied. When he would have moved, she gripped his hands as hard as she could and stared at him. Aric dropped his eyes and nodded, and Fae relaxed slightly.

"Oh! The curse!" Aric groaned and leaned into her, panting.

Stunned, Fae looked up: there, at the top of the stairs, was Burrage. He held a book in his hands, and now that she was looking beyond the power that burned in Aric, she could feel magic building as Burrage recited a spell.

And Aric was in that spell: she could feel him twisting it away from him. She put a protective spell around Aric and it swept past him. Then it was gone, changed by him into something different, something other than the curse, something that felt like the opposite of the curse.

Burrage screamed his rage from high up on the stairs and before he could recite the curse again, Fae siphoned the magic that was consuming Aric—Burrage's own power—into a shield that she placed around the conjurer. Sparks crackled when his spell—most likely the curse again—hit the barrier but couldn't escape it.

"Aric," Hewitt called from the prow of the boat. "Your friend . . ."

"Pax!" Aric called.

Fae followed as Aric scrambled to him, but instead of a man, Pax was . . .

Not a fish, although it had gills, and not a snake, although it had the flat mouth of one. Hair covered the head, and Pax's all too human eyes stared blankly up at the sky. The body had the shape of a seal but the fur that covered it was flesh coloured, not brown. And the flippers ended in webbed appendages that resembled the feet of a duck.

"He's dead," Aric said sadly. "From the curse . . ." Aric lifted what was once Pax and gently set him into the water.

"My fault," Fae said, her voice catching. "I didn't protect him." In her fear for Aric she'd forgotten to shield Pax.

"Not your fault," Aric said. "You did not do this."

Fae followed his gaze up towards Burrage, who was still at the top of the stairs, still magically battering at the shield she'd placed around him.

"We need to leave," Fae said. "He's almost broken through."

"No," Aric said. "We need to stop him. *Now*. Because he won't stop until we're all dead." He pointed his hand—his skin still shone with Burrage's power. "Create another shield around him, to give us time."

"Once I drain this magic from you," Fae said, hoping it wasn't too late, that it hadn't already damaged him. She closed her eyes against the glare and concentrated on the magic. She tugged it, and it resisted for a moment before it started flowing to her.

It felt almost familiar; a little bit like her own power, but there was a difference, and that small difference made it impossible for her to simply absorb it. So, she put it into a second protective spell and wrapped it around Burrage. She felt his surprise, and then his anger.

"Shiv!" Burrage called from above them. "Kill everyone in that boat!"

Fae looked up. Someone leaned out the door that led to the book bindery, but it was Oleda, not Shiv.

"Fae," Aric said. "You need to create a killing spell—but use my power. It can't be tainted by Burrage's. And then I need to somehow aim it at him."

"Yes," Fae replied. Burrage's power was of the Ten, and would fail if used against himself—a conjurer of the Ten. But would Aric be able to attack him with her spell?

Ignoring the conjurer, who was still throwing spells against the barrier that contained his magic, Fae studied Aric. There were still some traces of Burrage's power, she thought. Anything that felt similar to her own magic, she siphoned from him and not knowing what else to do with it, she fed it into the land; into the grass and flowers she'd encouraged to grow over the scars left by Burrage's destruction.

When she was finally satisfied that only Aric's power was left, she took a breath and created a killing spell.

"I have the spell ready," Fae said. "I think it will be better if we were on the pier."

The boat had drifted downstream a few yards, and Aric nodded and picked up the oars. As soon as they were beside the pier, Fae stepped out onto it. She looked up at Burrage, who had moved a few steps downward. Aric's hand gripped hers as he joined her on the pier.

The barrier was weak; she could feel the areas where the magic had thinned. Ah, there.

"Aric." She paused and tried to show him where the weak spot was. Then he was in the magic with her. He took hold of the killing spell, and she wrapped her own magic around him. When he flung the spell, she pushed his magic with her own.

The spell—created with Aric's magic and directed by him—hit the protective barrier—then with a burst of power it was inside. Burrage cried out in pain and rage when the spell struck him. It tossed him up against the stones of the bridge as magic flashed within the protective barrier; then the barrier shattered and Burrage was sent arcing away from the bridge.

Fae backed up against the base of the bridge as Burrage sailed out over the water. Small stones rained down on her and Aric: then Burrage hit the river and sank.

"Is he dead?" Hewitt called from the boat. "Is he really dead?"

Fae searched for any sense of power—of Burrage's power—but there wasn't even a spark. She stared out at the river but there was no sign of him, no sign of someone in the water, struggling to get to the surface.

"I think so, yes," she said and fell back against Aric. "He plunged into the river and he took the spell book with the curse with him."

"Good riddance to both," Aric said, wrapping his arms around her.

"Now tell me what you were doing," Fae said.

"I thought I could drain Burrage's magic," Aric replied. "That I could either kill him by doing that or render him powerless. I was hoping for something permanent."

Fae shook her head. "But then he found the curse."

"Because of Hewitt."

"I'm the last one," Hewitt said. "The last of the old conjurers. Shiv threw Sherston off the bridge because he was in his way, and Yaldon is dead because Oleda didn't like the way he smelled. And Maykin," he paused. "He thought Burrage would let him live if he gave him the curse. But I had it."

"You!" Fae glared at him. "You had it and didn't destroy it? What were you planning?"

"I . . ." Hewitt paused. "I am sorry I didn't destroy the spell. I meant to but . . ." The conjurer's voice trailed off. He took a breath and faced her. "I have spent all of my adult life hoarding spells. It is a habit I couldn't break when I should have."

Fae frowned at him. Pax was dead because Hewitt hadn't destroyed the curse. But also because she forgot to shield him. "We need to leave."

"No, WE NEED to go back up," Hewitt said from where he slumped in the prow of the boat. "And make sure the bridge is secured."

"Later." Aric pulled on the painter he still held, bringing the boat closer to the pier. "After we've checked on the village."

He helped Fae into the boat before jumping in and settling at the oars. His fear for what they would find when they reached the village spurred him to row faster. Eventually the huddle of boats came into view. It was quiet—was that a good thing?

"The protective spells are intact," Fae said, relief in her voice

"Thank Berhalla," Aric replied. He grabbed the painter and jumped to the closest boat and tied the line off. He helped Fae and then Hewitt scramble aboard. Then silently he led the way across the boats towards the centre of the floating village.

Everyone would be on Pax's boat, he guessed, waiting for him to return.

"Aric! Over here."

Aric turned to look in the direction of the voice. "Rand," he said, relieved. At least one person had escaped the effects of the curse. He gripped Fae's hand and headed towards the other Riverman, trying to determine if there was good news or bad.

"Is everything all right?" Aric asked.

"Did anyone . . ." Fae paused. "Feel anything?"

"You might say that," Rand replied. He scowled past them, and Aric turned to see Hewitt catch up.

"He helped us," Aric said. "He's on our side."

"He's a conjurer," Rand spat. "He's to blame. Where's Pax? I need to report."

"He's dead," Aric said. "He . . . changed, and then he died."

Rand's eyes narrowed and he nodded. "Some of the folk closest to the edge of the village noticed changes: small changes, though, and for the better. Less webbing for the most part. What happened to Pax?"

"Complete transformation," Aric said. "I was able to change the spell—I tried to reverse the curse—but not before it hit Pax." He didn't mention that Fae had shielded him from Pax's fate. "He died. I gave him to the river: I didn't want people to see him like that."

"Probably for the best. We're all scared enough as it is. Come on, folks will want to see that the shaman is alive."

Chapter Sixteen

HEWITT TRIED TO stay out of anyone's line of sight as Aric and Faelin spoke to the crowd of Rivermen about what had happened. When one of them did look his way, it was with suspicion.

He could hardly believe that Burrage was really dead, though he'd seen the man plunge into the river. Was there any way the Rivermen could find his body and make sure? Did they need to? Even if he'd been alive when he went into the water, even if he'd somehow survived the fall, Burrage couldn't swim; no one other than Rivermen could swim.

How he longed to return to the bridge, longed for his small home with its thick stone walls and familiar shelves of books.

Useless books—he would never again perform any of the spells they contained, not after seeing the true power of magic, the true power of conjurers—but comforting to him.

He watched Faelin take Aric's hand. They had finished their tale and now Rivermen shouted out questions. Faelin's children would be the start of a new dynasty of conjurers; if Burrage was truly dead, he had to make sure that happened. But all would be lost—all his plans would amount to nothing if those children were fathered by the Riverman.

He'd get her to return to the bridge, get her settled back into the book bindery. That was what she'd always wanted, to live on the bridge and take up her family's trade. That would be enough for her again, he'd see to it.

As for the Riverman? He'd have to tread carefully. He was Faelin's oldest friend, and the shaman, which turned out to be a powerful position. But he was still just a Riverman and had no place on the bridge. It would have been better if Aric had changed and died, like the other Riverman.

"What about the upstream village?" someone asked.

"We'll send a party to search for them," Aric said. "As soon as we secure the bridge."

"I'll go to the bridge," Hewitt said. "I am the last of the conjurers. The people will be looking to me for leadership. It has always been our way." He would need to find Shiv, of course, and get his co-operation. The rest of the people of the bridge *would* follow him. Faelin looked at him with gratitude, and he smiled. She might have the true power, but a conjurer had never been a woman. *He* would lead, and she would follow. That had also always been the way.

In less time than he expected he was being helped into a boat. Faelin, Aric, and half a dozen Rivermen carrying knives and poles with hooks, climbed in after him and soon they were rowing towards the bridge.

"Still no sense of Burrage," Faelin said. "Or his magic. He really is dead."

Up ahead the bridge looked as calm and solid as ever; the stones arching across the river the same as they had for generations. For the first time Hewitt noticed the barriers across all but one of the arches. The river ran swiftly through the single opening.

The men on the boat were quiet as they moored at the bottom of the stairs. One of them quickly tied a rope to the ring set in stone.

"Hewitt, you follow with Fae," Aric said. "I'll go first with the men."

Aric hopped out and scrambled up the stone steps, followed by five of the six Rivermen. Faelin stepped out after them, and then the last remaining Riverman was steadying him as he carefully placed one oversized shoe on the pier.

There was no choice, he had to follow them. But he went

slowly, taking extra care to place his large feet securely on each step. Soon Aric and his men were out of sight through the door into the book bindery.

Faelin paused at the landing, and he waved her on and she too disappeared through the doorway.

He delayed for as long as he could, but eventually he had to step off the top step and into the bindery. He clumped up the stairs and was in the small kitchen before he remembered.

She must be here. He'd seen her look out as her son battled Faelin. Now that Graylon was dead, she would have no friends on the bridge. She must still be here, somewhere.

He found her tucked into a tiny closet in the smaller bedchamber.

"Oleda, my dear," Hewitt said. "I fear it has been a tragic day."

"Oh, Conjurer Hewitt." The woman's face was streaked with tears as she lifted red-rimmed eyes to him. "My poor boy is dead. I saw him, on the stairs. Something hit him and then . . ." She paused to rub a knuckle across her eyes. "Then he flew off into the river. I couldn't see him—no matter how hard I looked, I couldn't see him."

"Yes, I know. Where is Shiv?"

"I don't care," Oleda spat. "My son asked him for help and Shiv just walked away. I hope he stays away."

"We must find him," Hewitt said. He didn't bother to say that the help Burrage had asked of Shiv included killing him—he had been on the boat, after all.

"I don't care," Oleda repeated.

"We'll need his help," Hewitt said. "*You* will need his help, unless you want the ones who killed Graylon to throw you off the bridge."

"Why would they do that?"

Hewitt sighed. "You know that not everyone liked your son." *Or you*, he finished silently.

"They were jealous of him."

"And afraid."

"As they should be," Oleda hissed. "Should have been," she amended, her head bowed.

"And he is not here to protect you," Hewitt said. "Shiv saw the way it would end so he chose not to side with Graylon at the last, but he had backed him earlier. He will not find friends among those who killed your son either. Help me find him so we can discuss both your futures." He looked around what had once been Faelin's room. And would be again; at least a room in her house, although she may not sleep here.

"Thank you," Oleda said. "You've always been such a good friend to me and my son."

Hewitt nodded and turned towards the stairs. She would not be allowed to stay here in Faelin's home. Would likely not be allowed to stay on the bridge, unless he helped her. But could she be useful? He turned back to her.

She'd given birth to one conjurer—she might have the blood. It was possible Oleda could become a conjurer herself, but how to test her when reading from either a Wailes or a Kellen spell book—or both if the bloodlines came from Graylon's father— might be her death? He didn't think Faelin would help Oleda Burrage gain magical abilities, but she might help a child of Oleda become a conjurer.

"Oleda, I hate to bring up such a delicate subject while you are mourning the loss of your son, and of course no one could take his place. But have you given any thought to marrying and having another child?"

"I'll have to, won't I?" she said, bitterly. "I need a home, and a man to tie myself to. A child will do that."

"Yes, it will." Hewitt headed down the stairs

THE DOOR TO Conjurers Hall was open. Aric held a hand up signalling the others to stop. A few whispered about being able to breathe on the bridge and he smiled. Here was proof that he *had* changed the curse when Burrage recited it.

He closed his eyes—there were traces of magic, but no sense of any spells set as traps. Fae was behind him and he opened his eyes and looked over his shoulder at her.

"I don't sense any spells," he said. He turned around and frowned. "Where's Hewitt?"

"He was taking so long on the stairs," Fae said. "Because of his . . ." Fae raised her hands. "He told me to go ahead."

"Of course." The conjurer's afflictions would make climbing the stairs difficult. "I suppose we won't need him unless we find Shiv and his Bridgers. Go slow," he told the Rivermen. He motioned them forward and two men brandishing fishing gaffs entered the hall. Aric followed them into the hallway with Fae close behind.

The door to the room he'd met Burrage in was open. He stepped past the other Rivermen and into an empty room. A book was open on a desk as though the person reading it was planning on returning any moment now.

"I don't think there's any danger in here," he said. "And no Bridgers."

"They're on the bridge somewhere," Fae said. She went over and peered out the window and he followed her. The sun shone on the river, belying the terrible struggle that had happened.

"You were the key," Fae said. "Your premonition: my spell created using your magic, wielded by you."

"But you defeated him," Aric said. "It was your spell."

"Wielded by you," she repeated. "And the other premonition: two conjurers meet and only one survives. Maybe that's you as well."

"But I'm not a conjurer," Aric replied. He was happy being a shaman. "You're the conjurer." He sighed. "The bridge might have been damaged."

She frowned. "From the blast when Burrage died?"

"And when he dammed the river," he said.

"Right. We'll need to look at it."

"And fix it," Aric said. "Like you fixed much of what Burrage did to the land and the river." He sighed again and turned to the Rivermen who waiting for direction. "We need to find Shiv and his Bridgers. Then we need to go upstream." He was worried about what he'd find further up the river. Had he changed the curse in time to spare them? They hadn't been protected, like the village downstream had been.

"I need to get word to Councilman Larwood," Fae said. "You find Shiv and make sure the Bridgers aren't going to cause trouble and then see to the upstream Rivermen."

"All right," he replied. "I'll come for you if I need you." If they'd been changed upstream, the way Pax had been, and there was anything Fae could do to help them. Praise Berhalla that Burrage had been so focussed on the village downstream that the curse had only been directed there.

Fae ducked into the bakery and Aric and his men went in search of Hewitt. And the Bridgers.

"IT'S A GOOD option," Hewitt said. "Maybe your only option. But you have to make your decision now. Aric and Faelin will be looking for both of you."

Hewitt and Oleda had found Shiv sitting alone in his house. Shiv's house was small, like all bridge houses, but the room seemed even more cramped in contrast to the size of the Bridger. Hewitt had tasked Oleda with making tea and opening the curtains so it didn't look like they were hiding.

"They will believe me when I tell them you were helping me help them," Hewitt said. "It's even almost the truth."

"Then why her?" Shiv asked, gesturing at Oleda, who stood silently beside Hewitt's chair.

"I don't like it either," Oleda said. "You abandoned my son. That's why he died."

"He was going to die anyway," Shiv said. "Why should I die with him? Rather die here, in my own home." He looked at Hewitt. "If I do this, what's in that for me?"

"Besides a woman who can cook and keep house for you?" Hewitt asked. "And warm your bed?" He saw Oleda flinch, and Shiv's half smile told him the Bridger had noticed as well.

"Because I am asking this of you. Do you need another reason? I want to save you both, and this is the best way. You, Shiv, were only doing as you were told, following the orders of the person you thought was in charge. But you struggled with determining who that was, so you tried your best to accommodate two masters who were at odds with each other." Hewitt paused. "There's enough truth in that for me to convince Aric and Faelin. And I would like Oleda to be spared. You can help me do this. That is how you help repay me for ensuring that you and your people stay on the bridge."

They were running out of time. If Faelin and Aric arrived before the Bridger agreed, before Hewitt could trust him, he would encourage them to turn Shiv and his Bridgers off the bridge. And Oleda as well. Let them find a new place to live. He would still have Faelin's bloodline to help shape the new dynasty of conjurers.

"I'll do it," Shiv said. "I'll take orders from you and keep the woman as long as all of my people can stay on the bridge."

"Thank you," Hewitt said. He heard a sound from out front. "I think your guests are here. Oleda, let them in."

Hewitt sat back and met Shiv's eyes and nodded. Aric and his Rivermen crowded into the room.

"Where is Faelin?" Hewitt asked.

"She's gone to visit some old friends," Aric replied. "Now that Burrage is dead." Aric took a step closer to Shiv, standing over him. "What are your thoughts about this one?"

"He'll be loyal to the conjurer in charge," Hewitt said. "But he was confused about who that was. He helped me. He's the reason I was able to visit Faelin in town."

Shiv looked up in surprise, and Hewitt nodded. "You see, he wasn't aware that I was meeting with Faelin, but he didn't question me. Or tell Burrage what I was doing. I think he can be trusted."

"As long as he doesn't try to think for himself," Aric said. He leaned over the Bridger. "But don't think for a moment that I have forgotten that you hurt me. And liked it. And *that's* not just following orders." He looked back at Oleda. "And her?"

"For some reason Oleda and Shiv have taken a shine to each other," Hewitt said. "He says he wants her as his woman."

"Really?" Aric asked. "I'll need to talk to Fae about this. Oleda is her relative, after all. She might not like being related to Shiv. I know I won't."

Hewitt relaxed when Aric turned his attention back to Shiv. "We need to go upriver. Remove the rest of the barriers and any grates that might still be in place."

"What do you want done with them?" Shiv asked.

"Sink them in the river," Aric replied. "I'll ask my upriver cousins to take them away. The bridge—and especially Bridgers— no longer control where Rivermen can travel on the river or off it."

"Of course," Hewitt said, before Shiv could react. "Shiv, see to it immediately. Aric, do you need anyone else to go with you?" He was curious enough to know what had happened to the Rivermen upstream to offer to go himself, but he needed to solidify his position on the bridge. Before Faelin had a chance to try to assert hers.

Shiv led the Rivermen out of his house, leaving Hewitt and Oleda.

"A drop more tea, if you would my dear," Hewitt said. The

woman turned—without a scowl, he noticed—and headed for the teapot still warming on the stove.

He had time. And he didn't expect to have any trouble—he *was* the last conjurer. And he was a man. Even if Faelin tried to gain authority, the bridge had never had a woman lead them. He was confident that they wouldn't accept her: not with all the turmoil and uncertainty of the last few months.

FAE POPPED ANOTHER piece of bread into her mouth and sighed. It seemed like ages since she'd eaten bread and this was fresh and warm from the oven.

"He'll be here soon," Mistress Pullen said. "My husband will see to it."

"Thank you," Fae said around another mouthful of bread. As soon as Fae had told her what had happened, Mistress Pullen had sent her husband off to fetch Councilman Larwood. Now the door to the shop was locked as they waited.

"Will things be better?" Mistress Pullen asked. "Now that the conjurers are gone? At least the bad ones?"

"As long as the Bridgers behave," Fae replied. She wasn't sure what would happen if they didn't. They could be forced off the bridge, but that would just let them loose on one of the towns, and that wouldn't be fair—or safe—for the townspeople.

"Don't trust Conjurer Hewitt."

"Pardon?" Fae said. "Has he said anything?"

"No," Mistress Pullen said. "But he didn't help my Thorpe. Or any of the others."

"I'm not sure he could have without being in danger himself," Fae replied. She would always wonder that about Hewitt. What could he have done—that he hadn't—without sacrificing himself. Or was she expecting too much of the man?

But he, along with the rest of the conjurers, had elected Quillan Wailes to govern them, thereby inflicting him on the rest of the people who called the bridge home. Without Wailes there would have been no Burrage. Hewitt bore some responsibility.

But how much blame belonged to the dead conjurers and how much to the one left alive?

A knock sounded, and Mistress Pullen got up and peered out the front window.

"It's them." She unlatched the door and Baker Pullen stepped inside, followed by Councilman Larwood and his wife.

"Thank you for coming," Fae said. "Did you have any trouble getting onto the bridge?"

"None," Larwood said. "The gate was wide open and there were no guards to be seen."

"Good. That means Hewitt and the Bridgers have done what Aric was going to ask them to." She looked at Mistress Pullen. "We don't trust Hewitt, but the Bridgers see him as the authority on the bridge."

"But not for long?" Mistress Larwood asked. "Is that why we're here?"

"Yes. The Bridgers will never take direction from a Riverman." She paused. "And I think they'll be reluctant to take direction from a woman."

"But they'll have no choice if you have the Rivermen and the towns behind you," Larwood said.

"Yes," Fae agreed. "They need to know that they have no place else to go. If we are united, they have no opportunity to settle somewhere else and continue their violent ways. And I certainly don't want to burden the towns with them."

"Thank you," Larwood said. "I'll talk to Cleric Kenway." He paused. "I imagine he'll be as grateful as I am to keep the Bridgers out of Durnham. I did hear he was thankful not to have to deal with the Burrages any longer. Where is Oleda?"

"I'm not sure," Fae said. "But she's another one we might be better off keeping on the bridge. We live close together here. I'm sure her neighbours could be counted on to keep an eye on her."

"We've been doing that already," Mistress Pullen said. "And I don't think anyone is ready to stop that, even if we're asked to. But we can let you know if we suspect she's up to trouble."

"Yes," Fae replied. "That sounds workable."

"I'm certain Cleric Kenway will welcome this as a solution," Larwood said. "I'll visit him right now if I have permission to cross the bridge and back."

"Of course," Fae said. "I'll come with you and make sure the Bridgers know it's allowed. And not just for you—it's allowed for everyone."

"Truly?" Mistress Pullen asked. "I've a niece in Durnham with a new baby I would dearly love to see."

"Truly," Fae said. "The bridge will no longer divide people. It will do what it was built to do—bring people together."

"THE THREAT OF the curse is gone," Aric said. He looked out across the boats that were lashed together in front of him. "Forever. The new Wailes conjurer is dead and the book that held the curse is in the river, hopefully on its way out to sea."

They'd found the Riverman village far upriver. Aric was told that they'd moved here when the river had been dammed, and had stayed as far away from the bridge ever since.

"I hope I can trust you on that," Chart said. "No one was harmed up this way, and I've even heard some claim that their old symptoms have improved."

"Good," Aric said. It seemed that poor Pax was the only fatality, and even as he mourned his loss, Aric was certain Pax would have been relieved.

He'd been able to change the curse: it seemed that he truly had reversed it a little. The Rivermen had been able to breathe on the bridge, and others had less webbing. Aric was tempted to try his luck on land but he thought it might be better to keep a secret or two.

He didn't trust Shiv, no matter how hard Hewitt tried to convince him that the Bridger would follow orders. Hewitt's orders, is what it sounded like. And he didn't trust Hewitt, either.

He and Hewitt had come to an understanding a while ago that Fae was worth any sacrifice. Aric wasn't sure Hewitt wasn't still thinking that way.

"The metal plates and grates on the bridge have been removed," Aric said. "From now on the bridge will not be a barrier between up and downriver."

"Hard to believe that." Safi Brookden crossed her arms. She stood just behind Chart and the scowl on her face was evidence that although Chart wanted to believe him, his second in command was more skeptical.

Aric looked at the people gathered on the boats in front of him. He shrugged. "Time will provide the proof," he said. "Today, the grates are gone. They're at the bottom of the river and you are welcome to move them anywhere you want. Bridgers can neither swim nor pilot a boat, so there will be no chance for them to recover them even if they know where they are."

"They can make new ones," someone shouted from the back.

"Not Bridgers," Aric said. "Conjurers made these ones long ago, and I think a conjurer would need to remake them and Fae won't do that." He sighed. He'd done all he could. They would believe him or not, trust him or not.

"That's all the news," Aric said. "Feel free to send someone downriver to check for yourselves."

He nodded, and one of his men untied Chart's boat and pushed them away from it. He felt for magic and smiled when he felt Fae.

"Chart, Safi. I'll be on the bridge if you need me. Rand is probably in charge downriver." Pax didn't have an official second, but Rand had been in his confidence.

"Thanks, Aric," Chart said. "It's good to have access to downriver. And to find out we still have a shaman."

Aric nodded and then turned to where the bridge would soon come into view. Would they still consider him their shaman if he lived on the bridge with Fae?

"OLEDA HAS ALREADY vacated the bindery," Hewitt said. "I don't believe she ever used the workrooms." Sitting across from his desk, Faelin frowned.

"Didn't Quillan Wailes have everyone traipse through when he brought Aric's mother there?" Faelin asked. "And what about when he dragged all the books out?"

"That," Hewitt said. "Yes. But it was before Oleda came to live on the bridge."

"Where is Oleda Burrage now?"

"She's . . ." Hewitt paused. He'd wanted a chance to lead into this, but Faelin wasn't going to give him that. He met her gaze. She knew the sort of woman Oleda was. "She's already moved into Shiv's quarters."

"What?"

"I did mention it to Aric," Hewitt said. "Oleda said she needed a man, now that her son was dead. And Shiv was willing to have her." He paused.

"Was he?" Faelin said. "How very . . . interesting. Well. As long as she's out of my home, what does it matter to me?"

She shrugged and Hewitt relaxed. It was the truth. At least part of it. There was no need to mention that it had been his idea.

"I'll wait until Aric returns before looking to see what repairs

I need to make. Both the blast of magic and damming the river might have caused damage to the bridge." Faelin smiled brightly. "Councilman Larwood stopped by for a visit. Testing the freedom to go from one side of the bridge to the other. And back home, of course. He's delighted."

"I'm sure he is," Hewitt said. He didn't care what the people in the towns did, although he would rather not have the peace and quiet of the bridge disturbed too often. "Perhaps at night we can have the bridge closed to traffic?"

"Don't you think it's too soon for that?" Faelin asked. "I should think it would cause unnecessary worry. We want everyone to trust us, don't we?"

"Yes," Hewitt said. He would talk to Shiv about this. If the Bridger said keeping the gates open was too dangerous—and he would make sure he did—Faelin would have to accept his decisions. After all, as the sole male conjurer, *he* was in charge.

"My offer still stands, Faelin," Hewitt said. "The one I made to you before all of this . . . unpleasantness. I would have you as my apprentice. It would signal to everyone that you are to inherit the leadership."

"But," Faelin started. "I am sorry, Conjurer Hewitt. It is, again, a generous offer, but Aric and I . . . well, Aric is shaman to the Rivermen, and that is something that none of this . . . unpleasantness has changed. The bindery is the perfect place for him to live. He has access to both upriver and downriver villages. I will be living there with him, as his wife."

"Of course," Hewitt said. He hadn't expected her to accept his offer, but neither had he expected her to be so blatant about her . . . relationship with Aric. "It was just a suggestion."

"I must be going," Faelin said. "Aric will be back soon and I want to remove all traces of Oleda Burrage from my house before nightfall."

Hewitt said something pleasant when she rose and left. He must have, because she nodded and smiled at him. She closed the door, and he swiped an arm across his desk, sending papers and quills flying.

How could she? How could Faelin marry that . . . what had Shiv called him? River rat! She was supposed to bring conjurers back to greatness, she was supposed to give birth to a new generation of powerful magic users. Not mongrels with webbed hands and feet who could barely set foot on land.

It wouldn't do, he would not allow it. But he was afraid that stopping it meant that Aric had to die. And it had to be in a way that did not point back to him; otherwise Faelin would never trust him again.

He would talk to Shiv. But not about closing the gates at night—no, he would let Faelin have her way on that subject. He would let her have her way on almost anything. But she would not have sons by that river rat.

Fae stared at the front door of the bindery. It had only been a few months since she'd run away, but so much had happened. She'd been back inside but only to pass through going to or from the stairs. She hadn't taken a good look at the kitchen and sitting room, and she'd deliberately stayed away from the bedrooms.

"It won't open by itself."

"Aric!" She flung her arms around him. "I was hoping you'd be back to do this with me."

"So, I'm the excuse?" Aric said. "Come on, time to see what damage Oleda inflicted on your home."

"*Our* home," Fae said. "And she inflicts damage everywhere she goes, so I am expecting the bindery to be no different." She followed Aric inside and stood, with the door still open, and stared around.

It smelled different. Not horrible, but different. Was it because Oleda had her own smell and ate different food or was it because no books had been bound, no leather had been worked, for so very long?

Upstairs was the worst. Her father's bedroom, the one place in the house that had truly smelled like him, now had a sweet, flowery odour to it. She pulled the bedding off, and Aric helped her flip the mattress. She blushed when he smiled at her. This would be their room—the bed in her old room wasn't big enough for two.

Although when she finally looked in her old room, the bed there didn't seem much smaller than the one on Aric's boat.

Once the bedrooms had been stripped of all bedding and the floors swept, Fae headed to the kitchen. A small spell sparked a flame and soon water was heating for tea.

Aric lifted the top off the larder.

"I ate her supper," he said. "When I came to prevent Burrage from looking for you. I stopped here and ate Oleda Burrage's fish pie." He looked up at her and grinned. "It was quite good."

"She would have been furious," Fae said. She frowned. "Hewitt said she's coupled up with Shiv. I don't like it."

"I know, he told me as well," Aric said. "Oleda and Shiv. A bad pair who will make dangerous enemies." Aric's voice sounded tight, and when she turned to him, he slid to the floor.

Fae dropped to her knees by his side, cradling his head on her lap.

"New forces have replaced the old on the bridge," he said, then he gasped and his eyes focussed on her. "I heard myself that time," he said. "I'm getting better at . . . not control, but awareness."

"Are you all right?" Fae asked. Now she was worried; a premonition probably meant there was still danger. "Did you hurt yourself?"

"I'm fine." Aric sat up and grabbed her hands. "I don't think I needed a premonition to tell me that Oleda and Shiv together mean trouble."

"I know," Fae said. "Oleda *is* the type of woman to find a man to support her, but she would never willingly align herself with someone she has no hope of controlling."

"Hewitt?" Aric asked.

"It has to be," Fae said. "He has assumed control, as we knew he would. He asked me to be his apprentice, again. This time his argument was that it would let everyone know that I was his heir to his leadership."

"You told him no?" Aric asked.

"I told him you and I were going to wed and live here."

"That's it," Aric said. "There's something about you and I together that initiated whatever event I foresaw. I'm Hewitt's target, although somehow Oleda and Shiv are his weapons."

"Should we kill them?" Fae asked. "I don't want to but I will if it's the only way we'll be safe." She blew out a breath. She'd hoped Burrage's death meant the end of the fighting. Why did Hewitt have to cause trouble? "What do you think he wants? Hewitt?"

"That's what we need to find out," Aric said. "He was willing to sacrifice himself to ensure that you lived. I *felt* that he meant it."

"He was also willing to have Burrage win," Fae said. "I'm not sure he cared that much which one of us survived, as long as one of us did. So, it's something we have in common."

"The old blood," Aric said. "It has to be."

"We're conjurers with the blood of the Ten," Fae agreed. "And Burrage has two bloodlines: Wailes and Keetley."

"And one or both of them could have come from his mother," Aric said. "Could we test Oleda? See if she can do magic?"

"The only way I know of to test Oleda would include showing her how to create a spell," Fae said. "Something I'm not prepared to do."

"So, if Oleda was to bear another child—by Shiv," Aric said, "that child could become a conjurer. Hewitt would control it in a way he would never be able to control you and your children. Especially while I'm alive. That's why I'm the target."

"So maybe we should kill *Hewitt*," Fae said. "Or confront him?"

"I don't think confronting Hewitt will change anything," Aric said. "He'll just be more careful. But I don't think we need to kill him. At least not right now. I don't sense this as an immediate threat but we do need to watch all three of them."

"And if Oleda becomes with child?" Fae asked. "Hewitt might feel he doesn't need either of us then."

"Still, we have some time," Aric said. "You can magically protect me. And I have some abilities of my own—I'm not the easy target Shiv would expect. Besides, if we solidify our alliances with the towns and Rivermen it will show how little real power Hewitt has. We may be in a better position to offer Shiv whatever Hewitt has promised him. And Oleda."

"I don't like it," Fae said. "But the alternative is worse. Shiv and his Bridgers—and Hewitt—are bridge problems. We can't banish them, and I don't want to kill them. Not unless they act first. Besides, any child Oleda may have will need us."

"How so?" Aric asked.

"Burrage had both Wailes and Kellen bloodlines," Fae said. "If only the Kellen bloodline came from Oleda, Hewitt could kill any child by having it recite a Wailes spell. I'm the only one who can teach a child with an unknown bloodline how to use magic safely, teach it to create its own spells."

"So, we wait," Aric said. "And watch."

Chapter Seventeen

"ARE YOU FEELING up to this?" Aric asked. Fae took a deep breath and stood up.

"The nausea is gone," she said. "Until tomorrow. I'll be fine."

"I don't like you doing so much when you should be resting." Aric tried not to hover over her, but he couldn't help it. She was carrying his child, and he couldn't be happier. Or more worried.

They hadn't told anyone—and certainly not Hewitt—but soon they wouldn't be able to hide it. And poor Fae, not only was she experiencing nausea in the mornings, but her exhaustion made working magic more difficult. They had yet to figure out how to hide that from everyone, but if today went well they should gain a few more weeks of secrecy.

"Hewitt has everything set up," Aric said.

"He does like to make a spectacle," Fae said. "It would be much better if I simply went out one night, cast a spell, and everyone woke up the next day to find the bridge fixed."

"We talked about this, about letting him feel important," Aric said.

"I know," Fae replied. "But it is at the expense of letting everyone know how important you are."

Aric sighed. Hewitt might have tried to undermine Fae if they hadn't acquiesced to some of his requests. And it was important that Fae be seen as an authority on the bridge, not him. He had the Rivermen behind him; that was enough, he hoped.

He could sense that they had to decide what to do about Hewitt soon but there was always the question of Shiv and how much trouble he would cause. He'd watch the Bridger today—try to gauge his reaction to the respect the people of both towns showed Fae.

Even if she was exhausted and her magic wasn't dependable, she still had authority. But if Shiv felt that could be overcome, that Hewitt could override Fae's ties with the towns, he wouldn't be safe.

As much as he loved the idea of this child, of Fae bearing his child, he was afraid that it would come into a world without him.

"I know," Fae said. "Let's get this over with." She stepped out and into the street, and Aric followed, closing the door to the bindery behind him.

People greeted them as they walked towards the small square. Hewitt was there, his white robe gleaming in the sunlight. Shiv stood behind him, scanning the crowd. His eyes narrowed when his gaze paused on him. Aric lifted his chin in response.

He didn't see Oleda—perhaps she'd stayed at home to avoid people from the towns. Even the ones she hadn't known before didn't like her. Not that the people on the bridge liked her either. Despite the fact that her position had diminished with the death of her son, Oleda Burrage, as Shiv's woman, had not learned any lessons in humility.

"Fae," Councilman Larwood greeted her, then leaned over and hugged her. He slapped a hand on Aric's shoulder as his wife kissed Fae's cheek. Next was Cleric Kenway and his wife. Their greeting was just as warm, although a shade less effusive.

Aric looked over at Shiv, who was watching Fae with interest. There hadn't been many opportunities to show just how highly the leaders of the towns regarded Fae: hopefully Shiv was realizing that Fae not only had more magical power than Hewitt, but she held more political sway as well.

Hewitt started to speak, and Aric gently guided Fae towards the stone railing. He peered down at the boats that ringed the footing, one weighted down with a block of stone.

With the metal plates and grates removed, and Rivermen able to travel freely through the arches, they'd been able to inspect the pier. They weren't certain if some of the damage had been caused by damming the river or if it was a result of the daily wear and tear, but the river had scoured one footing enough to cause a stone to crumble. Fae was going to use magic to replace the worn block.

She would have preferred to be on a boat, and he'd taken her for a close look at the footing yesterday, but the motion of the boat had caused worse nausea than usual, so they'd given in to Hewitt's demand that this be done from on top of the bridge.

Aric waved and Rand waved back. The Rivermen were ready. When he turned back to Hewitt, he met Shiv's gaze again. This time the Bridger nodded.

Aric leaned close to Fae's ear. "I think Shiv is starting to realize who has the power," he said. "Did I miss anything important from Hewitt?"

"No," Fae said. "A history lesson—but mostly made up history."

"The Rivermen are in place," Aric said. "Whenever you're ready."

"And now," Hewitt said, his voice rising. "As it has ever been since conjurers built the bridge, we will maintain it. Faelin?"

"Thank you, Conjurer Hewitt," Fae said. "I'll get started."

Aric and Fae both stepped up to the railing and peered down. Rand waved again, and Aric felt Fae take hold of the magic. He wrapped an arm around her shoulder as she drew more power towards her. There was a spasm in the magic, and without thinking, Aric reached into it, steadying it. Fae's hold on it slipped and then *he* was the one maintaining the power, *he* was the one making it do what he wanted.

"I lost it," Fae said softly. "I'm sorry, I'm not sure I can do this."

"I have it," Aric said. Even with Fae's instruction he'd only been able to create small spells—he suspected creating powerful spells was a talent his line of shamans didn't have, but he was getting better at manipulating existing spells. "I think I can do it but I would prefer to have your help." And then she was back in the magic with him, connected to him by a thread.

There was plenty of magic to allow Aric to move the stone into place. He stared down at the river and *forced* the undercut stone to crumble. In a few moments, the river had washed the remains away. He peered down at Rand, who clambered onto the pier and then back to his boat. A few moment later, Rand pointed at the stone, indicating which way it should be placed.

Aric looked at Fae, who nodded and waved at Rand.

"I can do this," he said, more to himself than to her. But he felt the truth of it. He concentrated on the stone, on lifting it out of the boat and turning it so that the designated end was pointing towards the pier. Then slowly, he pushed it into the vacant slot. It was a tight fit, and he thought the grinding sound was in his mind until people around him began to comment on it.

Finally, the stone was in place, and he let go of the magic.

"It's done," Aric said to Fae. "They need to think it was you."

She nodded and waved at the Rivermen before turning to the crowd. "The footing is repaired," she said.

"Thanks to you," Hewitt said. He looked around at the gathered people, his arms spread wide. "Conjurers created this bridge, and we will keep it sound for all who live on, below, and beside it."

"And thanks to the Rivermen for noticing and letting us know about the problem," Fae said. She smiled and stepped towards the crowd.

Aric kept his arm looped in hers. Fae leaned on him as people congratulated her. Finally, they stood in front of a beaming Hewitt; Shiv loomed behind him.

"Faelin," Hewitt gushed. "Thank you. This is everything I could hope for. Conjurers returned to greatness."

Now it was Fae who helped him stay on his feet. That was it—that was what Hewitt wanted! For conjurers to be revered: for *him* to be revered and honoured.

Once he steadied himself he looked up and met Shiv's eyes. He didn't nod, he didn't acknowledge that he'd noticed Aric's unsteadiness—he simply stared for a moment before looking away.

Aric supressed a shudder and turned his attention back to Hewitt and Fae. They'd been joined by Councilman Larwood and Cleric Kenway.

"I'm going to talk to Rand," he said to Fae. "Will you be all right?" She nodded, and he turned and made his way back to the bindery.

"THAT WAS A fine piece of work Fae did," Rand said when Aric was almost at the bottom of the stairs. The Riverman was standing on his boat a few feet from the pier. "Hop aboard and we'll take a look."

Aric pulled his shoes off—a concession to Fae when they were on the bridge—and leapt onto the deck of Rand's boat. He grabbed an oar and helped manoeuvre the boat to the section that had been repaired. It looked solid—the stone was snugged in tight. Algae would cover it soon, just as it covered the rest of them.

"Do we need to mortar it?" Aric asked.

"Nah. Did you hear the grinding when it went in? Don't think water will be getting in there." Rand smiled. "Like I said, Fae did good work."

"It wasn't Fae," Aric said. "She was too tired to do it. So, I did."

Rand's eyebrows went up. He leaned closer. "New shaman abilities?"

"Maybe," Aric said. "Or old ones. We've lost the knowledge of what specific powers each shaman bloodline had."

"I won't ask why Fae was too tired," Rand said. "But no one will hear about that from me. Do you want me to keep silent about the other pier that needs repair?"

"As long as it won't put anyone at risk," Aric said. "And no one on the bridge or land finds out."

"I'll tell the Rivermen," Rand says. "Most of us don't like anyone coming down here to look anyway. But we'll keep watch on the other pier." He pointed at the crack in the stone that led from the replaced block up towards the arch. "That crack didn't change when the stone block was replaced so I don't expect anything to happen with the other one."

"Thanks, Rand," Aric said. The other man nodded and silently they picked up oars and steered the boat back to the bottom of the stairs. Aric watched Rand row downstream before he turned and headed up the stairs.

"SHE'S WITH CHILD."

"What? No." Hewitt stared at Oleda. "How do you know?"

"I don't," Oleda said. "Not for sure, but there's speculation amongst the women. She's been feeling ill in the morning, and the Riverman has been even more attentive than usual. The women think it's *adorable*."

She spat the last word, making it clear that Oleda did not think that at all. But Faelin was carrying that river rat's child. Just when fixing the bridge had gone so well in showing everyone how powerful a true conjurer was.

Hewitt felt hurt—no, more than that—he felt *betrayed*.

"And you?" he asked Oleda. "When will you be with child?" Oleda's child would be his to control. Faelin's would only be his when Aric was dead.

"Not yet," Oleda said, her voice flat. "Although Shiv is most . . . diligent in his efforts to become a father."

"Shiv understands the realities of his life," Hewitt said. "Send him to me," he said, dismissing her. He watched as she hurried from his office.

No doubt Shiv was doing his best to father a child, but if Oleda was barren, she was no longer needed. He had no real knowledge of how long things might take, especially since Oleda was a little old to be a mother, but he had time to wait. Especially once Aric was out of the way.

In a few years, he would select a suitable father for the rest of Faelin's children. And it wouldn't be a Bridger—or a Riverman. He would look at pedigrees—at which families might have blood ties to true conjurers.

Shiv stepped into his office. "You asked for me?"

"Did your woman tell you the latest gossip?" Hewitt asked. "That Faelin is with child?" Shiv's face was unreadable. Did he already know? "She is at her most vulnerable if something were to happen to her Riverman."

"What exactly should happen to him?" Shiv asked. "An accident, you said, but not what type."

"You figure it out," Hewitt said. "What do you usually do?"

"Kill them and toss them in the river," Shiv replied matter-of-factly. "And say that they must have tripped and fallen off the bridge and then drowned."

"Then do it," Hewitt said. Why was Shiv asking him how to kill the river rat? He'd never asked questions before. "I told you I don't want to know."

"Yes, Conjurer Hewitt," Shiv said and turned to leave.

"And Shiv?" Hewitt called. "Get Oleda with child or I will take her away from you." The Bridger paused and nodded briefly before exiting the room.

Hewitt sat back in his chair, staring at the closed door. Once Aric was dead he'd be there to help Faelin through her grief. He'd hold her hand, make sure she ate and help her stay healthy until her child was born.

He would become her most trusted friend—hadn't he shown his loyalty by offering to take her on as his apprentice? Perhaps now she would accept that as well.

It would make it so much easier to have her bear sons for a man of his choice.

FAE CLOSED HER eyes and looked at the magic. A thin line connected her to Aric. She gripped his hands.

"Do you see it?" she asked.

"Yes," Aric replied. His voice was soft and she knew he was smiling. "Our child binds us together through magic. I can feel your power, and use it."

"And it does not sap my strength. At least not more than the child does all by itself." She opened her eyes to find Aric looking at her tenderly. She took one of his hands and placed it on her belly. "Oh!" she said, startled at the spark she felt.

"I felt that as well," Aric said. Suddenly he stood up, panic in his eyes. "It's started," he said. "Hewitt has decided that he wants me dead."

"Then we have some work to do," Fae said. She sat up and pulled Aric back down beside her. "I need to make sure that if you can't create the spells, you know how to control them. We'll need defensive spells. For me and you."

"He won't hurt you," Aric said.

"Shiv might," Fae said. "If I'm trying to kill him." And she would if he hurt Aric. She'd kill Hewitt as well; although she was pretty sure he assumed he was safe.

IT WAS LATE afternoon before Fae was satisfied.

The magical protections she'd placed on the book bindery the day she and Aric moved in were reinforced and new warnings had been added. If anyone came in they would know. And Shiv, Oleda, and Hewitt would be barred unless invited in.

She'd created a defensive spell for Aric, one that was triggered by an attack—including if someone threw anything at him—and now they were both wrapped in spells.

They weren't killing spells—Fae wasn't confident that her powers could differentiate between friend and foe, and she didn't want to cause permanent harm unless there was a need. But anyone who threatened either of them would be immobilized.

And Aric could change the spell into something more deadly, if it was needed.

"I think that's all we can do," Fae said. She watched Aric bolt the front door as well as the one that led to the workrooms below. They didn't expect an attack from the river but that didn't mean someone couldn't take the stairs from the fishmongers to the book bindery. Shiv would be stopped by their protection spell, but not every Bridger would be.

The workrooms had been repaired enough to keep the elements out, but not enough to keep out a Bridger in case the spells failed for some reason. Neither of them thought it a bad idea to rely on both physical and magical barriers to entry.

Aric stopped by the stove. Fae smiled when she felt the magic stir: a small spell that Aric could manage. In a moment, the fire in the stove was out, the only light left coming from the lamp in her hand.

"We'll be safe tonight." He smiled. "So say my shaman senses."

IT WAS THE spell that saved him. Fae had created it more than a week ago, and he'd almost forgotten that it was there. He was coming back from a late meeting on the river with Rand and Chart. Once the tide started to go out, Rand had dropped him off at the base of the stairs and left to ferry Chart to his own boat.

Aric was a few steps from the landing when the protective spell was triggered. A fist-sized rock bounced off it and fell to the river below. He looked up and saw a shadow on the landing above.

"Shiv," Aric said. "I've been expecting you." He climbed the stairs until he was a few steps below the Bridger, who glared at him. His back was pinned to the wall and his arms and legs were splayed. All he could move were his eyes.

"Give me one good reason why I shouldn't let you drop into the river," Aric said. "Like you've done to so many others." He tweaked the magic, freeing the other man's head. Shiv's eyes widened. "That's right," Aric sad. "I can do magic." He didn't feel the need to tell him he could only create small spells.

"I wasn't trying to kill you," Shiv said. "I needed to get your attention."

"You have it."

"Faelin has magic," Shiv said. "And the backing of the towns. I know that even if you are dead, Hewitt will never control her or her children." He paused. "Hewitt cannot win but I can lose if I side with him. I want to be on your side."

"Why should we trust you?" Aric asked. This was the best that he and Fae could hope for but could they ever trust Shiv? And if Shiv died, what of the other Bridgers? Fae said they were a bridge problem and should be handled on the bridge. He looked down at the river. Or tossed off it. But he couldn't kill them all.

"Oleda is also with child," he said. "I do not want her child—*my* child—to be controlled by Hewitt."

"You and Oleda." Aric shook his head. "That pairing I don't understand. Hewitt ordered it, didn't he?"

"He did," Shiv said. "But Oleda and I have come to . . . an understanding."

"One that doesn't include Hewitt? Then why haven't you killed him?"

"I can't," Shiv replied. "Not and protect Oleda from everyone who lives both on and off the bridge. Only you and Fae can do that."

"Hewitt would try to control your child," Aric said. "But he doesn't know enough about the old blood and magic. The first time he had your child recite a spell could kill it." He stared at the Bridger. Should he tell him the complete truth and allow him to make a fully informed decision?

"Fae and I have already decided that we will never let that happen. We would never jeopardize the life of a child." He shook his head again. "Even when we're pretty sure we don't want a child of Oleda's to have magic."

"She's gentler than my first wife," Shiv said. "And a lot kinder than my own mother. I'll kill Hewitt if you look out for Oleda and my child."

"No," Aric said. "We'll handle him another way. But Fae is the only one who can teach your child how to safely use magic. If you want her help, you and Oleda and your Bridgers must agree to be loyal to us."

"Yes," Shiv said. "I agree."

"Good. Tell Hewitt your decision and that I'll be waiting for him at the square." Aric stepped past the Bridger and up to the door to the bindery. Once there, he changed the spell enough to free Shiv. The Bridger scrambled up the stairs to the fishmongers. Aric waited until he was inside before ducking into the workroom and heading upstairs to Fae.

"What did he promise you?" Hewitt called out, but Shiv was already leaving Conjurers Hall. "No!" All his plans were gone because the ignorant Bridger decided to believe the word of a Riverman. Aric hadn't even spoken to Faelin. There was no way Hewitt believed he had the authority to promise Shiv whatever he'd been promised. Aric Rawley wasn't even of the bridge, let alone a conjurer.

He sifted through the books on the shelf—books that Burrage had assembled—looking for a familiar binding. He picked out a Hewitt spell book—an old one. All he needed was a small spell, one he could recite without it killing him or making his own deformities much worse.

Hewitt flipped through the pages. This one. It seemed small but it should be enough to take care of a river rat who had no magic of his own. He quickly memorized the spell before tucking the book into his robes.

He would meet Aric Rawley, and kill him. Then he would control Faelin, just as he always should have. If her father had only allowed her to become his apprentice, all of this could have been avoided.

Aric was in the square, as Shiv had promised.

"Foolish boy," Hewitt said. Then he started to recite the spell. He felt the familiar pain in his hands and feet, and then suddenly the magic was . . . gone.

"A spell?" Aric asked. "To . . ." He paused and closed his eyes. When he opened them, he shook his head. "To slowly draw all the liquid from me. It would kill me eventually, but not before I killed you."

"How did you know?" Hewitt asked. He shook his right hand. It was already far larger than it had been. Aric may have done something with the magic in the spell but he still felt the full effects of reciting it. "What the spell was for?"

"The river *was*, before the bridge *became*," Aric replied. His voice was strange, and when Hewitt peered closer, his eyes were unfocussed. "The bridge is *from* the river."

Hewitt took the spell book out from beneath his robe and rushed Aric, raising the book over his head to strike the other man. Suddenly, there was a blast of power, and he was suspended mid-step, one hand raised overhead. He watched in horror as his hand expanded in size until the book dropped from it.

What have you done to me? he tried to say, but he couldn't move his lips. Aric stepped into his line of sight.

"Give me one good reason why I shouldn't kill you," he said.

Suddenly, Hewitt could move his mouth. "What did you do?" he asked.

"Magic," Aric replied calmly. "I did magic." He smiled. "Now I know why I can do it. My premonition just now—the river was, before the bridge became? It means that Rivermen lived here long before the bridge was built. Rivermen most likely built the bridge—or at least helped build it—with magic. The magic of the conjurers *came* from the magic of Rivermen."

"No," Hewitt said. "That's not possible. *Conjurers* built the bridge. *Conjurers* held all the power."

"I sense the truth in what I said," Aric said. He glanced at the book at Hewitt's feet. "I don't need books to work with magic." Aric swept his hand out and the book flew into the air and over the railing.

It couldn't be true; Hewitt knew that conjurers were the great ones, not the smelly river rats this man came from. "I only wanted a return to greatness," Hewitt said. "For true conjurers to create powerful spells. Like Faelin did when she fixed the bridge."

"Sorry," Aric said. "I did that too. Fae was feeling tired. You got what you wanted," he continued, as though what he'd said hadn't just made Hewitt's life a mockery. "Powerful magic has returned to the bridge. Me, Fae, and our child—our *children*—will be called conjurers."

"Yes," Hewitt replied. "That is what I wanted." Faelin and her child, yes, but this river rat with his preposterous notion that conjurers came from the likes of him? That was not what he wanted.

"Good, now that we've reached an understanding, I'll let you go."

Hewitt fell to the cobblestones and groaned, his head bent downwards.

"Let me help," Aric said. He grabbed one of Hewitt's arms.

With a roar, Hewitt surged up, grabbing Aric around the waist and propelling them both towards the edge of the bridge.

Then he was lifted off the younger man, his larger than ever hands grasping futilely as his body flew off the bridge. As he went over the edge he saw Shiv's face staring down at him. Then he twisted in the air and the dark of the river loomed closer. He felt the cold water then he sunk into the darkness. He opened his mouth and gasped, and cold seeped into him.

"CAN WE TRUST Shiv?" Fae said. "And Oleda?" She'd felt Aric use magic but hadn't been able to reach him through it. He'd returned from his meeting with Hewitt, saying that the conjurer had tried to kill him but that he'd stopped his spell. Then Shiv had thrown him off the bridge.

Aric was safe, and now she was curled up beside him in a large chair by the stove.

It was hard for her to believe that Hewitt—that *all* of the old conjurers—were gone. It was just her now, and her and Aric's child.

"No," Aric replied. "He helped me tonight with Hewitt but we can never truly trust Shiv. Or Oleda. But we can manage them if we're smart."

"Their child will never be a conjurer—a magic user—without my help," Fae said. "We'll need to stay close to them in order to judge what's safe to teach the child."

"Yes," Aric replied. "Not a pleasant task, but necessary." He shifted to face her. "I had a premonition, when I was with Hewitt. Conjurers came from Rivermen—probably from the shaman bloodlines. Hewitt couldn't accept it."

"You did say there used to be more shaman families," Fae said. "I wonder if there were the same ten as the conjurers?"

"We'll never know," Aric replied. "But our child reunites conjurers and shamans."

"So many years of being divided," Fae said. "So many years of hate and suspicion and not trusting each other. All at an end. Because of us."

"Because of us," he agreed.

About the Author

Jane Glatt loves that along with creating original worlds, writing fantasy allows her to indulge her curiosity about an eclectic group of subjects. So far she's researched synesthesia, medieval guilds, tidal rivers, cities atop bridges, pirates and privateers, plants used for healing and the history of spying. For that last one she blames a visit to the International Spy Museum (yes it's a real place), in Washington D.C.

For news on Jane's future releases visit her website http://janeglatt.com/index.html and sign up for her newsletter.

www.ingramcontent.com/pod-product-compliance
Lightning Source LLC
Chambersburg PA
CBHW050510190726
48284CB00003B/764